Praise for the Darkwing Chronicles

"Exciting, fast-paced. . . . It has everything: humor, action, mystery, and romance."　　　　—Huntress Book Reviews

"Savannah Russe [lets] us know that there is more than one way to tell a good vamp's story."
　　　　　　　　　　　　—Victoria Laurie, author of
　　　　　　　　　　　　Demons Are a Ghoul's Best Friend

"Exciting . . . superior supernatural suspense."
　　　　　　　　　　　　—The Best Reviews

"Wonderful . . . with a sharp bite." —*Midwest Book Review*

UNDER DARKNESS

THE DARKWING CHRONICLES

SAVANNAH RUSSE

A SIGNET ECLIPSE BOOK

SIGNET ECLIPSE
Published by New American Library, a division of
Penguin Group (USA) Inc., 375 Hudson Street,
New York, New York 10014, USA
Penguin Group (Canada), 90 Eglinton Avenue East, Suite 700, Toronto,
Ontario M4P 2Y3, Canada (a division of Pearson Penguin Canada Inc.)
Penguin Books Ltd., 80 Strand, London WC2R 0RL, England
Penguin Ireland, 25 St. Stephen's Green, Dublin 2,
Ireland (a division of Penguin Books Ltd.)
Penguin Group (Australia), 250 Camberwell Road, Camberwell, Victoria 3124,
Australia (a division of Pearson Australia Group Pty. Ltd.)
Penguin Books India Pvt. Ltd., 11 Community Centre, Panchsheel Park,
New Delhi - 110 017, India
Penguin Group (NZ), 67 Apollo Drive, Rosedale, North Shore 0632,
New Zealand (a division of Pearson New Zealand Ltd.)
Penguin Books (South Africa) (Pty.) Ltd., 24 Sturdee Avenue,
Rosebank, Johannesburg 2196, South Africa

Penguin Books Ltd., Registered Offices:
80 Strand, London WC2R 0RL, England

First published by Signet Eclipse, an imprint of New American Library,
a division of Penguin Group (USA) Inc.

First Printing, May 2008
10 9 8 7 6 5 4 3 2 1

To
SUSAN J. COLLINI

*"A faithful friend is a strong defense:
and he that hath found such an one
hath found a treasure."*

—ECCLESIASTICUS 6:14

INTRODUCTION

A vampire is as a vampire does.
My mother didn't tell me that. I figured it out all by myself. Of course, it took me more than four hundred years.

I have passed for human for all these centuries. But upon close inspection (note my fangs, my translucent white skin, my overreaction to garlic), it is evident I am not.

Besides the obvious, let me explain what my being a vampire means.

I cannot die unless I get a stake in the heart (the preferred method of those who hate us), am exposed to the sun, or am shot in a soft and vulnerable place with a bullet made of silver. I shudder to think of it.

I must drink blood, preferably human, but animal will do.

I am, by my nature, addicted to immorality, pursuing pleasure in every form—no matter how much I try to be chaste. And I do try—to be chaste, that is. I fail miserably every time.

I live among millions of people in the greatest city in the world, but I will always be an outsider. I can never fit in.

Now you can understand why I have the proverbial snowball's chance in hell of making any committed, long-term, man-woman relationship work.

I keep trying at that too. Because more than anything else I need forgiveness, redemption, and, oh, yes, true love.

I live in darkness, but I do believe, deep in my heart, that I can find light.

Without further ado, let me introduce myself. I am a vampire through and through. But I am one who is paying it forward—trying to rack up some good karma. I have gotten myself a name, rank, serial number—and a government job. I am Agent Daphne Urban, American spy.

CHAPTER 1

"He that lives upon hope dies fasting."

—Benjamin Franklin

The footsteps—slow and measured, heavy and deter-mined—hit the pavement behind me with the steady rhythm of a funeral drum. The sound alone told me they belonged to a man of considerable size and consequence. I didn't have to look back. I knew he meant trouble.

At half past three a.m., night covered Manhattan like a shroud. A fast, hard June shower had just ended, leaving the stone buildings black with rain. As I passed, their windows stared at me with blank, empty eyes. Until the arrival of the man, only the occasional swish of a Yellow Cab's tires on the wet streets had broken the hush of the late hour. The cool air felt as sharp as a knife blade when I inhaled deeply, and I kept walking, my dog, Jade, on a leash at my side.

Glancing down I saw Jade's body tense, her tail going straight, her ears up. The footsteps became quicker, got closer. To anyone watching I appeared to be an ordinary young woman, taller than most and thin as death. Perhaps, as I strolled alone on the empty city streets, a mugger or a rapist had targeted me as easy prey.

That thought fled as quickly as it came. Who was I kidding? Sane people invariably drew back from me, giving me a wide berth. Some ancient instinct struck dread in their very bones, telling them that I was someone—no, not some*one*, but some*thing*—to avoid. As for the crazies of New York City, even they weren't that stupid: My huge malamute, looking more like a wolf than a dog, kept them away.

That meant the odds were 101 out of 99 that my stalker was a vampire hunter. If I didn't do something quickly, I was about to die.

West End Avenue intersected with my block about two hundred feet ahead of me. I broke into a run, Jade keeping up with my stride. I reached the corner, turned sharply, hugged the granite wall of an apartment building, and stopped. I turned, crouched, and quickly released Jade's chain. I readied myself to attack.

I never got the chance. The moment the man passed the wall of the building and appeared, Jade sprang so fast, her body became a blur of snarling rage. With a growl that made my blood run cold she knocked him flat, her teeth sinking deeply into his forearm. He swore loudly. The polished wooden stake he clutched in his ham hock of a hand arced up, catching the light of a streetlamp before spinning and falling into the street with a clatter.

My mind became a haze of red anger with no thought. Irrational and reacting, I raced after the lethally sharp implement, meaning to use it as a weapon of my own. I grabbed it from the asphalt. My long fingers tightened around its smoothness. I raised it high above my head and charged toward my assailant, seeing him clearly for the first time.

Fighting to push Jade off and struggling to stand, the hunter was a fearsome sight. Clad entirely in black, he was broad and solid. With no visible neck, his head appeared to sit directly on his body, so thick were the muscles of his shoulders. He had a wrestler's build and an assassin's face, flat and dull and cruel. A thick silver chain was wrapped diagonally like a bandolier across his wide chest. Three more stakes hung from it.

The sight of the stakes drove me toward madness. Throughout my centuries on this earth, too many of my friends had felt the piercing agony such an instrument delivers. And as a stake is driven into a vampire's heart, from the vampire's lips comes a last terrible scream—a heartrending, animal cry of pure terror. Then comes the fierce, horrible burning: the withering of flesh and bones crumbling to dust until nothing but a fine, dry ash remains.

These memories fueled my rage. My own bestial nature took control of my soul. My mouth widened to show the terrible whiteness of my pointed incisors. I think I was screaming as I leaped forward, intending to drive the glistening point into the hunter's slablike face. But as I struck he twisted away, and the stake grazed his cheek, leaving an angry streak of red. Shaking Jade from his arm at last, he gained his feet. My dog flew at his legs, her barks and snarls wild with fury. He ran then, but in the moment before he moved his dark eyes sought mine, and I felt their hatred.

I did not give chase. My chest heaving, my brain spinning, I stopped. I called Jade back and she returned to me, her mouth smeared with blood. I found her leash on the sidewalk and snapped it on. I still held the smooth, long wooden stake in my hand as my dog and I retraced my steps and headed home.

As I pushed my way through the glass doors into the lobby of my apartment building, I spotted Mickey, the doorman, asleep in a wooden chair. The *New York Post* lay spread on his lap; his hanging head bobbed up and down with his snores like a davening Jew at temple.

So much for security. I felt annoyed, and I walked over and gave a leg of his chair a kick.

"Huh?" he said, lifting his head, his eyelids fluttering. "Wha . . . ?" he muttered as his gaze fastened at knee level of my faded jeans. He tipped his chin up for his barely open eyes to take in my black tank top until he focused on my face and my eyes, which held no warmth. "Miss Urban? Wha' you want? Your dry cleaning?" His breath smelled of beer.

"You were asleep again, Mickey!" I gave the chair another kick out of pique. My voice sounded shrill even to my own ears.

Giving his head a shake, he stuck out a rubbery lower lip and said, "No way, Miss Urban. No way. Just resting my eyes."

I snorted. "Yeah, right. Listen, this is important. Has anybody been around asking about me? A big guy? Maybe earlier tonight?"

Mickey's bleary eyes got wider, and he stared at the long wooden stake in my hand. Suddenly he got it. "No," he said, and lumbered to his feet. "The Brits after you again, Miss Urban?"

Mickey's brain was scrambled eggs from drink, but he was a tough old guy. He had made up his mind I was working undercover for the IRA after taking a beating on my behalf a few months back. He wasn't that far off. I was a spy, but for a top-secret American intelligence organization, a deep-black operation called the Darkwings that was so hush-hush that even I didn't know which agency had hired me. I was one of the original three Darkwings; now there were five of us in this antiterrorist group, vampires one and all.

My completely nocturnal existence alone would have been enough to raise questions about my identity. I also received deliveries from a blood bank every week. Strange men and women showed up to find me at all hours of the night: They were furtive visitors who ran the gamut from a New York City police detective to a Mafia hit man.

Privy to some of the shadiest aspects of my life, the world-weary doorman had come up with an explanation for me that sat a lot better in his scheme of things than the truth would have. He could envision my being a spy, but a blood-drinking vampire who looked to be in her mid-twenties but was over four hundred years old? No way. So if my recent love affair with the proudly Irish St. Julien Fitzmaurice, who had often taken the time to listen to the doorman's stories and to discuss the troubles of Northern Ireland, convinced Mickey I was a Provo, that was cool.

I also would never forget that Mickey had put himself in harm's way for me. My voice was softer when I answered his question about whether I was in deep doo-doo once again. "To tell the truth, I don't know," I said. "Watch your back, okay?"

Fully awake now and ready for action, he shot back, "Don't you worry about me. I worked in Dublin, but I grew up in Ulster, y'know."

"I know, Mick, and a fine young lad you must have been," I said with a gentle smile. "Who's on days this week?"

"McDougal. I'll fill him in. We got you covered, Miss Urban," he assured me.

"Thanks, I appreciate it." I tugged on Jade's leash and

moved toward the elevator, my step lively but a heaviness weighing down my heart. I hoped my double life didn't get Mickey or somebody else in my building killed one day. I pushed the number of my floor, and as the door slid shut I thought, *Evil thwarted doesn't go away. It just waits for a more opportune time.*

CHAPTER 2

"There is the greatest practical benefit in making a few failures early in life."

—Thomas Henry Huxley, *On Medical Education*

At dusk the next evening I stirred awake, the faint rustling of unseen wings attending my arousal from sleep and the nightmares that troubled it. The air in my crypt smelled stale, the atmosphere humid even in this hidden room behind the bookcases in the hallway of my apartment. I sat up in my coffin and peered out into the surrounding darkness, which held not a glimmer of light. *This is the mirror of my soul,* I thought, and suddenly became aware that I was in a really pissy mood.

I climbed out of the satin interior, which, although perfumed, retained the distinct earthy smell of the Transylvanian dirt that lay beneath the mattress. I stood naked, flexed my back, stretched my thin arms high above my head, and decided I needed a surefire mood lifter: fresh-brewed black coffee followed by some serious shopping therapy.

Where to shop? I thought. Saks Fifth Avenue, which to me was a creaky old lady of a store anyway, was open only until eight. The much hipper Bloomingdale's at Fifty-ninth and Lex stayed open until ten every weeknight. Those were my kind of hours.

In truth, my favorite shopping mecca was Neiman Marcus, but the chain's best store was at the Houston, Texas, Galleria. Since I had nothing whatsoever penciled in on my social calendar (what would it read if I actually had one? *Type O blood at midnight*? *A tryst for anonymous sex at two*? *Searching for true love at three*?), I briefly entertained the idea of a red-eye flight, then nixed it. Airline cutbacks and lack of customer service coupled with oppressive yet ineffective security procedures had taken the fun out of commercial flying.

These days when I went airborne, it was usually under my own power. Since I transformed into a huge vampire bat in order to fly, I had to be highly selective about the times and places I lifted off into the wild blue yonder. Once, exhilarated by the moonlight and inattentive to what floated below as I flew along the Atlantic coast, I sent the *QE2* cruise ship into emergency status. Passengers strolling the upper decks had spotted me and panicked. They had the ship doctors convinced that someone had slipped a hallucinogenic into the champagne-cocktail fountain.

Despite the risks of discovery, I would never forgo flying. Flight in my vampire-bat form, that phantasmagoric breaking free from the bonds of earth, became a Zen experience, as close to nirvana as I was ever likely to get.

No, I just lied about the route to nirvana. I knew full well that there was another path. Why did I lie? The long life that I have lived, filled with disguises, subterfuges, and the hiding of my vampire nature, meant I lied a lot, to both myself and others. And I was lying to myself now, driven by my shame, for I aspired to be as chaste and moral as a nun.

However, the other path to satori, nirvana, or bliss—call it whatever you wished—was prolonged, uninhibited, completely satisfying tantric sex with the right man.

And if I dared to confess it, I knew exactly who that "right man" was—for sex, anyway. For a sustained relationship he had turned out to be Mr. Wrong: Darius della Chiesa, that gorgeous hunk of macho male who was also a lying, double-crossing, cheating SOB. A few months ago he stole my heart—and then what? He stomped on it and left me flattened, my soul steamrolled into a shadow of its former self.

Suddenly my crappy mood returned in full force. I slammed through the secret door from my crypt into my apartment, where tall windows revealed the perfect purple of a New York City early-summer twilight. I stopped at the hall mirror. My long, dark hair hung lankly around my pale face. My shoulders were stooped. My eyes had lost their twinkle. I looked washed-out. A night of shopping? Hell, I needed something more drastic: a total makeover. Maybe it would alleviate the depression that had dogged me since the Darkwings' last mission.

Having come down from the adrenaline high that sustained me when I was on active duty, and currently drifting between relationships, I once again found life to be without purpose or direction. Worse, a combination of boredom and sexual frustration had left me more and more haunted by memories of Darius.

What the hell was the matter with me! I scolded myself. I had been within days of marrying former Secret Service agent Julien St. Fitzmaurice, my post-Darius rebound romance. Fitz had actually proposed, made a commitment, been open and honest. He would have given up being human to become a vampire like me.

Did I bite him? Hmmmm, yes, but not enough to make him undead. Instead I called the wedding off and sent him packing—literally. Now he was on the run. My mother, no romantic, wanted him killed. Her motto is: "Dead men tell no tales"—and Fitz knew too much about the vampires of New York.

Instead of mooning about over the loss of that truly good guy, I was thinking, *Darius, Darius, Darius*. His blue eyes. His strong hands. His laugh, his charm, his passion. Even though I knew he was currently on tour in Germany with his hot new rock band, Darius DC and the Vampire Project, I found myself watching people on the streets with the illogical hope I'd see him walking toward me. When I closed my eyes at night I was back in his arms. We had been fighting like cats and dogs when he left, but all I remembered was that we made love like animals—wild, crazy, and no-holds-barred.

Boy, I better get a grip. I needed to get Darius out of my system. Maybe a colonic cleansing would help. I walked into the kitchen, absentmindedly giving Jade's head a pat as she pulled herself out of her doggy bed and tagged along next to me, ready to be fed. From the bedroom where I did not sleep but kept my clothes I heard the squeaking of Gunther, my white rat. My pets' needs were simple: eat and drink, poop and pee, sleep and play. I wished mine were so elementary.

A few minutes later I sat at my kitchen island, grasping a coffee mug in one hand, sipping the black coffee, and turning the pages of this morning's *New York Times* with the other. Scanning the news stories, I got a chuckle from a Metro Briefing piece about a man in Connecticut who pleaded guilty to blowing up portable toilets in three towns.

He threw himself on the mercy of the court and said a presciption drug he had been taking made him think the privies were spying on him.

I also laughed at the stupid criminal in Alabama who had donned a ski mask before carrying out a home invasion and yelling at an elderly man, "Give me all your money and valuables. And, Paw-Paw, I mean it!" His grandfather called the police to tell them his grandson had robbed him of fifty bucks.

I was about to turn to the Arts section to start the cross-word puzzle when I noticed another innocuous news story buried in the back pages of the first section:

> On Monday, June 5, the Intrepid Sea, Air & Space Museum will leave its home berth at Pier Eighty-six at Twelfth Avenue and Forty-sixth Street in Manhattan to be towed to Newport, Virginia, for an $8 million renovation. The ship will be repainted and undergo a complete exterior refurbishment. New areas of the interior, including the anchor chain room, general berthing quarters, and the machine shop, will be made accessible to the public for the first time. The museum complex will reopen in the fall.

Although the great World War II aircraft carrier *Intrepid* had been docked a short cab ride from my apartment, I had never taken the time to visit it. I had seen Michelangelo's *David* in Florence, the Colosseum in Rome, the Eiffel Tower in Paris, and Big Ben in London, but like most people I had ignored the history in my own backyard.

The thought flicked through my brain, *Well, guess I won't see the* Intrepid *this summer*, just when my cell phone started ringing. I let it play my current ring tone, the theme song from *The Sopranos* TV series, while I located the crossword puzzle; then I lazily reached over and flipped on my phone. I figured it was my BFF, Benny Polycarp, calling with news of a sample sale or something equally as urgent.

I figured right. It was my fellow Darkwing, a pretty, buxom blond vampire from Branson, Missouri, of all un-likely places. Her cheery voice gave me a "hey and a holler," as she'd say, and then burbled on about her rocky affair with a vampire named Martin.

Benny's relationships tended to have an expiration date shorter than that of a gallon of milk. They soured quickly and left a bad taste in one's mouth. I half listened while I worked on the crossword and murmured agreement when-ever it was appropriate.

"Benny," I finally said when I could get a word in edge-wise. "What's the name of the hot new hairdresser you use?"

"You mean Nick? The guy from that TLC television show *What Not to Wear*?"

"Yeah, him. Do you think I can get an appointment fast?"

"Not a chance. He's got a waiting list a mile long. Some of his assistants are real good, though."

"I don't know. This is a big thing for me. I've had my hair long for what? Four hundred years? If I get it restyled, I need to love it."

"Maybe you should just get a trim," she suggested. I could hear running water. Since she didn't cook, she wasn't doing dishes. I guessed she was about to take a bath.

"A trim won't cut it," I said, snickering at my own wit. "I have to do something drastic. I've been going nuts lately. I don't know what's the matter with me. I can't seem to shake these blues."

"Sugar, it's understandable." She talked loudly above the gurgling water in the background. "I mean, Fitz was gor-gee-o-sis, and you were practically walking down the aisle when you told him to run for his life. Who would have thought any of us would find a guy willing to spend eternity with the same woman? It can't be easy to have given him up. Anybody would be bummed."

I had to bite my tongue. Actually it had been a lot easier to give up Fitz than I would have thought. I loved the guy, but I wasn't *in love* with him. In fact, just days before accepting his engagement ring I had cheated on him with somebody else—and the very thought of who that had been still embarrassed the hell out of me.

My "slip" had not been a good sign that I was serious about marriage, and I knew it. I would never have dreamed of cheating on Darius. I had been so gaga about him. Oh, shit, there I was again, thinking about Darius. I murmured, "Yeah, Benny, I know," into the phone. "It was the right thing to do."

"Of course it was! You were so noble about it." Her voice was filled with empathy, and I felt like a turd for deceiving her. "Whatever you need to do to make yourself feel better, you should just go right ahead," she said. "Now, let's think about this new 'do you want. Should I ask around for another stylist, or do you want to forget your hair and come down to the vampire club with me?"

I knew what she was suggesting: a quickie, a zipless fuck with a good-looking vampire. Our kind could be poster children for Freud's principle that we spend our lives seeking pleasure and avoiding pain. With no consequences for promiscuous behavior—no kids, no disease, no commitment—vampires just did it with whomever, whenever they wanted.

But that wasn't for me. I had been there, done that, had the T-shirt. Compared to making love with someone I truly cared about, anonymous sex was no more exciting than sneezing. Okay, I'm lying again. Sometimes it felt good in the moment, but afterward I hated myself. And that's the truth.

"Thanks, Benny, but no, thanks," I said. "You know what? You're right. I need to forget about the hair for now. Let's just shop instead. Can you meet me at Bloomie's around eight?"

"Sure. Should I call Audrey?" Audrey Greco, a vampire *librarian,* of all things, was a newbie to the Darkwings. She had joined us for our previous mission. Audrey, a shadowy wraith in heavy black glasses who had been sucking blood in Greenwich Village since the mid–nineteenth century, had become a friend to both Benny and me.

"Absolutely. And another thing, Benny . . ."

"What?"

I took a deep breath and exhaled hard. My heart was starting to race. I just had to spit it out. "I was attacked by a vampire hunter last night."

"What!" I could sense her getting upset as the words spilled out of her in a rush: "Are you okay? You must be okay. You're talking to me. Did you kill him? Who was he? What happened? Holy shit. Holy shit. Holy shit." Her voice rose with incipient hysteria. "How did he find you? What are you going to do?"

"Benny, calm down. I'm okay. It wasn't even a close call. I didn't kill him. He got away. And I don't know what I'm going to do. Just be careful, I guess."

"You have to call your mother. I know you don't want to.

But promise me! You need protection." Her words were tinged with fear.

Benny was right. I should let my mother know about my attacker. The problem was that I didn't like to tell my mother *anything*. Worse still, Marozia "Mar-Mar" Urban was not only my mother; she was my boss—the invisible puppeteer who pulled the strings on many an intelligence operation, a woman who had the ear of our nation's presidents (and with Bill Clinton often a more intimate body part), and was a true believer not only in making the world safe for democracy, but also in running my life.

Naturally she was a vampire too. A master at deception, Mar-Mar looked like a cute, body-pierced, neo-hippie type who was twenty or, tops, twenty-two years old. In reality she had lived over a thousand years. Her eyes gave her away if someone had the audacity to look closely. Through them one could glimpse her soul, and that soul was wizened, suspicious of everything, and very old indeed.

Before I hung up I vowed to give Mar-Mar a call and told Benny I'd see her at Bloomingdale's. I assured her I'd make sure no huge, dark man carrying a wooden stake was following me. I could tell she was nervous about that.

After Benny's phone call I didn't do anything for a while. I sat there staring at nothing, my foot bouncing nervously. I was in trouble; I knew I was. Somehow the vampire hunters had identified me. More precisely, the people who sent the vampire hunters had identified me. My best guess was that those people were Opus Dei, that secretive, cultlike group within the Roman Catholic Church that had figured so largely in the best seller *The Da Vinci Code*.

I couldn't verify whether any of Dan Brown's fictional account was true. But I knew a lot of genuinely scary things about Opus Dei: Their members, or *supernumeraries,* practiced "corporeal mortification," which meant they used whips for self-flagellation and wore around their upper thighs a cilice, a metal chain with spikes that bit hard into the flesh. Their founder, Josemaría Escrivá, once wrote about suffering: "Let us bless pain. Love pain. Sanctify pain. Glorify pain!"

I could think of a lot things to love. Pain wasn't one of them. But Pope John Paul II canonized Escrivá, and so Rome made him a saint.

The organization embraced killing vampires with a similar fanatical relish. They kept in their Manhattan headquarters meticulous files on vampire sightings and incidents around the world. My fellow spy Cormac O'Reilly, who had been planted in the building as a receptionist until recently, my "handler" and spymaster, J, and I had risked our lives to retrieve as many of those files as we could. But our thievery had evidently not deterred the group. Opus Dei vowed to eradicate all of us "demons" and aggressively recruited and trained vampire hunters to do it.

My chances of survival were fast plummeting from slim to none. I had to weigh my options. I knew I would be attacked again. Maybe I should leave town for a while.

Finally I got myself together enough to phone Mar-Mar at her home in Scarsdale, the staid, posh enclave in Westchester County, twenty-four miles north of New York City. She didn't use cell phones. Landlines were more secure, she always said. Now her voice was brusque when she answered my call, as if she were in the middle of something important. Then again, she probably was.

"Hello, Mar-Mar," I said flatly.

"Sweetheart! I was going to call you later. No, really, I

was. But I'm right in the middle of something, I'm afraid." I heard her cover the phone receiver with her hand and talk quickly to another person.

"You're obviously busy," I said. "Look, I won't take long. Can you give me, your only daughter, maybe two minutes of your time?" I asked with an edge to my voice.

"I'm never too busy for you, dear. You know that," she responded. It was such a crock. I was frequently way down on her priority list. "Your voice sounds funny. Is something wrong?"

I twirled the phone cord around my finger. "Yeah, sort of. Now, don't get all upset, but I was attacked by a vampire hunter last night."

There was silence for a moment. Then Mar-Mar asked, "You were attacked? A vampire hunter? Are you sure?"

"Of course I'm sure! I know a vampire hunter when I see one. He tried to kill me!"

"Calm down, dear. I need to think for a minute. A vampire hunter in Manhattan is a serious situation. They rarely operate alone. It's never a random event. How did they find you? I need you to tell me what happened. From the beginning. Where were you? What time was it?" She had begun to sound less like my mother and more like a police investigator.

I answered her questions. She grilled me about what he looked like, if he was alone, and if I had been followed previously. She never once asked if I was okay. But she did throw out one final zinger: "The last time we had vampire hunters in New York, that boy you were involved with—you know who I mean—brought them here."

"Darius couldn't have had anything to do with this. Why would you even say that? You never liked him, that's all.

He's not in the city. He's not even in the country. He's touring Europe with his rock band." I noticed I was beginning to whine.

I heard something like a snort from the other end of the line. "Are you sure about that?" she asked.

"Yes! No. Okay, I can't be one hundred percent sure. I haven't talked to him since . . . " I hesitated. Did she know Darius had come back to New York looking for me after I started seeing Fitz? " . . . for a long time."

"Well, I wasn't going to say anything to you," my mother said, immediately snagging my total attention. "I heard something from my old friends down in Greenwich Village about Darius DC and the Vampire Project canceling some tour dates and having to refund a pile of money. So maybe he's not in Europe."

My heart started thudding in my chest. "Did . . . did you hear anything else?" I choked out.

"No, of course not. I would tell you if I had."

Sure you would, I thought.

"I might regret saying this," she added, her voice tight, "but you'd better find out where he is. We need to get to the bottom of why you have been targeted by the hunters."

"Okay," I said, immediately thinking about whom to call to get information. Then I said as an afterthought, "Oh, yeah. I wanted to tell you—if I'm a target, maybe I'd better leave town for a while. I was thinking of Texas. I was thinking I could leave tomorrow night. I might drive down. I don't know. Do you think it's a good idea?" I felt unsettled and distracted.

My mother didn't say anything.

"Mar-Mar? Are you there? Do you think it's a good idea?"

"No, Daphne, I do not," she said crisply, then called out to someone else, "I'll be through here in a second. That altar looks great. Get the smudge pots going."

"Why not? Because it was my idea? You always shoot down *my* ideas." I was definitely whining now.

"Stop being juvenile. The fact is, you cannot go anywhere. The Darkwings are being called in for a new mission. I thought J would have contacted you already. You have a meeting about it tonight."

CHAPTER 3

While I waited for J to call, I sat on my high stool at the granite countertop nursing my second cup of black coffee. I finished off the puzzle and went back to thumbing through the *Times*. I spotted an ad for a Juicy Couture terry tennis jacket and pants on sale at Bloomie's, as well as a 7 for All Mankind denim skirt that would be just right for this variable June weather. I was ripping out the advertisement when my home phone finally rang.

As I expected, J was on the line, ordering me in for an emergency meeting. J never asked; he barked out demands. I was to get down to our office in the Flatiron Building at Twenty-third Street by seven, and he did mean *sharp*.

I am *so* not good at following orders. Maybe in reaction to Mar-Mar's controlling hand trying to steer my life at all times, I buck authority as a reflex reaction. So I dug in my heels. Instead of saying, *Aye-aye, sir,* I said in the sweetest voice possible, "I can't get there at seven. I'll try for seven thirty."

J's response had that strangled tone of someone about to blow a gasket. "You are going to *try* to get here? We have a red alert. A national emergency. Drop everything and get your ass here. Now."

"Nope. I can't. Really. See, my mother, *your boss*, also gave me an order. I have to make a few phone calls for her before I leave here tonight. I assume her request is also a matter of national security."

Okay, I was lying again, sort of. I would make a few calls—on my cell on my way over to Bloomie's. The shopping wouldn't take long. What was the harm? Like another half hour was going to make any frigging difference. J obviously took his time before calling me, so I wasn't about to go running because he decided it was now convenient *for him* to hold the meeting.

J missed a few beats before he answered me. He couldn't very well countermand Mar-Mar's order, so he had to concede the point. "Roger. Finish up what you need to. Get down here as soon as you can. Remember," he growled, "early is on time. On time is late. I can't hold the meeting for you more than fifteen minutes."

"Well, you just do what you have to do," I said. I hung up before he started yelling. He was probably ten shades of purple. I enjoyed yanking his chain.

Benny called next, canceling our shopping, her voice high and twittering, excited at being called back to work. I didn't tell her of my small rebellion against J, or my plans to be late. I needed neither her silent disapproval nor a lecture.

Afterward I dressed quickly in cropped yoga pants, cross trainers, and a French terry workout jacket. I slicked my hair back into a tight chignon and secured it with a clip. As I emerged from the elevator into the building's lobby a few minutes later, I noticed that Mickey had created firing points in the lobby. He had brought in a heavy metal desk to replace the fragile French provincial reception table. Strategically placed wing-back chairs covered in silk brocade now provided him with cover should the Black and Tan come bursting through the front doors, guns blazing.

Mickey, gray hair askew under his cap and his shoulders stooped, stood on the far side of the room, absorbed in a conversation about a missing FedEx delivery with the stockbroker who owned the rottweiler in 9B. But as I walked by, the doorman surreptitiously lifted the hem of his uniform jacket to reveal a pistol stuck in the back of his pants. He shot me a quick glance and wink. I gave him a thumbs-up.

I stepped out of the apartment building with caution. I surveyed the street in both directions and watched for movement. I peered at the parked cars, even taking the time to check out a black SUV, the deeply tinted windows of which aroused my suspicions. When I was satisfied that I wasn't under surveillance, I hailed a taxi.

A Yellow Cab with a dent in the rear fender pulled up. I opened the door but didn't enter until I took a careful look at the driver. He was a scrawny black guy with grizzled white hair and a pack of Camel no-filters in his shirt pocket. According to the ID displayed on the dashboard, his name was Myron Jones.

"Where to?" he asked as I ducked in. I told him, and he grunted something unintelligible, picked up a clipboard, wrote down my destination, then started smacking the staticky radio with the flat of his hand as he pulled out into traffic. The announcer's voice was distorted by an occasional pop and hiss, but the cabbie had a Yankees–Red Sox game playing and totally ignored me. All his hostility, homicidal urges, and bad vibes were directed at Boston, which was leading by two at the top of the seventh. That was about as good a guarantee that he wasn't a vampire hunter as I was going to get.

From the gloomy interior of the taxi whose lumpy backseat pinched my butt with its sprung springs, I began making calls. I had a few contacts who might give me some news of Darius, but not many. He was a more experienced spy than I and had managed to hide even the most basic details about his life, including the address of his apartment, the identity of his family, and, of course, the location of his base of operations.

But when I became frantic after Darius was shot in front of my eyes and taken away to some secret hospital somewhere, J, of all people, had an officer from Darius's agency contact me. The guy was pretty decent. Although he never gave me his name, he did give me a contact number to call. Professional courtesy and all that. Later, when Darius and I reconciled and were again doing the horizontal rumba every night, I snooped through his stuff after he dropped into a postcoital sleep. His wallet held the numbers for his tour manager, PR guy, and what I discovered when I dialed was his bass player's mother out in Jersey.

Am I proud that I went through his pockets while he snoozed? Sure as shit I am. I never would have found out that the band's singer, a curly-haired, tattooed hussy named Julie, was also a spy and Darius's ex-girlfriend if I hadn't poked around. Fool me once, shame on you. Fool me twice? That's not going to happen. I'm not a trusting person. If I were I would have been killed centuries ago. Bottom line, I found whatever scraps of information I could and I kept them to use when I needed to. Now I did.

Consequently, as Mar-Mar suggested, I made inquiries. I discovered that after the band played a gig in Hamburg, Germany, Darius announced to his entourage that he was suffering from exhaustion and was worried about damaging his vocal cords. He canceled the rest of the Germany dates and said he was taking some R & R. The tour manager had a vague idea that Darius might be in Turkey. He overheard Darius asking about renting a villa in Bodrum. Evidently Julie also suffered from exhaustion, since both she and Darius packed their bags and drove off together in a white Mercedes. I felt my face setting in hard lines as I listened to that bit of news.

By the time the cab pulled up in front of Bloomingdale's, I had determined that nobody really knew where either Darius or Julie had gone. Nobody knew when they were coming back. Nobody had heard from them for nearly three weeks. Everybody I spoke to was aware of Darius's depression after our breakup and his strong feelings for me. Everybody kept assuring me that his departure with Julie wasn't what it looked like: He was *not* sleeping with her. Yeah, right. And the pope wasn't Catholic.

I turned rigid from head to toe when I thought about that woman. The murderous little bitch had tried to kill me twice, and those attacks had gotten fobbed off as misunderstandings. The official explanation that Mar-Mar passed on to me was that Julie didn't know I was a fellow spy. She was an experienced, highly regarded operative. She was invaluable to her agency. Anybody could make a mistake. She didn't even get a slap on the wrist.

I sometimes dreamed of meeting her one-on-one in a dark alley. I didn't want to kill her. I just wanted to have it out with her fair and square.

Now, after paying the cabbie and before heading through the doors into the department store, I made one last call to a service I used. I requested a trace of activity on Darius's credit cards (of course I had lifted the numbers from them) and asked for a search of the airlines to see if he and/or Julie had taken a commercial airline out of Germany. If they had traveled by military transport, I'd be out of luck.

I sure didn't buy Darius's exhaustion story. I didn't know what he and Julie were doing, but the thought of them being together landed like a kick to my solar plexus. I couldn't get my breath. When I did finally gulp in a lungful of air, I wanted to strike out with my fists at anyone or anything until the hurting inside me stopped. Since knocking down the nearest passerby would have been stupid, I sublimated and looked around for a shopping target I could attack with a vengeance.

I ignored the perfume counters. I forgot about clearance sales. I headed for the escalators and zeroed in on the latest designer collections. I stepped out onto the floor, my eyes bright, my blood high. I saw women bunched up three deep around a rack of cocktail dresses.

I didn't hesitate. I ran over, waded into the crowd, and viciously snatched an embroidered halter dress by Mandalay off the rack, stopping the reaching hand of another shopper with a malicious glare and a body block. The dress was a showstopper: backless with a plunging V neckline and a killer rhinestone inset in the empire waist. Fifteen hundred bucks for a dress I might never get a chance to wear might sound like a shameful indulgence. Not so. Emotionally I needed this dress, and I needed it right now.

I followed up my dress purchase with shoes and a clutch purse. By the time I finished I had gone well beyond the estimated time of arrival I had envisioned earlier. A niggling of guilt started moving around in my brain. I shifted my packages to one hand and hailed a cab. I got in, sighed deeply, and closed my eyes. Why couldn't I be all bad or all good and not have to cope with this gray interior landscape of indecision that seemed to lead me to nowhere but trouble?

Fifteen minutes later I finally pushed through the door leading to the Darkwings' office on the third floor of the old Flatiron Building. Ornate gold lettering spelled out ABC MEDIA, INC., A HARVARD YARD CORPORATION on the frosted glass. The door was old, the lock outdated. No one would think that spies—vampire spies, at that—were meeting behind it.

Inside, low-wattage bulbs left the familiar conference room in shadows. Nevertheless I could clearly see J's scowl. Wearing his class A dress uniform garnished above the heart with row after row of fruit salad, he stood ramrod straight at the head of the long rectangular table. To me he always looked as if he had a poker up his ass. Tonight his lips pressed together so tightly they were white. His eyes shone like shiny blue marbles, cold and angry, as he watched me enter.

"Agent Urban," he snapped. "I trust you completed your *phone calls.*" He gave a baleful look at the three Bloomingdale's Big Brown Bags in my hands.

My other teammates—moody Irish dancer Cormac and burly biker Rogue, good-natured Benny and scholarly Audrey—sat two and two, divided by gender, on either side of the table. They all stared at me without smiling. I felt a frisson of shame at my selfishness for keeping them waiting. Benny, who had after all canceled her shopping to make sure she arrived at the meeting on time, appeared especially peeved.

I pasted on a smile. I said to J, "Yes, sir, mission accomplished." I flopped into the seat next to Benny and hissed at her, "These are *returns.* I thought I might get a chance to take them back after the meeting."

She shook her head and rolled her eyes. Then she put her lips, bright red with lipstick, close to my ear. "That is so lame."

I had seen Benny and Audrey on a regular basis since our last mission, but I hadn't talked with Cormac O'Reilly since the party that I had thrown about a month ago in lieu of what was supposed to be my wedding reception.

My eyebrows rose in surprise as I took in his altered persona. Cormac had been a longtime Broadway hoofer who spent years in the chorus line of *Cats.* He usually favored tight shirts and Italian shoes and a man-purse, and sometimes he penciled on eyeliner.

No more. A few days of unshaved stubble darkened his cheeks. He wore a black horsehide biker jacket despite its being June. A T-shirt with the neck ripped out and black jeans completed his new look—which was a carbon copy of Rogue's, who sat next to him. Imitation is the sincerest form of flattery. Either that or Cormac had a man-sized crush on the big, brutish Rogue.

I put Cormac down a lot. I'm entitled. I've known him for two hundred years. We've moved in the same circles. We've fought over the same lovers. We didn't talk for twenty years after an incident with a gorgeous young boatman in Venice.

My compadre was a complex, difficult, irritating, contradictory vampire whose brooding, fine-featured countenance turned the heads of men and women alike. He didn't turn mine. I knew him too well. But I had to cut my old friend some slack. He and I were kindred spirits when it came to facing an undead eternity, and since we had already lived centuries, we knew better than newbies Benny or Rogue that eternity was a very long time.

I also hadn't seen Rogue, the shaved-headed vampire biker who sported a mashed nose and a rough demeanor, since the night of my party. Truth be told, Rogue had been the cause of my "slip" and my shame. I had cheated on Fitz with this uncouth barbarian. Then when the deed was done, we were both sweaty, and I was feeling rather fine, he had smirked and told me he had seduced me just to prove he could. That pissed me off.

The night of my party I planned my payback—premeditated with malice aforethought. Cormac and all the other guests had departed a little after two in the a.m., but I had encouraged a drunk and randy Rogue to stay on. Then, after hiding his clothes, I had left him naked, unsatisfied, and handcuffed to my bed during the predawn hours.

Rogue had broken the bed's headboard in order to free himself, but my satisfaction had been worth the price of replacing it. I heard from Mickey the doorman that a big, bald guy who had been at my party left the building before daybreak wearing a bath towel around his waist and nothing else. I had declined to offer an explanation, but Mickey laughed and said the way the guy was trying to hide the dangling handcuffs when he borrowed ten bucks for a cab was funny as hell. I gave Mickey a twenty for his trouble and my thanks.

Tonight Rogue kept his face devoid of expression as he noted my entrance. He gave me a curt nod in return for the one I offered him. To me my prank meant we had leveled the playing field. I hoped he looked at it the same way. Bad blood between us would have been unfortunate. I figured we were both professional enough to work together without rancor. At least, I hoped so.

As for Audrey, I couldn't tell what she was thinking. An angular, emaciated vampire of Greek descent, she had until recently worn Coke-bottle-bottom glasses that made her eyes look small and deep set. Last weekend she had had LASIK surgery and thrown away her spectacles.

Now she lifted huge, doelike brown eyes and peered at me myopically, as if I still weren't in focus. I assumed she was preoccupied with her thoughts, not really seeing me at all. Her left wrist was wrapped in a stark white bandage. I thought that was odd. Vampire wounds heal quickly, so this injury had to be severe indeed.

At this point J cleared his throat and his commanding voice broke into my reverie. "Now that Urban has arrived, let's get started. We have a highly unusual situation confronting us." He linked his hands behind his back and aimed his eyes above our heads as he began speaking again. "It's a matter of grave concern to U.S. intelligence, the Joint Chiefs, and to those privy to the situation in the Department of the Navy. We have, in fact, a serious threat to national security." He paused. His eyes flicked uneasily from team member to team member.

"But to be quite frank," he said, "at this point we don't know what we're dealing with."

Excitement poured like quicksilver through my veins. This job gave me a reason to wake up and climb out of that damned coffin every night. I might not have volunteered to become a spy, but I loved it. This was what I lived for: the knowledge that I, along with my friends, had the power to be protectors of the common good, and that I, a vampire created to be bad, could be something more than a despicable pariah and the stuff of nightmares. This had become the basis of my self-worth.

I kicked myself for the stupid one-upmanship I had played with J tonight. Chalk up my foolish behavior to my emotional immaturity. I had been turned into a vampire when I was merely eighteen by the bite of a Gypsy king. Deprived of normal access to maturity, I had lived nearly half a millennium with my hormones raging like an adolescent's and my judgment often marred by teenage rebelliousness.

I wanted to be better than I was. I made a mental note to try harder and to think before I reacted to J. He pushed my buttons, same as my mother did. I was smart enough to see the red flag. I just had to discipline myself to stop, look, and listen.

While I was woolgathering, J passed out the manila folders we always received at the beginning of a new assignment. This time they were so stuffed with paper they were over an inch thick.

Benny, the first to get the folder, opened hers and began reading some of the material inside. She quickly closed it, slapped her hand down on it loudly, and piped up. "J, sugar, can't y'all just spit out what's going on? I ain't too set on reading this here boring stuff about that old navy ship that's been turned into a museum and docked over at the river."

J's body went from stiff to rigid. Calling him, our superior officer, *sugar* no doubt pissed him off, as Benny knew it would. She sometimes acted as ditzy as Marilyn Monroe in the old movie *Some Like It Hot*, but her IQ was in the Mensa range. She had a tongue so sharp it could carve a

Thanksgiving turkey. She had her own issues with J and didn't take orders any better than I did. That's a vampire for you. We don't play well with others.

I took a quick peek in my folder and rifled through the sheets. I estimated at least fifty single-spaced typed pages. From what I glimpsed, the content appeared to be World War II naval history, including scale drawings of an aircraft carrier. It might take an hour to wade through this stuff.

J squared his shoulders, dropped his hands to his sides, and barked out, all military to the core: "The consensus from those higher up is that background data will speed the resolution of this case."

"Well, Lordy, now, doesn't that just take all. I may just be a po' lowly hillbilly from Miz'ora, but in my mind that there *consensus* is jist a pile of cow pucks," the Branson native drawled while tapping her perfectly manicured forefinger on the closed folder. "And, honey-chile, maybe them higher-ups don't know our biker friend Rogue ain't what you call 'print oriented'—no offense, darlin'."

"None taken," Rogue said, and turned to J. "I'd appreciate a verbal rundown."

"Ditto," said carbon-copy Cormac.

We all nodded our heads in agreement, including Audrey, who, with her expertise in New York City history, might already be familiar with some of the information.

I discreetly closed my folder and nobody else opened theirs. Together we stared at our commander. J faced mutiny in the ranks and decided that discretion was the better part of valor, as Falstaff once said. He cleared his throat.

"Simply put, the USS *Intrepid* is missing."

"That so?" Rogue grunted and leaned back in his chair,

stretching his tree-trunk legs under the table, kicking my chair accidentally on purpose.

I ignored him, trying to make sense of J's pronouncement. "Missing?" I asked. "I read in the *Times* that the ship had been moved to be refurbished. Where was it they said it was going? Newport News?"

J nodded. "That much is true. The *Intrepid* was scheduled for renovation. It was heading for Virginia. It never made it. It's gone."

"What do you mean, 'it's gone'?" Benny asked. "Gone where? You can't lose a World War Two aircraft carrier. What is it, as long as a city block?"

J locked his fingers behind his back again, stood square, and answered without consulting his notes. "The USS *Intrepid* weighs twenty-seven thousand one hundred tons. It is eight hundred seventy-two feet long. It took sail with a captain and a skeleton crew under its own power two days ago. The harbormaster and three tugs escorted it out of New York Harbor. The ship set sail on a southern course. It was last sighted off Asbury Park."

"Okay. So what? They can't find it? It must have sunk or something," Rogue said, lacing his fingers over his flat belly.

Audrey hopped in. "Any SOS? What were the weather conditions?"

"No distress signal. Early morning haze. Calm seas," J responded.

"Maybe a rogue wave?" Audrey ventured.

"Not likely. This was a mile or so off the Jersey shore," J responded.

I cut in, impatient, my excitement having ebbed away, feeling let down. "J, what's going on here? The *Intrepid* is missing at sea. How is that a national security problem?

We're talking a creaky sixty-year-old ship that had been turned into a museum for tourists. If it hadn't been, it would have been scuttled anyway. It has no military value. No working ordnance on board, right? It probably leaked like a sieve. It sank. Its wreck will be located by sonar sooner or later. What are we really doing here tonight?"

J shook his head back and forth very slowly. "I hear you, Agent Urban. I repeat, we are here to find the *Intrepid*. It is a matter of national security. I am not at liberty to say more than that at this time. As to its possible sinking—it didn't.

"The ship—which you must understand is a symbol of American military might—*was* seaworthy. It had withstood a torpedo attack and two kamikaze hits by the Japanese in the Pacific. Those attacks didn't sink the *Intrepid*. A massive explosive might send her to the bottom, but nothing less would do it—and there wasn't one. Believe me, all the other scenarios you suggested have been investigated, without positive results."

He took a deep breath and stared each of us in the eye before speaking again.

"We don't know much, but here's what we do know. The ship was spotted off the Jersey shore early Monday morning. Lots of witnesses. Sport fishermen. People on boats in the area. Their stories concur: Mist, haze, fog, or smoke, *something* moved in for a few minutes and obscured the ship. When the air cleared the ship was gone. It had been there. Then it wasn't. The navy tried to raise the captain by ship's radio. No response.

"In addition, the ship was within cell phone range. Efforts were made to phone the crew. No contact could be made with any of the mates aboard. The navy scrambled jets from Long Island. The coast guard arrived on the scene within twenty minutes. They found nothing. No debris. No wreck on the bottom.

"After an official investigation we can positively confirm only one thing: The *Intrepid* is gone. It appears to have vanished into thin air."

Chapter 4

*"I want to know what it says . . . The sea,
Floy, what is it that it keeps on saying?"*

Charles Dickens in *Dombey and Sons*

"Well, my-oh-fucking-my. It's the fucking Philadelphia Experiment all over again." Rogue snorted loudly and sat up, scraping his chair against the floor.

J glared at Rogue, then responded to him, his voice all frost. "That never happened."

"What never happened? What are y'all talking about?" Benny leaned forward, unable to repress the smile playing on her lips as she watched both men. She enjoyed what she saw: two alpha males trying to piss on the same tree.

Rogue turned his shaved head toward J, his chin thrust out. "Maybe it didn't happen and maybe it did. But we should look at it. Put the information out. What's the problem with that?"

"Waste of time," J said dismissively.

"I think the gentleman doth protest too much," Cormac broke in, prissy even in his biker garb. "I would like to make a motion: Let Rogue talk. Any seconds?"

"I second the motion," Benny chirped.

J slammed the flat of his palm on the table. "Enough! We

don't vote in this room. I am in command. Not Rogue. Not any of you. So listen up. The Philadelphia Experiment is bogus. No records have ever been located to confirm the event or to confirm the navy's interest in such an experiment."

"Which was . . . ?" Benny asked.

J let out an exasperated sigh. He had backed himself into a corner and had to answer. "In the fall of 1943 the battleship USS *Eldridge* supposedly was made invisible and teleported from its berth at the Philadelphia Naval Shipyards to Norfolk, Virginia. Supposedly members of the crew of the civilian merchant ship the SS *Andrew Furuseth* witnessed the *Eldridge* materialize in Norfolk. I say *supposedly* because no records exist confirming that the *Eldridge* had ever docked in Philadelphia or that the *Furuseth* ever docked in Norfolk. The whole thing is a myth."

Rogue scoffed. "Sure it is. 'Cause the *government* says it is. And we know the ships were never in either place 'cause the *government* says there are no records of it. Right?"

"That is correct." J nodded.

Rogue insolently leaned back in his chair again, pulled a toothpick from his shirt pocket, and stuck it in his mouth. He cocked an eyebrow at our "commander." The pissing contest continued. "Well, now, *sir*, the government *never* lies or destroys records, does it?"

Rogue crossed his arms across his chest and looked at Benny. "What J is leaving out, little lady, are a few known facts. One: Albert Einstein was a consultant with the navy's Bureau of Ordnance at that time.

"Two: A lot of people knew they were messing around with the *Eldridge*, installing cables, doing *something*. Sure, when people asked, the navy explained away eyewitness accounts by saying they were just degaussing the ship, in other words, putting electrical cables around a ship's hull to cancel out its magnetic field. That made it 'invisible' to detecting devices. People must be confused, that's all, they said.

"Three: A witness from the merchant ship *Furuseth*, a guy named Allen or Allende, talked to the media. The navy retaliated. Their top brass told the media Allen was a crank or a crackpot. Allen then conveniently committed suicide. Some say he was murdered.

"Four: A reputable scientist has since demonstrated that an electronic field could create a mirage effect of invisibility by refracting light. Course, he only did it with a spool of thread, not a battleship. But he showed it could be done, you know?

"You ask me? The whole thing reeks of cover-up. Always has."

While Rogue talked, J's color was rising, crawling like a wine stain up his neck, suffusing his face with an ugly, dark blush. The man was a coronary waiting to happen.

"Anyways," Rogue continued while he wiggled the toothpick up and down between his teeth, "now here's the *Intrepid*, another World War Two military vessel on its way to Norfolk, vanishing into thin air. Come on. You really believe in coincidence?"

"This discussion is over," J interrupted. "You want to discuss UFOs and nonsense like this, tune in to late-night radio and listen to Art Bell. The government did not make the *Intrepid* vanish, and that's that."

"Shit, J," Rogue said, nonplussed, giving a clenched-teeth grin. "I'm not saying the government's behind the *Intrepid* vanishing. I'm just saying it probably has the technology to do it—and now maybe somebody else does too."

Silence descended on the room. Then Audrey, paying some attention at last, came down on J's side of things. "I don't agree with you, Rogue. It's not the same situation at all. That old World War Two tale? People love conspiracy theories. UFOs. Alien abductions. Men in black—"

"But there are men in black," I interjected in a soft voice.

Audrey shot me a quizzical glance. "Whatever. I think we have to consider some other cause," she insisted.

Benny agreed. "Yeah, Rogue, honey. That was a real nice story, but it's what? Over sixty years old. Besides, that there *Eldridge* didn't just disappear. It moved. And that teleportation stuff is too woo-woo."

I drew my index finger in lazy circles on the tabletop while I listened. I didn't look up as I began to speak softly, as if I were thinking out loud, which I was. "Woo-woo? The teleportation stuff, yeah. Not the rest of it, you know." I raised my eyes and searched the faces of my colleagues before letting my gaze rest on J's grim face while my brain kept spinning out ideas.

I thought that the Philadelphia Experiment could be a myth. That didn't mean it was completely bogus. Myths allowed us to accept events or ideas we couldn't explain, events that challenged the status quo, that didn't fit into our worldview. Hey, I was a myth. All vampires were. But here I was, flesh and blood and real.

I guessed everybody was waiting for me to speak, so I did. "Rogue has a point," I said to J at last. "He gave us a theory for how the ship vanished. Maybe somebody has the technology to make it become, for all intents and purposes, invisible. Maybe the ship was simply camouflaged and moved. I'm not sure it's important to know *how* they did it. What is essential is to find out *who* did it and *why* they did it. We need to figure out *cui bono*—who benefits? And where in the world one hell of a big ship is right now."

J, honest to God, didn't seem to know what to tell us at this point. That alone was enough to make me suspicious about the whole assignment. The vanishing ship was weird. Our involvement was weirder.

And therein, my dear, lies the rub, as Shakespeare once told my mother. Someday some historian with an open mind—a contradiction in terms—should take a new look into the identity of the dark lady of Willy's sonnets. That loose thought flitted through my undisciplined mind before I forced myself to focus on the here and now. And the here and now was J.

At the moment I was staring at him. He bent down to pick up an attaché case and pretended not to notice me. I knew he did, though, because whenever I irritated him a muscle in his jaw started to jump. I watched it doing a tap dance.

J put the attaché case on the table and clicked it open as he told the Darkwings without looking at any of us to check back here tomorrow. He'd contact us if any information came in later tonight. Meanwhile we should—he shrugged at that point and dropped papers into the case—investigate, he added.

The Darkwings, including me, stood up. We had formed a habit of getting together after meetings. Without saying so, we knew we'd talk amongst ourselves downstairs, out in the street, where no listening devices could pick up our conversation. Yeah, we were paranoid. Even paranoiacs have enemies.

Besides, none of us liked the office. None of us ever used our cubicles or computers. We gathered there to get our assignments. It was a rendezvous point. But it wasn't ours. It wasn't anybody's. No pictures hung on the walls. No filing cabinets bulged with records. The dingy meeting room with its faded ocher walls and grime-coated windows appeared to be an anonymous place, as impersonal as a post office box.

Almost. For me the office had one singular characteristic: It contained J. He was a blank slate of a man, a person who had never revealed his name, address, past, or personal life. He showed us a very narrow band in the spectrum of his existence, yet some things couldn't be hidden. From the start he acted as if he hated me. *Acted* is the operative word. He might not like me, but he did desire me; I was sure of it.

I had read his jealousy of Darius della Chiesa in every word he said about my ex-boyfriend. Then, when I became engaged to St. Julien Fitzmaurice, he had given me a direct order *not* to marry Fitz. I awakened J's rage—and his lust. Don't tell me I'm wrong. A woman knows when a man wants her, even if he denies it to the world—and himself.

Tonight I had pissed J off once more. It was always so easy. I ignited his emotions like a match to dynamite. Now I intended to play with fire.

The new best buds, Rogue and Cormac, were already out the door. Audrey and Benny were coming around the table and walking past me. I reached out, tugged at Benny's arm, and whispered, "I want to talk to J. I'll catch up with you downstairs. Five minutes, tops."

Benny gave me a look that clearly said, *Don't do anything stupid,* and whispered back, "Sure."

I looked over at J. He flicked his eyes away but not fast enough. He had been watching me. He started closing the briefcase. I walked over to him.

"I want to apologize," I said.

His head snapped up. "What do you really want?" he asked.

"No, seriously. I was out of line tonight. No excuses. It won't happen again; that's all."

J stared at me, his face set hard. "Fine."

"And I'd like to ask you something."

His eyes narrowed ever so slightly. "What?"

"Why are the Darkwings in this? I can't figure it out. What are we supposed to be doing?"

"Finding the *Intrepid*," J shot back.

"No," I said, shaking my head. "No. I don't think that's it. What's the real link? To us, I mean."

J avoided my eyes then, so I moved a little closer to him, forcing him to either move back, which he didn't do, or to look at me. Which he did. "I don't know," he answered.

I leaned just the smallest bit toward him, and suddenly I felt his body heat. I smelled the musky male scent of him. "Guess," I said in a low voice.

His eyes held me fast. Now we were opposite poles of a magnet, and the pull drawing us together was becoming irresistible. "I don't know," he said very slowly. "Why don't you ask your mother if you want some answers?"

The bitterness was there. I heard it. J didn't like Marozia's manipulations any more than I did; I would bet on it. "Believe me, J," I said, my voice intimate and the words themselves just a small part of the game we were suddenly playing. "I'd be the last to know. That's how it is with her."

His breath, lightly scented with menthol and tobacco, moved the air around my face. "Like I said, Agent Urban, I don't know why the Darkwings were brought into this." I watched his eyes move to my lips ever so briefly before returning to my eyes. Did he want to kiss me, or was he thinking about how close he once came to my biting him?

We stood there without speaking for a long minute, both breathing a little harder than we had been. I thought about making the first move, about kissing him. It would have been so easy. But J was a man obsessed with control. Sex would be all about domination—either his or mine. I decided to piss him off instead.

"I have another question," I said.

"Which is?" he asked.

"Have your people heard anything about Darius?"

A door slammed between us. "*I* haven't heard anything," he said, then moved away and reached over to pick up his briefcase.

"Hey, I didn't ask it to piss you off. I need to know. It's not anything personal; it's business."

J shot me a cold look. "Your business is being a spy. And that's my business. So talk. Why are you asking about della Chiesa?"

"I don't have anything solid, J. He left Germany, maybe for Turkey . . ." I hesitated. How much could I leave out? I wondered. "He seems to have disappeared. Then last night I was attacked on the street by vampire hunters. If they're connected to him in any way—either because he sent them or because they're looking for him through me—I need to know."

J's face was different when he looked at me then. "I'll make inquiries. I'll tell you what I find out." He just looked at me for a moment. "Daphne . . ."

"What?"

I didn't expect it when J grabbed my arm with his free hand and pulled me to him so tightly that his medals pressed into my breast. His lips were very close to mine. "Don't play with this. If he contacts you, tell me. Don't trust him. I told you that before. Listen to me this time. Don't trust him."

Then J released me, turned very quickly, went into his office, and shut the door. I stood there, shaken and not knowing quite what to think, except I knew for sure that I didn't have the whole story. Not about the *Intrepid*. And not about Darius della Chiesa.

Downstairs, out on the sidewalk, the soft air of the June night caressed my face. Four vampires waited for me, standing close together, divided two by two. I was the fifth wheel, the odd man out. It had never been more obvious than now, when I, my only companions the Bloomingdale's shopping bags drooping from my hands, strolled over to join them.

"Guess what Macky did," Benny said.

I looked over at my longtime friend Cormac. As much of a chameleon as Johnny Depp, he wore his new persona well. His hair was long, his body wiry, his stance duplicating Rogue's. Cormac was the smaller, darker shadow of the bigger man, but not fey, not insubstantial. He was a vampire. He was dangerous all the time. Now, in his black leather biker clothes, he allowed the world to see something of the seductiveness of our evil, the turn-on of our dark side. I raised my eyebrows.

" 'Macky' did *something*? No, don't tell me. I want to guess. Oh, I know. He got a tattoo. Forearm? Shoulder? Or do you have to drop your pants to show us?"

Cormac scowled at me.

"You're not even close," Benny said. "Tell her, Macky."

"Yes, tell me. Really, inquiring minds want to know."

"I got a bike," Cormac said.

"A bike?" I echoed. I didn't get it. Had Cormac decided to do the Tour de France or something?

"A *motorcycle*. Come on; I'll show you." He went back to the Flatiron Building and pushed through the entrance door.

All of us followed, including Rogue, who had thrown down his cigarette and ground it out with his boot heel first.

Behind a frosted-glass door at the back of the lobby, parked on the granite floor, were two Harley-Davidsons, one black with chrome fenders, one all white.

"This one's mine." Cormac walked over and straddled the white bike.

"They look old," I said, not knowing what to say.

Rogue hooted at my ignorance. "They're classic bikes. Cormac has a 1940 knucklehead with a suicide shift. Mine's a 1954 panhead."

I stood there clutching my Bloomingdale's bags like a suburban matron and tried to sound enthusiastic. "Uh, cool."

Benny squealed. "Daph! They're worth tens of thousands of dollars! Don't you think they're beautiful?"

"Mine will be," Cormac said, "when I get it repainted. It was a police bike; that's why it's white. All stock. Rare as hell."

Rogue had already pushed his bike through the doors and into the lobby. He got on. Audrey climbed behind him, riding bitch. He gave it a kick start, and the roar of the engine hurt my ears.

"I'm riding with Cormac," Benny yelled over the noise. Cormac had more trouble pushing his bike than Rogue, but he got himself set, and Benny mounted his bike to sit behind him.

"Open the front doors for us," Audrey yelled to me as she

put one hand on Rogue's shoulder and pointed to the Fifth Avenue entrance with the other.

I did, propping open one side of the double doors and holding the other side wide with my shoulder to give both bikes easy passage through them. Rogue and Audrey moved by me and drove down the sidewalk until they reached a driveway cutting through the curb onto the street.

Cormac was having a little trouble getting his bike to start. I guessed the "suicide shift" was the problem. Benny sat perched behind him, grinning. I hoped he didn't dump her into the street once they started down the avenue.

"I thought we were going to talk?" I said to her.

"We are." Just then Cormac got the engine going and they headed out the door. Benny turned her head back toward me and yelled to me over the engine's roar, "Take a cab and meet us over at Charlie's Harley Hangout. You remember where it is, right?"

I remembered, all right. The seedy biker's bar on West Street was where I nearly got my head busted the night I first met Rogue.

Charlie's Harley Hangout, frequented by vampire bikers and just plain criminals, was no place to go carrying three big shopping bags. None of the clientele shopped at Bloomingdale's; most of them had never even heard of it, I bet. It was bad enough I was wearing yoga pants, for Pete's sake. I certainly wouldn't fit in. I decided to return upstairs to the office, leave my stuff by my computer, and return for it later.

The elevator doors slid open on the third floor. All lights had been extinguished. The hallway had become a dark tunnel. I exited warily and made my way on silent feet through the murky gloom. At the farthest end of the corridor I reached the office door.

Benny, Cormac, and I—the original Team Darkwing—had been "hired," if that's the right word for being given the choice to work for the U.S. government or be killed, at the same time. We had each been assigned a tiny office and a computer. We had been issued genuine government IDs stating that we worked for the Department of the Interior. We received a biweekly paycheck. We even had a TSP, the government's pension plan. But we had never been issued keys to "our" office.

I expected the door to be locked. It was. I pulled out the set of lock picks that lay among my other important "stuff" in the bottom of the well-worn Louis Vuitton leather backpack I carried everywhere.

With practiced movements I fiddled with the old lock. It was a lead-pipe cinch. Seconds later the doorknob turned easily.

I stepped into the shadowy conference room, the one we had left just minutes earlier. Looking bleak and deserted, it was illuminated only by the weak light of the city leaking through the tall windows.

"J?" I called out. "You still here?"

No one answered.

I walked past the conference table where we had lately been sitting and opened the door into the small side room that served as my office. Bare of any personal items, since I had never brought any here, my desk sat forlornly in the space. I looked at it, feeling a little puzzled. The computer that had been on the desk was gone. Then I mentally shrugged. I figured that since I never used it, it had been removed. I pulled out the desk chair and stowed my shopping bags way under the desk, out of sight. The cleaning staff vacuuming the floors might see them, but I doubted it. Why would they bother to clean my office when I was never there to get it dirty?

I went back into the conference room. It dawned on me that it too looked emptier than it usually did. I glanced around. The old card table with the coffeemaker and Styrofoam cups that usually sat in one corner was gone. Had it been there earlier? I couldn't say for sure.

I was about to leave and catch up with the others when a thought popped into my mind and I stopped. *Why not?* I reasoned as I made a U-turn and headed for J's office. I figured I'd snoop a little. Maybe I'd find out something about him. Like his name.

I knocked on the door first. No one answered. I tried the knob. It was unlocked. Good. I didn't have to break and enter.

"J?" I called out again as I pushed it open.

No answer.

I strode in, planning to search the drawers of his desk. I halted in my tracks. With windows on each side of the triangular-shaped room letting in the light from the street, the interior was clearly visible. But I couldn't believe what I saw. I blinked.

There was no desk. No chair. No wastebasket. None of the furnishings I had seen the last time I was there remained. In fact, there was nothing in the room. Nothing at all.

CHAPTER 5

"Know thyself."

—Socrates

Back on the street I pondered what I had discovered. Did J leave the building by some secret route? Or was he still there, on another floor, with others unknown to us? After all, someone—or more likely a whole crew of technicians—must have scurried into the office after our departure, removing any sign that ABC Media was occupied and erasing any evidence that we Darkwings existed. Our entire enterprise was all smoke and mirrors—lies and deceptions. I should have expected no less.

I smiled with no joy at the contradictions of my existence. I was not to trust Darius, according to J, but I certainly could not trust J. I could not trust my own mother. I wanted to trust my fellow Darkwings, but putting any faith at all in Rogue, at least, was beyond me. My best option was to trust no one.

Out here in the open my nerves jangled, and my fight-or-flight reflex had me wound tighter than a clock. As I was a creature of the night, it was not the lateness of the hour that disturbed me. It was the fact that I had been targeted, but by whom I didn't know. My encounter with the vampire hunter had affected me more deeply than I wanted to admit.

I could not blame the Roman Catholic Church and its sinister minions in Opus Dei for hunting vampires. They saw us as creatures of darkness, aligned with the devil. In truth I was a demon only metaphorically. My sole connection to Lucifer was my guess that we vampires were perhaps dark angels cast out of heaven, just as that fallen archangel had been. But I knew I was a monster—a thing phantasmagoric and terrifying.

Yet many creatures who walk this earth are monsters. Most are human; a very few are not. I was not. I believed, however, that I had a right to exist. Although I was inhuman, I did possess a heart. And I did have a soul, even if it was one deeply stained and terribly defiled.

I shook my head at the irony of my life. It is easy for those born good to be good. For me, transformed into a vampire, a thing innately bad, it was difficult. Yet I strove to be principled. I tried for goodness, despite my nature. You must believe me: I tried.

It was not easy for me, and sometimes I failed—terribly, tragically. Tonight, as on all nights, the darkness without and within concealed the deadly impulses that I did not want, but that to my lasting sorrow I so undeniably had. They raged up in me now as I spotted a lone figure standing not fifty feet away on the corner of Twenty-third Street and Broadway.

A man, appearing to be so young that he was more a boy than man, dallied there. He seemed to be in no hurry to either hail a cab or cross with the changing traffic light. He pulled a cigarette pack out of his shirt pocket. He lit it with a lazy motion, then drew in deeply so the tip glowed red. He exhaled slowly, the smoke trailing upward in the windless night. He appeared engrossed in the enjoyment of smoking, unaware or uncaring of all else.

Desire surged through me. How simple it would be to approach him. He would see only a pretty woman coming his way, not a threat, not a reason to feel the dread he should when a vampire came for his blood.

As I watched him, he raised his head and saw me. My heart lurched. My body urged me to go now, quickly, and take him. But my mind and my scruples stopped me. I looked away and forced myself to step toward the street to hail a cab. The young man's luck held that night. A taxi pulled over. I got in and gave the driver the address of the biker bar on West Street.

As the cab accelerated and began its journey down the avenue, I turned my head and glanced through the back window. The young man was gone. Only then did I feel a frisson of fear. I had been watching him, but had he been there, at that time and place, for the purpose of watching me? Had he been spying on me? Was he an agent of Opus Dei: a vampire hunter trained to assassinate us? Or was he one of J's men, for as I just said, there was no trust in our business, and of all the Darkwings I believed J, because I resisted him, trusted me the least.

Now, a solitary vampire making my peripatetic way through the streets of New York, I promised myself to be vigilant. I did not intend to die with a wooden stake through my inhuman, but so often broken, heart.

When I alighted from the cab on West Street, dampness enveloped me. The smell of rot and mud infused the air. I heard water slapping the pier on the other side of the ugly scar of roadway that rims this side of Manhattan. I, true to my vow, carefully surveyed my surroundings, getting ready if necessary to fight for my life.

Nothing living moved. I saw only the blank, sightless windows above me and the dull brick walls of the aging tenements that lined the block. A mist had risen from the river and crept on silent feet along the ground. It crawled up the buildings and swirled around my ankles. This was a night for foul things, for mischief makers, and for death to roam. After all, I was here, was I not?

I crossed the sidewalk and mounted the few stairs leading to the battered, gouged door of Charlie's Harley Hangout. I pounded hard with my fist. After a moment the door opened a few inches. Eyes filled with suspicion peered out at me. Then the door swung wide and a bald man with a soft, wide belly said, "Your friends are sitting in the back." He shut the door behind me and walked away.

I stepped into the room; cigarette smoke had turned the air a hazy blue. My eyes burned. The voice of Stevie Ray Vaughan wailed over the sound system about being a good Texan. I wished I were someplace else.

Vampire males filled nearly every table. Their distinct odor made me stiffen with distaste. I detected their breath, tainted with blood, and the muskiness of their animal spoor. Those who looked up at my entrance viewed me with a predatory interest, their eyes reflecting gold like a cat's, their pupils as dark as the black realms of hell.

These creatures were my kind, but they were not what I wanted to be.

I gathered my courage and started toward the horseshoe-shaped bar, trying to avoid contact with any of these fiends. Nevertheless a hand brushed my thigh as I threaded my way through the closely arranged tables. I reacted and turned angrily to face the intruder. A good-looking biker wearing cowboy boots and a Stetson winked a green eye at me.

I flipped him the bird and he laughed.

You and me, he mouthed.

"In your dreams," I snapped, and continued on.

A skinny woman with pale blond hair and purple smudges under her eyes tended bar. "Don't mind Sam none," she said, her accent rich with a Western tang. "He's a good guy when he's sober. Course, that's none too often," she added, then asked, "What'll you have?"

"A Virgin Mary. I need a clear head."

"I hear you," she said, and pulled a bottle of Bloody Mary mix from the refrigerator under the bar.

"I remember you." She set the drink down in front of me and I handed her a ten. "Don't often see a woman who can fight like that," she said, smiling.

I smiled back. "Well, I was in a bit of a bad mood that night, and getting hit with a chair pissed me off."

"Only a damned fool would mess with you again real quick. You take care, you hear?" she said as I walked away, looking around for my friends.

My four teammates had an empty chair waiting for me. It made me feel a little better, a little less lonely.

"How was your bike ride?" I asked as I moved the chair over next to Benny.

She held up her arm, revealing a long tear in her jean jacket. "Little spill going across Fourteenth Street," she said. "Otherwise it was almost like flying. I'm thinking about getting a Harley of my own."

"Probably safer than riding with Cormac," I muttered, which earned me a dirty look from him. I flipped my chair around to sit on it backward, straddling it with my legs and leaning my arms on the back. The ambience of the place kicked my adrenaline up a notch, and this position made it easier to move fast if I had to.

The big bulk of Rogue filled the chair across from mine. Audrey sat tight against him. I noticed her bandaged wrist again and nodded toward it. "What happened?"

"You know the competition we hold at the vampire club every night?"

I did know. Audrey spent her off hours at a funky club on lower Second Avenue called Lucifer's Laundromat. Part of New York's vampire underworld, a demimonde of debauchery, the patrons of this club specialized in what they called "blood sports"—an organized nightly hunt, not for foxes, but for young, fresh victims with smooth, white necks and rich, red blood.

Audrey held up her wounded arm. "It was the oddest thing. I went out with my team, the Chasers, the way I always do. I swooped down on a big guy on West Eighth Street. He pulled out what I thought was a knife. Turned out to be a wooden stake. I blocked the blow, but it penetrated my wrist right into the bone."

All of us stared at her. I frowned. "Was it a vampire hunter?"

Surprise crossed Audrey's face. "No. I don't think so. Not that I ever encountered one. I never have. I mean, if this guy was a vampire hunter, he wasn't after any of us at the Laundromat. He was just walking down the block. I think he was simply a weirdo. It was a fluke he had a stake on him."

Benny was looking at me, a question in her eyes. Did she think I should tell the others I was attacked? I gave my head a little shake no in her direction, keeping it so subtle that I hoped nobody else would notice it. I remembered what Mar-

Mar had said—that a vampire attack was never a random event. Of course, this hadn't been an attack by a vampire hunter. If anything it was Audrey's attack *on* some guy who carried a wooden stake around with him. Yet it seemed too coincidental to be a freak accident.

I thought for a moment, then said, "He could be one of those humans who take us seriously. You know, they carry crucifixes in their pockets and wear garlic around their necks. That's why he had a stake on him. If he was a hunter, it was really bad luck to choose him, or . . . "

"Or what?" Audrey said.

"I don't know. Just a thought. Maybe the hunters have heard about the human capturing contest you and your friends run nightly at Lucifer's Laundromat. They could be searching the area for you."

Audrey pulled a face, obviously not agreeing. "Oh, come on. How likely is that? We vampires keep our game really quiet, and the humans don't remember what happened when they wake up the next day. You're just being paranoid. Truly I think the guy was one of the world's crazies. They all seem to end up down in the Village. He probably thinks carrying metal will attract radio waves or something."

"You'd better keep your eyes open," Rogue said, "but I agree. It was a random thing."

Benny gave my shin a hard kick with her Manolos. I ignored her. If I said anything now, Audrey would tell everybody in the club there were vampire hunters in New York. Before long panic would set in. Vampires would be fleeing the city. I felt it would be premature to say anything. The vampire hunter the other night had targeted me and me alone. If I found out otherwise, I'd warn the others.

But Benny was talking now. Was she going to rat me out?

"Audrey, can I ask y'all something?" she said, a furrow between her brows.

"Sure," Audrey answered.

"Was Martin there last night?" Benny's current heartthrob usually led the Chasers.

"No, he wasn't. I thought maybe he was with you, to tell the truth. He called in and left a message with the bartender that he wasn't coming."

"Oh," Benny said, and got very quiet.

Rogue picked up his bottle of beer and chugged it. Benny's love life interested him not at all. He took the bottle from his lips, belched loudly, and said, "So what the fuck was that meeting with J about?"

Nobody said anything. Finally I spoke. "Not what it seems to be, that's for sure. Something doesn't sit right."

"Yeah, that's what I think too," he said, finishing up the last of his beer and whacking the empty bottle onto the table. "So do we go looking for this ghost ship or what?"

I didn't answer right away, but I looked back at him. He was so much smarter than he played. He also knew a lot more about the spy game than he let on, having worked for the CIA in the past. Finally I said, holding his dark, hard eyes with mine, "I think we go looking for the ship and turn up whatever it is they really want us to find."

"Now y'all are taking turns I don't rightly follow," Benny said. "Spit it out plain and simple, will you?"

"I just meant that they don't need *us* to find a missing ship. I'm sure the navy put their own intelligence people on it the minute it happened. But they already know we're connected to this somehow."

"How?" Benny asked, her eyes widening.

I shrugged.

Rogue said, "I sure as shit don't know, but I'd rather find out before it comes up and bites us in the ass."

Cormac had a tall draft beer in front of him. He moved his fingers up and down the condensed moisture on the outside of the glass. "Any suggestions on how we do that?" he asked.

"Gather intelligence." Audrey, the shy, quiet one of us, stated the obvious. "I'll fool around on my computer later. See if anything else strange has happened lately. Anything that might connect the dots from the *Intrepid* to us. And I'll check out the technology Rogue mentioned and do some research on military cloaking devices."

"Good idea," I said. "And I'm thinking of gathering some humint. You game, Benny, or are you busy after this?"

She paused, then said, "I want to go someplace later. But I've got some time. Who did you have in mind to talk to, or can I guess?"

I smiled at her. "Guess."

"Our favorite NYPD police lieutenant?"

"Right the first time."

Her sudden laughter rang out like silver bells. "We sure do make him as miserable as a hound dog tied out in the rain, now, don't we?"

"How about you boys?" I asked. "What are your plans?"

"Well, now," Rogue said. "I think we can find something to do tonight. We didn't come to this here bar down at the piers by accident."

I had sold him short again. I was beginning to realize that no matter how he looked, Rogue acted deliberately. In my estimation he went up from the level of something that crawled out from beneath a rock to just a slimy son of a bitch. He seemed to read my thoughts.

"You're not better than me, you know," he said to me in a low voice. "We proved that not so long ago."

My mouth got hard. I glared at him. I was so annoyed, I didn't notice somebody behind me until I felt a hand slide down my back with too much familiarity. I didn't even look to see who it was. I got up, whirled around, and sent a right cross into a jaw.

Sam, the cowboy biker with green eyes, went down like a toppled tree into a drinker with a handlebar mustache at the next table. Dandy Dan the mustache man jumped up and started throwing a punch in my direction. A shadow came between it and me, and the blow bounced off of Rogue's sleeve.

But a chain reaction had started. The brawl rippled out across the room. Screams and yells ricocheted off the walls. The canned music over the sound system changed to a fast zydeco, which egged everybody on.

Out of the corner of my eye I saw Audrey like a wild-haired Valkyrie, standing on the table swinging a chair, her eyes gone a little crazy. Benny and Cormac had chosen to get out of Dodge and were heading for the exit. I landed a kick in the solar plexus of some dumbass wearing a backward baseball cap, and he bent over double. Then I launched myself onto the back of the yahoo fighting with Rogue.

His opponent now occupied, Rogue took the opportunity to grab Audrey by the waist while he dodged her chair and dragged her off the table. As he carried her past me he took my arm in an iron grip.

"Hey!" I yelled, and let go of the neck of the guy I was trying to choke.

"Time to go, Rambo," he yelled, and gave me a mighty heave, literally tossing me toward the front of the room. I didn't need to be told twice. I gained my footing and sprinted for the door.

When we got outside the streets had become blanketed in a dense fog. Benny and Cormac waited there until they saw us emerge. They took off down the block. We followed on their heels until all of us were swallowed up by mist. In the doorway of a brick building we finally stopped.

I didn't know what had come over me in the bar; I sort of snapped. Now, without expecting it, I started laughing my fool head off.

"You know," Rogue said, "they're not going to let us back in there if you keep starting shit."

I sat right down on the sidewalk and howled. It struck me that I felt better. In fact, I felt good. I guess I had been pissed off at everything and everybody, and getting into a fistfight with total strangers had been a release. Not just a release: It was fun. I started laughing harder. After I'd spent more than four hundred years on this planet, my life had reached a point that getting into a free-for-all in a biker bar had become my idea of a good time.

Maybe I didn't know who the hell I was after all.

And maybe my heart was finally healing. The sadness had lifted; the sense of loss had dissipated. Suddenly I got up, brushed myself off, and started at a trot back to the bar.

"Where are you going?" Benny called after me.

"Just be a minute," I called back to her. "Hang on."

A number of guys were now standing around in the street in front of Charlie's. I saw who I was looking for and went up to him.

"Sam?" I said.

The cowboy biker gave me a questioning look. He had one eye swollen shut and a bruise starting to darken his jaw.

Despite the damage, his strong face with its wide mouth, straight nose, and high cheekbones retained its good looks. He had pulled his sandy hair back into a ponytail. He looked rugged without the wear and weathering of a real cowboy; his waist was small, his chest broad. By every estimation he was a real hunk and a half.

"You ain't gonna hit me again, are you?" he drawled, and smacked his hat on his thigh in a practiced way, as if to get any dust off. He glanced at me with a look all lazy and sweet. He didn't seem the least bit worried for his safety.

I grinned at him and stuck out my hand. He took it and we shook.

"I'm Daphne," I said.

"Sam," he said.

"Look, Sam, I just wanted to say, hope there's no hard feelings."

Sam smiled. "Nah. I was outta line. You hit like a god-damn mule, though."

"Yeah, I know," I said, enjoying this. "I have to go," I added.

"Maybe next time, Miss Daphne," Sam answered with a warm smile.

I started to walk back to my friends, but looked back at him and winked. "Sure, Sam. Why not? Maybe next time."

Benny called Det. Lt. Moses Johnson from her cell phone. He told her that he'd drive to West Street to pick us up in five minutes. He didn't say where he was, but he had to be some-where close, in Chelsea or the Village.

Meanwhile Audrey caught a cab. She would go home and get to work, but was stopping off at her vampire club first. Rogue and Cormac headed back toward the bar after telling us they intended to make "inquiries" into any suspicious activity down along the waterfront or in the vicinity of the *Intrepid*'s dock. I watched the fog swallow them up. Rogue didn't spell it out in so many words, but it was understood that he would ask his criminal friends about any talk on the street that might give us a lead.

We needed one. Right now we were looking for a ghost ship and had nothing more than ideas as insubstantial as air. We needed to figure out who had the *Intrepid*, for I was sure someone did, before we knew what the Darkwings could possibly have to do with the situation. A shudder caused my body to quake with such force that Benny noticed.

"You cold? You can borrow my jacket."

I shook my head. My cold was spiritual, not physical. "No, I'm okay. I was thinking about what Rogue said."

"Which was?" she said as she opened her purse and brought out a tube of lipstick. She applied the bright red to her full lips without using a mirror.

"That something is going to bite us in the ass if we don't stop it first."

"That's true, sugar. You ask me, we've been barking up the wrong tree. I don't think we've been thinking too straight on this."

"What do you mean? How else can we think about it?"

"We ain't gettin' the right answers 'cause we ain't asking the right questions. First off, why would somebody steal an old aircraft carrier? Come on, brainstorm with me. Anything come to mind?"

"Um . . . to use? To take planes near a target and attack?" I mused.

"That's a thought. But who would have the planes and not a ship? Al Qaeda doesn't have an air force. Hamas in

Palestine? I guess Palestine might have some fighters. The Saudis have quite a few. Could they be behind this?"

"Not the Saudis. They have a navy. They're rich enough to buy an aircraft carrier if they wanted one," I countered. "And why would they want one? They're allies of the U.S."

"Okay, it's not the Saudis. Think of another reason to take the ship. And why that ship? That particular ship?"

I swear I felt a lightbulb click on in my brain. "That's it! That particular ship. Why that ship and no other?" I felt as if I nearly had an answer. I was seeing through a glass darkly, but I was seeing something. Excitement raced through me.

"Why? Let's see now," Benny mused. "I can think of three reasons. Its location. Its accessibility. Its symbolism."

"Yes! Yes! Yes!" I said, punching the air. "Location: New York City. Accessibility: easy. She was right offshore but in the open ocean, not a dock. Carried only a skeleton crew. No security. No weapons. Symbolism: U.S. military greatness. You hit it, Benny." I was twirling around, feeling euphoric.

"Not so fast, Daph. Why did the terrorists, if indeed it was terrorists, take it and not blow it up?"

"Obvious. They need it," I said.

"Why?"

I thought for a moment. "Like I said before, to use in some way. Or . . . or to bargain with. That could be it. What could they want in exchange?"

"I think we're back to who 'they' are. Maybe we have to find the ship to find them."

My spirits faltered. We had gone in a circle. Were we any closer to the answer?

"Don't look glum," Benny said. "We figured out a passel of things, and it was as easy as sliding off a greased hog

backward. Let's talk to the Looie and see if we can get
something more to go on. There he is."

Almost exactly five minutes to the second from Benny's
call, a white Chevy pulled up to the curb. The driver's window lowered. I had seen happier faces at a funeral. In fact,
Lieutenant Johnson looked like he usually did when he saw
me—as if he had bitten into something that had gone rotten.

"Get in the back," he growled in lieu of *hello*. "Then tell
me what the hell you want."

CHAPTER 6

*"Enter by the narrow gate; for the gate is wide
and the way is easy that leads to destruction."*

—Matthew 7:13

"And good evening to you too, Lieutenant," I said, pushing aside some crumpled McDonald's bags and sliding into the backseat.

"This isn't a date," Johnson said, killing the engine and turning around in the seat so he could see us both. "Cut the small talk. Who's dead, kidnapped, or about to be assassinated?"

"None of the above, at least as far as I know," I said sweetly to my nemesis in the NYPD.

"So why'd you call me?"

Benny looked at me. We should have rehearsed some joint approach to the grumpy lieutenant. He wasn't going to help us out of the goodness of his heart. For one thing he openly didn't like me. He barely tolerated Benny. He had an old grudge against Rogue.

For another, he didn't believe in vampires. He'd seen both Benny and me in bat form. He evidently put that experience in the category of spotting a UFO: If you tell anybody, they'll think you're nuts. If you believe it's a spaceship, you probably are nuts. That means you'd better make up your mind that you saw swamp gas or a weather balloon. We weren't quite swamp gas, but he wasn't buying that we were I've-come-to-drink-your-blood vampires.

I kept my voice light. "We want to work out an arrangement with you. A mutually beneficial one."

"Spell it out," he said.

"An exchange of information. We keep you in the loop when we know something. You tell us when you pick up on a situation we should know about."

Since Johnson bitterly resented other agencies pulling off operations in New York without working jointly with the city police, he didn't say no. He didn't exactly say yes either. He grunted. I took that as a maybe.

Benny jumped in with a reference to our last mission. "Remember what happened with the kidnapped girls? We made sure you got the credit for that, didn't we? We caught hell for it too, but both Daphne and I feel—don't we, Daphne?"

I nodded vigorously, although I had no idea where she was going with this.

"—that we could accomplish more and safeguard against anybody getting caught in a cross fire if we *coordinated*— that's the right word, isn't it, Daphne?"

I nodded again.

"—our efforts." She smiled widely, which probably didn't have the desired effect, since I'm sure Johnson spotted her fangs. His complexion was such a deep chocolate I couldn't tell whether he got pale or not, but I suspected he did.

"You have anything specific in mind?" he asked, lifting up a can of Coke and drinking the contents. Fear can make a throat dry up fast.

"Let me cut to the chase," I said.

"Please do; I'm all ears," Johnson said, crushing the Coke can in his hand.

"Has anything highly unusual been reported lately?"

"Why? What's going on that I should know about?"

"Nothing. At least, not yet. We, um, have been put on alert. Something may be about to happen. We don't know what."

"Terrorism?"

"That's the best guess. But we don't know what form the threat will take. We're trying to connect some dots here."

Johnson gave me a hard look. "Narrow down 'highly unusual' for me. This is New York. We get weird shit happening every day. Yesterday a guy tried to mug a lady by siccing his pit bull on her. The dog ran over and hid behind the woman. She called nine-one-one and the perp tried to press charges to get his dog back. The lady kept the dog."

"I mean something different. Bigger. How about anything around the piers, New York Harbor, something like that?" I suggested.

Johnson thought a moment. "Not in the harbor. Out at Arthur Kill. The Outerbridge Crossing. The other morning, right at rush hour, something hit a support column. Must have been fifty drivers in cars going over the bridge that called in. The weird part of it was that nobody saw anything.

"No ships in the area. Nothing under the bridge. But the Port Authority people sent a boat out and found evidence of a collision on the bridge support. Something scraped it. And it must have been something big."

"How big a boat can pass under that bridge?" Benny asked.

Johnson snorted. "A ship. Big as they make them. You got

over a hundred, maybe a hundred fifty feet of clearance. Merchant ships, freighters go through there all the time."

"The Arthur Kill is a narrow passage of water, right?" I asked. I remembered flying over it months before, when terrorists were trying to get a nuclear device into Port Newark.

"Yeah. It's between Staten Island and Perth Amboy, and it runs between the Goethals Bridge upstream and Raritan Bay downstream."

"Where's this Raritan Bay?" Benny asked.

"Off Jersey. North of Sandy Hook," Johnson said.

"And what's that near?" Benny asked. She was from Missouri, and the state of New Jersey, sometimes called the armpit of the East Coast, was a foreign land to her.

"You keep going south and you hit Asbury Park," Johnson said.

Where the *Intrepid* disappeared. *Bingo.* Benny gave me a furtive pinch.

"Anything else?" I asked.

Johnson's eyes flicked away from mine. He pulled another can of Coke out of a soft-sided cooler on the passenger seat, popped the top, and took a long swig, obviously stalling, as if he knew something but was having a tough time deciding whether he was going to say anything to us. Finally he lowered the Coke can and said, "Might have something, but it's probably nothing. Bunch of drunks on the beach last night at Coney Island."

"What about them?" I asked.

"They called nine-one-one. Said they spotted a giant bat flying above the surf."

Neither Benny nor I said anything. Any of New York's more than five thousand vampires could have been out there. Sure, most of us didn't do solo flights over anything bigger than a lake or stream. We need places to land and land quickly sometimes, so ocean flights of any distance would be deadly. And most bat-form flying is done strictly for hunting and/or abducting humans. This vampire no doubt hoped to swoop down for a quick meal from somebody walking alone on the beach. Anyway, that was what I figured.

By this time I could feel Johnson's agitation. I watched him open and close the fingers of one hand. He lost eye contact. His glance kept straying toward the street. We had him upset. He broke into my thoughts, wanting to know if the terrorist threat had to do with the bridges, a vulnerable target that worried most inhabitants of the city.

Both Benny and I shook our heads no, so he pushed for more information.

"So the threat's got to do with a ship or a boat? Pleasure craft? Lots of talk lately about regulating them near Manhattan."

"Look, we don't know," I said. "But if I had to guess, I'd say a ship."

Johnson's eyes narrowed, his impatience increased. "Just a guess? Bullshit. What else don't you know?" he demanded.

"That's it. Honest. I need to ask you one more thing. . . ." I was thinking fast, taking a shot in the dark, hoping to hit something.

"What? Look, make it fast; I've got to be someplace."

Yeah, like going right back to your office and sounding the alarm that they'd better start watching harbor activity, I thought while I asked, "Has anything been going on in the local mosques? The more radical ones, like those out in

Brooklyn associated with the Blind Sheikh, the guy who planned the first bombing on the World Trade Center?"

Johnson's eyes got hard. "You mean the mosque on Foster Avenue? That's Abu Bakr. The other one is al Farooq on Atlantic Avenue."

"I guess. I don't know that much about them," I admitted.

"We keep an eye on them. Talk to informants. You think somebody's planning another bombing somewhere like the 'ninety-one bombing?"

I shrugged. "I have no reason to think that, or anything. I'm just throwing out a wide net. All we know for sure is that this threat probably, but not positively, has to do with New York City, and maybe it's coming by water."

"I'll find out about the mosques. Look, you two," he said. "Don't fuck with me on this. You find out anything—I do mean anything—I want to know."

"Of course, Lieutenant," Benny said. "A deal's a deal."

"So, what now, Sherlock?" Benny said to me after we climbed out of Johnson's Chevy and found ourselves back on West Street, alone in the fog, which was now as thick as cotton.

I said I needed to go to the office and get my stuff. I asked Benny to come along with me.

She hesitated and asked, "Why? I was thinking about going downtown to the Laundromat. Maybe I'll do the hunt tonight. If Martin shows up I want to ask him back to my place afterward."

I bit my tongue and didn't voice what I was thinking: that Martin was another vampire loser and Benny was sure to get hurt if she got involved with him. Sleeping with a guy was one thing; caring about him was another. That was where

Benny usually made her mistake. But I should talk. I said to her, "Take a detour and come with me. There's something you have to see."

"What?"

"It's better if you see it," I said. "Trust me; it's worth the trip."

By now the fog had besieged the streets along the river and was battling its way across the island. The hour had gone past midnight and no cabs were in sight. On clear nights cabbies cheated death driving in the insanity of New York traffic. With the lack of visibility and few people venturing out on the streets, most them had probably quit early.

The streets deserted, sounds muffled by the mist, and the fog enfolding us in its damp embrace, Benny and I started walking uptown toward Fourteenth Street. Somewhere between there and here we might find a subway to get to Twenty-third Street.

We might as well have been trekking toward the Yukon. We could barely see the buildings lining the sidewalk. If there was a subway entrance on any of the corners, we missed it.

Before long the hairs on my arms were standing up. My instincts were warning me that someone or something was watching me. Yet when I looked back over my shoulder I saw nothing but the swirling mist circling around the street-lights, snaking along the curbs, and closing in on us like a gray wall.

My scalp kept crawling. My nerves jangled. I made Benny stop for a moment and listen. No sound. No footsteps behind us. I didn't like this. Maybe I was just spooked, but I had an uneasy feeling.

By the time we got to Twelfth Street, Benny said she was

"plumb tuckered out" and her feet hurt like a toothache. She was wearing a pair of Manolo Blahniks, and those boots were not made for walking.

Determined to flag down a ride, we positioned ourselves right out in the street and stood there. When headlights finally approached I could see it was a Lincoln Town Car, a car service, not a city cab. Both of us waved frantically, and it pulled over. Benny threw herself into the backseat. I hung back a moment, checking out the driver. He was a young guy wearing a white shirt and tie, his livery jacket hung on a hook by the back window.

He didn't look dangerous, so I joined Benny. The guy charged us a flat rate: fifteen bucks for the ten-block ride. Benny didn't quibble. She whispered to me that she was willing to pay twice that to take a load off her feet. I didn't care either; I was glad to get off the streets that held something I couldn't see, yet I knew was there.

The car accelerated and raced up the avenue. I leaned back against the cushions and took a deep breath, feeling relieved. Whoever was following us had been left behind.

We got out of the Lincoln at the Flatiron Building and went over to the lobby doors. I tried them. They didn't budge. I rattled them a little. They held fast. We couldn't get in.

Benny looked at me. "I guess they lock them up after a certain hour. What time is it?"

"Heading for one a.m." I rang the night porter bell to see what would happen. At first nothing did. I leaned on the bell a few more times. I glanced over at Benny. She shrugged. We were about to leave when a uniformed guard—a tall, white-haired man with suspicion written all over his face—came to the door.

He didn't open it. He shook his head and motioned for us to leave.

I pulled out my government ID and held it up to the glass. He finally cracked the door a couple of inches.

"What do you want?" he said. His dentures clicked when he talked.

"We need to get upstairs. I left some things in an office."

He opened the door and let us in. He said we needed to sign the register. We followed his lumbering shape through the lobby and past the bank of elevators. A podium with a light held a large open book.

"Put your name, company, and floor right there. Then the time," he instructed. "And let me see your ID again. Yours too," he said to Benny.

I handed him my ID, which says I work for the U.S. Department of the Interior. I signed in while he looked at it. When I finished I handed the pen to Benny. Along about then the guard glanced at what I had written.

His face darkened. "What are you trying to pull?"

"What are you talking about?" I said.

"There is no ABC Media in this building; that's what I'm talking about."

Benny rolled her eyes. "Are you new or something? Of course there is. The name's on the office door and everything. Look over there. It's right on the building directory." She pointed to the black sign with the white magnetic letters that hung between the elevators.

The guard was angry now. "Are you two deaf or drunk? I told you, there is no ABC Media here."

Benny insisted, "Oh, yes, there is too." She went over to the sign and stood there. Then she turned around, her eyebrows raised, her eyes wide open. "Daph? It's not here. It was here before; I saw it. I saw it tonight." Her voice shook a little when she said to the guard, "Our company, ABC Media, is on the third floor. It really is. We were just there a couple of hours ago for a meeting."

The security guard, whose shoulders were rounded and his back bent as if he didn't like being tall, could see that Benny was genuinely upset. His voice was kinder when he repeated that there was no ABC Media in the building. "I told you ladies, it's not here. The entire third floor is empty. No tenants. It's been that way for months. They can't rent it out. A radiator leak flooded the place. It's got to be completely renovated."

Benny looked at me, bewilderment on her face. "I don't understand this. Do you?"

I didn't answer her. It was time we got out of there before we ended up facing the men in blue who protect and serve. I turned to the guard, doing my best to look puzzled. "I don't understand either. I'm sure our meeting was at 173 Fifth Avenue."

"Ladies, this is 175. The Flatiron Building."

"Oooooh, no! I'm so sorry," I simpered.

Benny jumped in with her ditzy-blonde imitation and said indignantly to me, "I told you not to let me have that there Acapulco Zombie drink. I swear, it's just made my brain all mush. If'n I had another one it would take three men and a fat boy to carry me on home."

Then she looked up at the guard, her brown eyes limpid, artful tears like crystals on her lashes. "Mister, I sure am dumber than a box of rocks. Our building's on the next block. I do hope you ain't too mad at us. Come on, Daphne. We've troubled this gentleman long enough." She hooked her arm in mine and we beat it in double time to the door.

As soon as we were back outside, we walked in a down-town direction toward the next block just in case the guard was watching. The fog was so intense we disappeared quickly from his view. We stopped midblock. Benny asked me what the hell was going on.

I explained what happened earlier when I went back up-stairs to leave my packages under my desk. I told her that I suspected that the premises had been "sanitized" once the Darkwings left. I also told her I thought J probably had an office somewhere else in the building, and so did a staff of operatives from whatever intelligence agency we worked for. Maybe they occupied the rest of the third floor. Anyway, they were there. They were no doubt watching us at all times.

Benny appeared dumbfounded. "You mean the whole thing is a stage set? They put it up when we're going to be there, and once we leave they remove everything?"

"Exactly."

"Now, don't that beat all," she said. "I guess it's to give them that there 'deniability' if anybody finds out about us."

"Yeah. Any exposure and they can say they never heard of us. They have nothing to tie them to a team of vampire spies. They'd be the first to say, 'Go ahead and terminate them.' They'd leave us hanging out to dry in a New York minute."

Benny shook her head. "Us, maybe, but not you. Your mother would protect you, Daphne. You have nothing to worry about," Benny said.

"Yeah, right. That's what you think. My mother loves me in her fashion. But as the poet Richard Lovelace wrote, 'I could not love thee, dear, so much, loved I not honor more.' If the mission were important enough, my mother, the spymaster, would deny she ever met me. It sounds harsh, but I know that if she felt I had to be sacrificed for the 'greater good,' she'd do it."

"You don't mean that," Benny said. "Not your own mother."

"You don't know the half of it. My mother could teach Machiavelli a thing or two. Hell, she probably did. No, Benny, I was thinking earlier tonight how I couldn't trust anybody. That includes my mother."

"You can trust me," Benny said.

"Thanks," I said. "That means a lot." I hoped it was true, but in my heart I wasn't certain even of that.

Benny gave me a hug and left, hoping to hook up with Martin. With a wave she disappeared into the stairwell leading from street level to the downtown trains on the Broadway line forty feet below.

I had no interest in going clubbing. I wanted to go home. I wanted to pour my blood-bank blood into a lovely wineglass, sip it delicately, turn on the TCM channel, hope for a Hitchcock film, and veg out. I wanted to forget about missing ships and the funhouse-mirror life I was living, where everything was deception and illusion. I wanted the comfort of my pets. I wanted to feel safe.

Since a cab ride was unlikely, I faced a long subway journey: catching the train here at Twenty-third Street, then changing to the number one at Forty-second Street. I needed to go uptown, which meant crossing the wide expanse of Broadway to the subway entrance on the southeast corner.

The traffic light looked like a green moon suspended in the mist as I stepped into the broad thoroughfare, moving at a trot to get to the other side before some reckless driver came barreling into the intersection. The opposite side of the street lay unseen behind a thick wall of fog. I felt wrapped in a cocoon of white mist, my visibility reduced to an arm's length around me. I finally spotted the curb, saw the railings of the subway stairs, and arrived at the stairwell to begin my descent.

Suddenly the hairs on my arms bristled. A tingling skittered up the back of my neck, and my scalp crawled uncomfortably, as if a low current of electricity ran over my skin. I didn't have to turn around to know someone was coming up behind me and meant me harm. I just had to pay attention to my instincts.

I quickened my pace, having no choice but to continue going down into the earth, into the tunnels that honeycombed the rock beneath the city. I reached the subway station and dashed with my MetroCard in my hand to the turnstiles. I pushed through and rushed onto the platform. No one else waited there; the space stretched forlornly in either direction until it dead-ended in a tile wall. Before me lay the deep, forbidding trench of the tracks.

Now I could hear heavy, clattering footsteps coming down the stairs. My heart beat a staccato. My mind raced: fight or flight?

If a train pulled into the station now I could hop on and get away. I darted over to the edge of the tracks and peered into the unremitting darkness of the approach tunnel. I saw nothing. I'd have to fight.

I was in the security area of the platform, the part monitored by cameras. But at this late hour the token booth on the other side of the turnstiles sat unlit and unoccupied. A fat lot of good my being videoed was going to do me. If I were overcome by the vampire hunter, by the time help came I'd be a pile of dust.

Pushing those thoughts from my mind, giving myself over completely to instinct, I mentally readied myself to face my attacker. I had no weapons but my wits and strength. Yet when I saw what was coming for me, I knew neither would be enough.

Not one vampire hunter appeared on the stairs. Not two. Three of the leather-clad hunters emerged from the clouds of fog that flowed like thick honey down the stairs and swirled around the floor. They were gigantic men, each well over six feet tall and broad as grizzly bears. Each carried a bandolier filled with sharpened wooden stakes slung across his chest. Each had wrapped a thick silver chain around one arm.

I doubted they had MetroCards, but the illegality of vaulting a turnstile was not going to deter them. Bottom line: I couldn't fight them all and win. I had to take the only other option I had. Without hesitation I jumped the four or five feet down onto the tracks, avoiding the deadly third rail. It wouldn't have killed me outright but would have stunned me long enough for the hunters to get me.

I didn't look back to see what was chasing me. I sprinted between the rails toward the next station, five blocks away at Twenty-eighth Street. I still had on my Nike cross trainers. That was a lucky break. My speed would mean the difference between existence and extinction.

I splashed through the puddles of the filthy, refuse-strewn water that lay stagnant in the trough between the parallel tracks. I raced into the narrow tunnel.

Black, grime-encrusted steel plates formed the walls of these subway tubes. They rose up on either side of the tracks, leaving only inches of clearance when the train passed through. Every dozen feet a bare lightbulb fought back the darkness without much success.

I ran on with death at my heels. I heard the squeaking of rats. I heard the thuds of the three hunters hitting the ground after they jumped off the platform. I heard the dull thumps of their footsteps as they pursued me. Then I heard something else: a low rumble followed by the squealing of brakes.

I knew what that ominous sound was: A subway train had just pulled into Twenty-third Street. Within moments it would pull out of the station, and its unstoppable tons of steel would come roaring toward me and the hunters too.

Having ridden the trains for years, I was well aware that safety alcoves appeared in breaks in the tunnel walls at regular intervals. Track workers ducked in there to wait for trains to go by. I needed to find one.

It was true that, being what they call "undead," I could survive the terrible impact of the subway hitting me, shattering my bones, tearing my flesh. But I'd *feel* it. Recovery would be long and arduous, and I would never, not ever, be quite the same.

I intended to avoid the ordeal if possible. I looked frantically ahead for an alcove, trying to judge the intervals at which they'd appear. The trick would be getting into one right before the train reached me. I was desperate to run as far as I could before I stopped. Once I was pinned in the small indentation, unable to flee until after the train had gone, my pursuers—the train having passed them first— would be able to gain on me.

But if I was lucky, these vampire hunters wouldn't know about the safety alcoves. Hopefully they were out-of-towners who had come to Manhattan for the sole purpose of exterminating me. While I stood unharmed in the shelter, they'd be like dead bugs on a windshield as the speeding subway train smashed them flat. It was a cheery thought.

As I reached deep inside myself for the energy to run faster, I distinctly heard the creaking and squealing of the train pulling out of Twenty-third Street and the clacking of the wheels as it picked up speed. I bolted forward with every ounce of power I had, spotting an alcove a few hundred feet ahead of me. Suddenly the train's headlight lit up the tunnel with a blazing intensity, catching me clearly in its bright beam.

The hunters could see me now, but I could only hope they were in a state of panic. Even if they had spotted the haven of an alcove, it was large enough for only one of them to use it. The other two might survive if they threw themselves flat between the tracks and let the train pass over them. *Might* was the operative word. They *might* survive. But bulky as they were, with their supply of stakes and their oversize muscles, they might not. Like the peeling back of a sardine can with a key, the train would violently flail them lengthwise from heels to head.

Just then screams of terror rang out behind me before the harrowing sounds were swallowed up by the roar of the train. The noise deafened me. The train's headlight wrapped me with its brilliance. I had no time left. I threw myself toward the alcove, and my body smacked hard against the filthy wall. I pressed my face against the adamantine steel as the train rumbled by. A cacophony crashed and echoed like a thousand struck cymbals. Turbulent air buffeted my back, tearing at my clothes and pulling my hair loose from its once-neat chignon.

Then the air stilled. The gloom returned. The noise receded. The train had gone.

I peeled myself off the wall in time to see the R on the train's back window fading into the distance. I heard nothing from the tunnel behind me, but I didn't wait to see if any of the hunters lived. I began running as if the hounds of hell were chasing me until I saw the glow of the station at Twenty-eighth Street. Once I reached it I pulled myself up on the platform and darted for the exit.

Up the stairs two at a time and onto the sidewalk I went, and then, in the fog-shrouded city, I melted away into the mist, glad now for its cover, grateful to be invisible as I hurried onward through the vacant city streets.

As I entered the lobby of my apartment building forty minutes later, having first run, then jogged the more than fifty blocks uptown, I looked disheveled enough to cause Mickey to hurry over, his face showing alarm.

My chest was heaving as I sucked in air, and a wave of dizziness made the room spin. A cold sweat broke out on my forehead. I found myself limping badly too; I must have turned my ankle during the chase. Only in the final moments of my journey, as I came down off my adrenaline high, did I feel its pain.

"Lean on me," the tough old Irishman said, offering his arm. I did.

"You hurt bad?" he asked.

"No. It's nothing. Really. Just a sprain. I was jogging home."

Mickey gave me a knowing look. "Yeah, like I used to jog when the Brits were shooting us down. You sure you're okay?"

"I just need to catch my breath." I took long, deep inhalations for a few minutes to steady myself. Finally the vertigo passed, and the darkness stealing my consciousness receded.

"Trouble out there?" Mickey asked.

"Some." I looked at him and said in a quiet voice, "It may be following me. Keep a close watch, okay? Call upstairs if you spot anybody hanging around out on the street."

"Aye, a fog like this invites trouble. Don't you worry none. I have your back." He walked me over to the elevator, but I refused to let him accompany me all the way upstairs. My ankle throbbed now, but I didn't mind the discomfort. It meant I wasn't dust. Not yet anyway.

When I opened the door to my apartment, the light from the hallway spilled into the shadowy interior. I could see my dog padding over, her tail wagging. My hand, now cold and white from needing blood, rested on her huge head. I stroked her ears as she leaned against my legs. I closed the door behind me, letting myself be surrounded by the comforting darkness.

I started toward the kitchen, my body sagging with relief at arriving home. Then I stopped. My entire being stiffened with alarm. Something was wrong. I could sense it. To be more specific, I could smell it. And of all the scents in the world, this one I knew well. Another vampire was in here.

CHAPTER 7

"I am also called No-more, Too-late, Farewell."
—Dante Gabriel Rossetti, Sonnet 97, "A Superscription"

A breeze touched my face with gentle fingers. I moved cautiously into the living room. The window had been thrown open wide. The velvet curtains swayed and undulated. Tendrils of fog were slipping over the windowsill and rolling across the floor. The figure of a huge bat, its great arched wings a curious shadow in the mist, stood not ten feet before me.

"Hello, Daphne," the vampire said.

"Hello, Darius," I answered as calmly as I could with my heart going like a trip-hammer in my breast. "I've been expecting you."

"Sorry to drop in unannounced. You have a dragon downstairs guarding your door. Besides, I'm not officially here." He made no attempt to come closer.

"Only unofficially then? Why are you here at all?" I stayed where I was, although I had begun to shiver, a tremor shaking me from head to toe.

"I had to see you."

I was feeling unwell. My legs had turned rubbery and weak. My voice faltered. "Okay, you see me. Now what?"

"I never want to stop seeing you," he said. Or at least I think that was what he said, because all of a sudden the world went sideways. I slid to the floor thinking, *Oh, it's so dark and I'm so cold.*

The first thing that I could clearly determine afterward was that I lay prone on the floor, and my cheek was next to a naked man's chest. The next thing that registered on my consciousness was a man's voice saying, "Daphne, wake up. Do you hear me? You have to wake up."

A cold washcloth touched my eyelids then softly patted my temples. The voice commanded me again to wake up. I opened my eyes. The voice said, "Drink this." A trickle of blood poured into my mouth; then the flow paused as I swallowed. This continued for five or six swallows, and I felt my strength return. I struggled to sit.

"Give that to me," I said, snatching the clear plastic bag of blood-bank blood from Darius's hand. "I am not an infant. I can feed myself!"

"It's good to see you back to your old self already," he said.

I drank long and deeply, emptying the bag. When I was finished I stood up. Darius remained reclining on the floor, propped up on an elbow, grinning at me.

"Why the hell are you naked?" I demanded. "Where are your clothes?"

"I am naked because, if you think back a few minutes, I flew into your window as a giant bat. My clothes? I left them in the rental car. It's in the Park 'n' Lock under your building."

"You need to put something on," I said, striding toward the bathroom.

"Why?" he called after me. "It's not like you never saw me without clothes on before."

"That was then. This is now," I said, coming back into the room and tossing him a terry cloth robe. "Put this on."

"It's pink," he said, deftly catching it in one hand.

"Don't tell me your manhood is threatened by the color." I glared at him. "Just put it the fuck on."

"Hey, no need to start swearing. I come in peace." He stood up and slipped his arms into the sleeves. They were too short. The robe wasn't just pink; it was flamingo. He looked ridiculous.

A smile twitched around my lips. I turned my head away, trying to stifle the merriment rising up in my throat.

"You're laughing. Don't pretend you aren't. You are," he said.

I was. I couldn't help myself. Darius was here. Just when I had convinced myself I was over him, I knew without a doubt that I wasn't. Oh, boy, I wasn't. Suddenly an alarming sensation radiated through my body, as if my passions were awakening from a deep sleep.

I had never wanted any man more than I wanted Darius—and I didn't want to want him. This was the absolutely perfect goddamn end to one hellacious night. What else could I do? I could laugh or cry. I let loose and laughed until the tears rolled down my cheeks.

"It could be worse," Darius said. "You could have started to point and laugh *before* I put on the robe." He walked close to me then, his voice lowering, becoming seductive and disturbing to me. "But you were looking, weren't you? We both know that may be a dangerous thing to do. 'We must not look at goblin men, We must not buy their fruits: Who knows upon what soil they fed / Their hungry thirsty roots,' " he said, reciting as he so often did the poetry that colored his words and made me delight to listen to him.

Caught between mirth and sorrow, I fought for self-control. I got the hiccups instead. Darius went into the kitchen and brought me back a glass of water. He handed it to me. I took a sip.

"If you have some fuzzy slippers I'll put them on too," he said, and grinned. The smile put deep dimples along each side of his mouth. He looked at me with hooded, sexy bed-room eyes. A ragged scar ran along his cheekbone, curving downward. It gave him a rakish look, like a pirate. Without it he might have almost been too pretty. His hair, once long, was now the pale, sandy-colored stubble of a military buzz cut. It made him appear tough, almost savage.

Mixing memory and desire, as Eliot wrote, I thought about the past as my eyes searched his face. I remembered our first close encounter. I had been a newly made spy, checking out a billionaire arms dealer on Fifth Avenue. After I finished for the night I strolled over to Madison Avenue, looking into the shop windows. Some jewelry attracted me. I stopped and lingered. A mirror inside the display case reflected my startled face—and the one of the stranger who had come up behind me.

The barrel of a handgun poked into my back. A man's voice whispered a warning into my ear. Darius didn't intend to hurt me. It was his way of getting my attention. I laughed at him that time too, but I thought there was no better-looking man on earth. I still thought that.

Now, Darius took the glass from me and set it down. He put one strong hand behind my head, gripping my hair hard enough to hurt, and pulled my face to his. "I've been dreaming about doing this for far too long," he said as his lips came down on mine.

I didn't resist. I kissed him back. Soon I was lost. He tasted of violets and wine. I melted against his body, pushing the stupid pink terry-cloth robe off his shoulders so I could touch his flesh. Smooth and warm, it pulsed under my fingers, breathing life back into the passion I had left for dead.

I kissed him for a very long time, drinking my fill, needing more, not wanting to ever let him go. Eventually we ended the long caress and he pulled me tight to him, wrapping his arms around me.

"I'm sorry," he whispered softly. "I'm sorry for everything. For blaming you for biting me. For hating becoming a vampire. Most of all for leaving you."

I sighed deeply. *Sorry* didn't cut it. I wished I could have kept silent. My tongue moved faster than my brain.

"Sorry for Julie?" I said. "Sorry for lying? Sorry for bringing the vampire hunters to kill me?" Bitterness had an astringent taste. It filled my mouth. I pushed away from him.

"We can talk about all of that. Later. Not now." His voice was coaxing. He reached out and took my hand. He pulled me back to his sheltering arms. I didn't resist as much as I could have.

"Listen," he said in a voice ragged and torn. "I made mistakes. But I didn't make a mistake in loving you. Don't you understand? It all doesn't matter. Nothing does except us and this." He ran his hand up under my soft jacket to find my breasts. He cupped them as he lowered his lips to take mine again.

I didn't stop him. Nothing else did matter at that moment

except merging myself into the being of him. If my body could have become diaphanous and transparent so that I could have entered into his very bones, I would have. Instead I let him pick me up and carry me into the bedroom and lay me down on the bed.

I let him strip off my clothes, carelessly and in haste, before he flung himself full-length atop me. There was no finesse in this joining. He had arrived already naked, and now, with my garments torn aside, I was ready to receive him.

I gasped as his long, stiff member pushed violently into me, sliding upward with force before drawing back and ramming into me again. In those few moments before I forgot to think, it occurred to me that anger as much as desire drove his lust. But then I became insensate to all else except Darius and me thrusting and turning, moving in a hard, driving rhythm together.

After a short while he flipped me so I was on top. I rose up and sat on his shaft, rocking my pubis against his. A whimper escaped my throat. His hand reached up and stroked my face for a moment before he put both hands on my hips and pushed me down as powerfully as he could, entering more deeply inside me than I thought possible.

I cried out and tried to draw back. He held me fast and began a pumping motion. My head flung back; my eyes sought the darkness. I was filled with a crescendo of intensifying feelings. Higher and higher they took me until I climaxed and felt him empty his seed inside me. I moaned and hung my head. I was damp with perspiration and limp as a rag.

Yet still Darius did not take his hands from my body. He did not release me. He kept me sitting tightly astride him.

"I hunger for you. In every way," he said, his voice hoarse and almost cruel.

My heart fluttered. I did not want him to bite me tonight. I did not want my blood pouring out to fill his mouth and my free will pouring out with it. Like a human caught in a vampire's thrall, I, though a vampire too, would be bound to Darius with ties beyond emotion.

I shook my head. "No, no. Not tonight. I am too weak, my love," I pleaded, feeling worried and upset even as a dark force urged me onward, coaxed me to give in, to turn my chin and offer my white neck with its blue vein to him.

Darius's grip on me loosened as he pulled me off and laid me, like a doll, next to him. "Of course. Not now," he conceded.

He traced his finger over my lips and down into the hollow of my throat. He spoke no more, but lowered soft, seeking lips to my breast and suckled, putting one arm around my waist as he did so. Once again he took away my movement and my ability to escape him. He was controlling me. It was wrong; it was right. I no longer cared.

I was drowning in sensations. I felt his other hand slip between my legs. He stroked me there with his fingers. After a sweet time of pleasure and forgetfulness, he took his mouth from my breast and trailed kisses down my body. My belly tingled along a shivery path. He moved his hand, opening my lower lips with his fingers. He lowered his head farther. I gasped as his tongue licked down the cleft of me. Soon his mouth teased me into a breathless excitement.

This was a seduction. I knew that, and even as I knew it I surrendered.

I lost my reason. My mind went somewhere outside me, flying toward nirvana, carrying me on an ocean of rocking desire to no thought. I felt the brushlike stiffness of Darius's hair beneath my hands. I pressed his head against me. I made noises like a dove cooing, like a beast lowing, like a wild thing.

And when his fingers, first one, then two, then three, slipped inside my velvet shaft, I slipped completely away from consciousness and ran free across the glistening vales of ecstasy.

"Don't stop, don't stop," I urged, and let him tantalize me. No matter what the consequences, even my demise, they seemed worth it at this moment. I not only surrendered; I gave him the gift of myself. Rolling with wave after wave of orgasm, I put my hands on either side of his head and gently pulled him up. I let go long enough to find his shaft and put it where his mouth had been.

"Darius," I breathed. "Drink." And I lifted my chin, exposed my neck, and pulled his face down to the smooth blue vein.

I felt the sharp pinch of his fangs piercing my skin. I felt his lips encircle the wound. I felt an electric current surge through my veins as my blood poured out. I climaxed again, moaning loudly and thrilled beyond imagining. And then I knew no more.

I didn't expire, of course. A vampire is not easily exterminated, and then only by ancient and very exacting means.

Instead I woke near dawn with something knocking inside my head like a twenty-pound sledgehammer. I sat up in bed and groaned. Beyond the painful thuds of the hammer, an annoying tapping came from the windows. I swung my legs to the floor, stood, and made my way, bleary-eyed, to check it out. A thunderstorm had moved in over Manhattan. A slanting silver rain beat against the glass.

"Ohhh, please shut up," I moaned. In reply the wind threw a spray of raindrops big as jellybeans against the window where I stood. The noise smacked against my eardrums like a handful of ball bearings. *Well, fuck you too*, I thought.

This was the worst hangover I had ever experienced. I hadn't consumed any alcohol. I was hungover from Darius.

I pried my eyes open wide enough to look carefully around the bedroom. The pillow still bore the imprint of his head, but he wasn't here. I moved sluggishly into the living room. Jade jumped up expectantly, excited to see me, hoping to go out.

Otherwise the room was empty. Darius must have left some time ago. He had brewed a pot of coffee. A mug sat forlornly on the granite counter. The brown liquid was cold when I dumped the remains into the sink.

I rationalized that he had to return to his car under cover of darkness, and the June nights were short. *He could have left a goddamned note at least,* I thought. *He flies back into my life. He flies out. He leaves behind the wreckage and detritus of my heart.*

I swear to God, after more than four hundred years you'd think I'd learn.

My entire schedule had gone to hell too. I usually retired to my coffin early in the morning, when the sun lit the eastern sky or shortly thereafter. I rose again when the sun sank below the rim of earth in the west. The lengthening days already played havoc with my routine. I had developed insomnia from oversleeping, and of late I tended to wander from room to room from five o'clock in the evening until dusk, the thick velvet curtains blocking the persistent daylight.

The last thing I needed under the circumstances was a nap, even if it had been more akin to a coma than sleep. As a result I was sure to lie awake, tossing and turning, most of the long June day. I'd feel like crap by evening. Actually with the pounding in my head I guess I couldn't feel much worse. Where had I put the ibuprofen, anyway?

As I headed for the bathroom to search through the medicine cabinet, I picked my light jacket off the floor where I had dropped it a few hours ago. I fished my cell phone from my pocket to check my voice mail. A click on the message center reviewed that I had three new voice messages and one text message.

First, Audrey, her voice excited, said she found something really interesting and would fill us in tonight. Benny came on next; her words tumbling out frantically. Martin hadn't shown up at the club. He didn't call in. He didn't answer his phone. She was going to go looking for him. I grimaced and hoped she didn't find him in flagrante delicto. Third was J. He offered no hellos, just stated without preamble: "We've had contact. Be here at eight thirty. On time."

Contact from whom? About what? I wondered.

The fourth message was a text message that read: SOTMG CUL8R RUOK LY BYKT BFN. Translated into plain English, Darius had written, *Short of time, must go. See you later. Are you okay? Love you. But you knew that. Bye for now.* Evidently during his days as a rock star, he learned it was no longer cool to put pen to paper.

The devil on my shoulder spoke then. *Of course he left a text message. Julie would have overheard him otherwise.*

The angel on my other side countered with, *He was proba-bly somewhere in public. Give him the benefit of the doubt.*

I wasn't sure what to think, but I had, at least, a commu-nication from him. It wasn't one that I could fold away and put under my pillow, but he had written he loved me. Sort of.

And when was "later"? And something else nagged at me. When earlier tonight I had accused him of not being sorry for Julie or lying or for sending vampire hunters to kill me, he never denied it. He just said we'd talk about it.

I mean, what the hell was there to talk about? Causing my imminent death was not a negotiable item. I was flipping mad all of a sudden.

I was fast working myself up into a generally pissed-off state. Besides my ambivalence about Darius's behavior, I knew from the steady racket outside the window that the rain still came down like walls of water. Day would be dawning in what? Fifteen minutes? And my dog had to go out.

That wasn't a negotiable item either. When Jade took a dump, it was by the shovelful. I grabbed my supersize pooper-scooper, snapped on her leash, and limped out the apartment door.

When I came back minutes later from the slick-splashed streets of the city, my hair was wet. My clothes were drenched. My dripping dog left a wet trail across the parquet floor. I barely noticed. My emotions still reeled. My mind was in chaos.

My cell phone beeped. A text message waited. JTLUK CU PM KOTL. *Just to let you know. See you tonight. Kiss on the lips.* It wasn't much. But it was better than nothing. Fleetingly I had the idea that Darius might not have written it himself. Anyone could have sent it. A stupid thought. The suspicious idea would not have occurred to me at all if J hadn't spooked me earlier with his warning.

I answered this second text message. AAS LY2 L8R. *Alive and smiling. Love you too. Later.* I hesitated; then I typed in, MUSM. *Miss you so much.*

I am a fool for love.

I stripped off my sodden clothes, took a shower, and headed for my secret room. My headache had receded into a dull throbbing. I downed two more ibuprofen and climbed into my coffin. Darkness enveloped me. I smelled the loamy Transylvanian earth beneath my pillow. I sighed and shut my eyes. I had survived for one more day. Surprising myself, I quickly drifted off into sleep, experiencing neither joy nor sorrow, not even in my dreams.

CHAPTER 8

*"I look upon this world as a wrecked vessel.
God has given me a lifeboat and said, 'Moody,
save all you can.'"*

— Dwight L. Moody, evangelist

I awoke at twilight, sorely troubled in mind and spirit. The night stretched before me, filled with uncertainties. I would soon venture forth to save the world. Yet how could I save the world when I couldn't even save myself?

Always the drama queen, the voice of my mother echoed in my head. She was right, as usual. What had really happened? Darius had returned, we had sex, he left. Same shit, different day. *Get over it,* I admonished myself. Besides, he didn't really leave this time. I'd see him tonight. Maybe.

Yet I had an uneasy feeling that Darius had an ulterior motive for coming here, and our spontaneous combustion had been just a fringe benefit. *You really are getting paranoid, Daphne girl,* I said to myself. *Can't you just believe the man loves you?*

No. No, I can't.

I dressed with more care this evening than last. I didn't say I dressed *better*; I just thought more about it. I wore soft, faded jeans and a black cotton T-shirt. Instead of the Nike cross trainers I wore last night, I put on a pair of

Adidas running shoes. I retrieved my Louis Vuitton back-pack from the back of a chair. Inside I placed a well-oiled, well-made Beretta Tomcat Laser Grip: small enough to be comfortable in my hand, outfitted with the latest laser technology, all I had to do was point and shoot. I would not be found unarmed the next time the vampire hunters came for me.

On my way out I stopped in the lobby to tell Mickey to let Darius into my apartment if he arrived before I got back.

"You think that's smart?" Mickey asked.

I nearly snapped at him that it was none of his business, but I bit back the retort. "What's the problem?" I asked.

"Trouble and your old boyfriend both show up at the same time. I gotta ask why."

I had been thinking the same thing, of course, but I didn't like Mickey saying it out loud. "I'll take it under advisement. I know you preferred Fitz," I added in a gentle voice, and put my hand on his arm.

Mickey's rheumy eyes seemed to tear up. "Now, there was a man. You could have trusted Mr. Fitzmaurice with your life, Miss Urban."

"I know. And I did. But he had to go into hiding. He can't come back. There's a price on his head. He told you that himself before he left."

"Aye, and he asked me to watch out for you. That's just what I'm doing."

"You're a stubborn old Irishman," I said, removing my hand and turning to leave.

Mickey's shoulders straightened and his chin thrust forward. "That I am."

"But let Darius go upstairs anyway," I said, giving him a meaningful look as he held open the front door for me.

With a reddening complexion, Mickey nodded his head. As he ambled over to his desk I could clearly hear him muttering. "Aye, I will, but I don't like it none."

Daylight, although weak and fading, made it uncomfortable for me to venture out at this hour. Necessity drove me, and to tell the truth, my foray into the outside world was hardly fatal. Not only had the sun disappeared below the horizon, but Manhattan's canyons of steel kept me in the shadows.

I hugged the deeper shadows near the buildings as I walked. The rain had ended sometime earlier. I took a deep breath of air washed clean by the downpour. Nevertheless, it still smelled of car exhaust and Chinese food. At the kiosk on the corner of my street and Broadway I picked up two newspapers to read on the way downtown. Then I disappeared into the stairs leading to the Seventy-ninth Street station like Alice going down the rabbit hole.

The subterranean gloom quickly enveloped me. I felt at home in the man-made caverns beneath the city streets. I could imagine myself hanging by my toes from the girders in the roof. I smiled to myself. Wouldn't that be a sight for jaded New Yorkers? Chances were that most of them would glance up, see a giant bat hanging upside down, figure it was a publicity stunt, and continue hurrying along to their destinations. No oohs or ahhs, no fear, no curiosity. That's New York. It has to be something truly spectacular to impress this city . . . like the Yanks beating the Red Sox in the playoffs and then winning the World Series.

The squealing brakes and deafening roar of the number one local coming into the station made me pale with the memory of my narrow escape last night. As soon as I was seated in the nearly empty car, I scanned the *New York*

Times to see if the demise of the vampire hunters had made the paper. I saw nothing in the Metro section, but I wasn't surprised to find no coverage of the incident. I did spot a story on boutique ice creams being made in Brooklyn. That's the *Times* for you: "All the news that's fit to print." I ripped out Will Shortz's crossword puzzle just in case I had time on my hands later, a vain hope, and tossed the rest of the pages on a nearby seat.

The *New York Post* didn't let me down, however. On page twelve I spotted a short two-column article titled, "Gruesome Subway Mishap":

Two men met a violent death on the tracks of the Broadway local near the Twenty-eighth Street station around two a.m. this morning. The driver of the R train, Richard J. Hawkins, reported he could not avoid hitting the men who had been running through the uptown tunnel in front of the approaching train.

No charges have been filed against Mr. Hawkins, who was taken to the hospital for chest pains.

The Broadway local line was taken out of service while emergency workers recovered the remains. The tracks were reopened before the morning rush hour without causing any delay to morning commuters.

No evidence of terrorism has been linked to the dead men, but a police spokesperson said they were checking their fingerprints in the FBI database.

Hawkins, a twenty-five-year veteran with the MTA, reported seeing a third man in the tunnels, and he believed a fourth person, possibly a woman, was being chased by the others.

Police are theorizing that the incident was gang-related. The investigation is continuing.

I ripped the article out of the *Post* and threw the rest of the paper on top of the *Times* on the next seat. I made a mental note to ask Lieutenant Johnson if the men had been identified or if anyone had claimed their remains.

I learned an important fact: A Vampire hunter remained alive. He was still out there looking for me. And I had the bad feeling that vampire hunters were like cockroaches in a city apartment: You never have just one.

A listing for ABC Media, Inc., was back on the building directory in the lobby of the Flatiron Building. Fancy gold lettering still adorned the door to the office on the third floor. When I walked in, so early I had beat everyone else except J to the meeting, I noticed that the Mr. Coffee machine, as usual, sat atop its rickety table in the corner. Having the carafe half-full and some used Styrofoam cups in the metal wastebasket next to the table was a nice touch.

Looking out one of the tall windows, J stood with his back to me. After I entered, pulled out a chair from the table but did not sit, and dropped my backpack on the floor next to a chair, he finally turned and nodded with the smallest of movements. He was a cold man, with a cold manner.

"You telephoned me?" I asked, standing with the table between us.

"I called all the team members," he answered. "Something happened, but I'll wait for the rest to get here to talk about it."

"Right. Since we have a moment before the others get here, can I ask you something?" I wasn't going to ask him about the skullduggery with the office. If nobody had spotted my shopping bags, I didn't want him to know I knew. I had something else in mind.

"You can ask." He looked at me with those blue marble eyes of his. His self-control was a well-practiced art. The only sign that he felt anything at all when he spoke to me was the ropy vein throbbing along his right temple.

"Is Darius connected to our current mission in any way?" Even as I said it, it sounded absurd. Darius was back, but it had to do with me, not a missing ship.

"I have no evidence of that. Do you think he does?" J gave me a searching glance.

"Not really. I can't see how he could. I was just wondering . . ." I said, my voice trailing off.

"Why were you wondering?" J probed.

"Something my mother mentioned. Then you warning me off him. It just put the idea in my head, that's all."

J didn't answer right away. He seemed to be weighing his thoughts. "If I were you, Agent Urban, and I was concerned about Darius della Chiesa, I know what I would do."

"Which would be?" I said, my eyebrows raised in surprise.

"I would speak to your mother again."

At that point the other team members began entering, and I took my place at the table. Cormac and Rogue, dressed alike and ready to star in the latest buddy film, came in together. Benny pushed through the door next. Wearing the same clothes she had been the night before, she apparently hadn't slept today. Where she had spent the sunlit hours I didn't know. The tip of her nose was red. Her eyes were puffy. I guessed she had been crying. I mouthed, *What's the matter?*

She sat down next to me and whispered, "Martin's gone. I couldn't find any trace of him." Her breath caught and her voice trembled. "Help me find him. Please."

I said I would and squeezed her hand.

She lifted worried eyes to mine. "Daphne, I'm afraid something's happened to him."

Audrey was last to arrive. She would have heard me gasp if Cormac's and Rogue's wolf whistles hadn't drowned me out. Her thick hair cut short, her tall, thin body showing off a strapless denim minidress, she looked like a runway model. While the makeup was a little much for a spy meeting, her appearance certainly had shock value. When had the ugly duckling turned into a swan?

Noticing us all gaping at her, Audrey ducked her head in a manner that reminded me of Princess Di and said, "I came straight from a fashion show on Seventh Avenue." A shy smile lit up her face. "Elite's representing me."

A vampire as a runway model? Why not? We're everywhere, doing everything from brain surgery to truck driving. We have no restrictions except for avoiding exposure to sunlight, so, sure, none of us will ever win the U.S. Open or Wimbledon. But one of us did win the Nobel Prize and the International Poker Tour.

Looking at Audrey's new self-confidence, I felt some satisfaction. I had suggested that she give modeling a try. She hadn't recognized the potential of her angularity, her high cheekbones, her strong features. She had been worried about coming out of her shell. She had protested she'd be bored.

But there she was, doing it.

"That's excellent cover for a spy." J nodded. "Good

work. Now, let's get this meeting started. First, can I get your reports? Agent Urban? Why don't you begin."

"Benny and I spoke to an informant in the New York Police Department. A report of a mysterious collision between an unseen vessel of some type and a support column of the Outerbridge Crossing on Monday morning leads us to believe that the missing ship, still either camouflaged or invisible, turned north and was sailing toward the Goethals Bridge in the Arthur Kill shipping channel."

J looked visibly surprised. "Well done. Anything else?"

I looked at Benny. She shook her head.

"No," I responded. *Anything else?* I thought. So much else had happened, but I wasn't willing to discuss either the attack on me or Darius's appearance in my apartment. Chances were neither had anything to do with the *Intrepid*'s disappearance. I had learned long ago never to volunteer information. Answer just the question. Saying too much is a leading cause of getting fucked, and not in a pleasurable way.

Rogue and Cormac took their turn next, with Rogue doing the talking. Cormac sat with papers in his hand, ready to supply any details Rogue forgot, I guess. The two of them had made queries along the waterfront. No one had seen any suspicious activity along the river or in the harbor.

They had covered most of the West Side piers when they finally encountered a retired sanitation worker who ran a twenty-one-foot cruiser out of City Island. He had heard a rumor that about a month ago, a guy's fifty-seven-foot wooden ketch disappeared from its mooring at the Miramar Yacht Club in Sheepshead Bay. The missing ketch caused a big commotion.

Rogue showed some animation as he said, "Boaters in

the area said it was there one minute, gone the next. The marina called the owner—"

Cormac broke into Rogue's narrative to say, "He runs a tire store in Hempstead. Name of Ahmed Saud."

"—who didn't want them to even look for it. Said he sent somebody to take it out. Two days later the ketch—"

"It was named the *Petrel*," Cormac interjected, now beginning to annoy the bigger man.

"—was back in its berth. Same thing. The mooring was empty one minute, and the next thing the sailboat was back. Nobody saw it coming into port. One yacht owner said there was a mist or cloud, and a few minutes later he noticed the *Petrel* had anchored in its slip as if it had never gone." Cormac opened his mouth. Rogue glared at him.

"We're going to track down the owner and talk to him," Rogue finished up.

"So are you suggesting that this incident with the ketch was a practice run?" J asked.

"Could be."

"There's a world of difference between a fifty-seven-foot sailboat and an eight-hundred-seventy-two-foot aircraft carrier. However, you might be onto something. If that was a rehearsal, there might have been another one. With a larger ship. Check into incidents involving barges or cargo freighters."

"Right," Rogue said.

"Audrey?" J asked. "You have anything to report?"

Audrey hesitated, clearing her throat. "I don't know if what I found is relevant, but it's interesting, you know? I was doing an online search, fooling around, focusing on the Middle East. I was looking for an entity or a group having taken something of ours and wanting something else in exchange in order to give it back. You follow me so far?" She looked around. I nodded and so did the others.

"What I found sort of surprised me. Remember when Iran captured fifteen British sailors in March 2007? It was headline news at the time. Iran claimed the British had trespassed into their territorial waters. It was pretty clear from the start that the sailors were over a mile from Iran's boundaries. Britain even produced satellite photos of the sailors' position to prove it.

"Two weeks after Iran took the prisoners, following some very secret talks back and forth between Iran and Tony Blair, Iran released the sailors unharmed. Britain carried out no retaliation. The U.K. didn't even demand sanctions against Iran. Outside of some meaningless bluster, Blair and his government basically hushed up the incident, buried it as quickly as possible. Why? What was it all about? I found it baffling." She looked at all of us again.

"Then I found the key to the whole incident!" Audrey's voice rose and her face lit up. She glanced down at her notes. "Listen to this. In February, a month before the taking of the sailors, an Iranian diplomat—his name was Jalal Sharafi—was snatched off Baghdad's streets by men in Iraqi defense force uniforms. Immediately Iran blamed the U.S., made all kinds of threats. They really jumped up and down in the press about it. The U.S. vehemently denied having anything to do with it.

"Now, here's the fun part. After Iran released the British sailors, Mr. Sharafi was spotted at his home in Tehran. Isn't that neat?" She smiled at us.

Cormac shook his head. "I don't get it."

"It's so devious it's brilliant," Audrey said. "See, I think British forces disguised as Iraqis took Mr. Sharafi. It's not unusual, by the way. Our people—Delta Force, maybe CIA people, you know—do it too, almost routinely. We kidnap a diplomat and question him. 'Does Iran have nuclear weapons? Are they developing them?' That kind of thing.

"Now, the Iranians knew from the start that intelligence operatives from the West snatched their diplomat. There were plenty of eyewitnesses to the kidnapping, and not a lot of Iranians are blonds, as at least two of the perpetrators were.

"Iran blamed America, naturally, but somehow—I wouldn't be surprised if our embassy told them—they found out British intelligence forces had carried out the abduction. A month later Iran found an opportunity to take the fifteen British sailors into custody. It gave them the bargaining chip that they used to secure Sharafi's release.

"The public had no clue what was going on. The way the media reported the seizing of the sailors, it seemed as if the Iranians were just acting crazy. Sure they were. Crazy as foxes!"

"Okay, I see that," Cormac agreed, leaning back in his chair like Rogue always did, crossing his arms across his chest, and stretching his legs under the table. The trouble was, Cormac was shorter than Rogue. Only his head poked up above the tabletop. It was comical. Something was definitely lost in translation. "But how is all that relevant to the *Intrepid* going missing?" he challenged her again.

"It's the same thing," Audrey insisted.

"Hold on there, girlfriend," Benny said. "You're sounding one can short of a six-pack, if you catch my drift."

"I mean," Audrey said, "somebody took the *Intrepid* because we took something of theirs."

"Well, now, it must be a mighty big something," Benny said, still skeptical.

"Actually, Audrey may have a point." J took over the conversation. "As I informed you all, we have had a communication that may relate to the *Intrepid*'s disappearance. It came through our embassy in Pakistan. An international cricket star named Shalid Khan has asked to meet with U.S. intelligence officials when he arrives in New York City tomorrow. He says it has to do with returning a national treasure."

Audrey's brown eyes sparkled. "I told you!"

"Here's his photo. It's a Reuters press photo taken at a fund-raising gala for a hospital charity." He passed out some eight-by-ten glossies. "As to what the communication concerns, let's not leap to any conclusions," J warned. "But the director of our agency must be thinking along the same lines as Audrey, since the message has been passed on to the Darkwings.

"One of you is to meet with Mr. Khan. Audrey, you would be perfect to take the assignment. We'll set it up and let you know when and where. There's only one problem," J added.

"What's that?" Audrey asked.

"To the best of my knowledge—and that's after talking to our people and the officials of the other intelligence agencies—we do have some 'persons of interest' from the Middle East in custody at the moment, but none of them is important enough to warrant an operation of the magnitude of stealing the *Intrepid*."

"So what do they want?" Audrey asked.

"That's what has everybody nervous," J said. "Maybe they want us to empty Gitmo. Maybe they want a troop pullout from the Middle East. Your job is going to be to find out who's behind this, and then learn what they're really after."

The meeting finished up. Audrey was like a kid about to get a pony as she anticipated meeting with Shalid Khan. She chattered to Benny. She bounced around in her chair. Her energy level exhausted me just looking at it.

J's mandate to the rest of us was to keep trying to find the ship. *Fat chance of that happening*, I thought.

Before we dispersed I ducked into my office to retrieve the Bloomingdale's bags. They sat undisturbed where I had stashed them. But the computer was back on my desk as if it had never been moved. I was impressed by the layer of dust on the keyboard. It was subtle, but it showed some nice attention to detail.

I came back out into the meeting room, my hands laden with packages. It was going to be awkward to tote them down to Lucifer's Laundromat, the vampire club on Second Avenue in the East Village. But Audrey, a well-entrenched regular, said she'd get the bartender to put them behind the bar while we were there.

We all decided to start the evening at the club, then plan our next moves. The boys had their toys with them—in other words, Cormac and Rogue were still riding their Harleys—but this time Benny said she'd join me in a taxi. The men on bikes went roaring down Fifth Avenue while we flagged a Yellow Cab. Audrey was coming along with us too. She definitely wasn't dressed for riding bitch.

As we settled ourselves in the backseat, with Benny in the middle, I leaned forward and said to Audrey, "You're not in the right clothes for team blood hunting, but you look fabulous. What designer are you wearing?"

"Juicy Couture. Their summer collection. Isn't it precious?"

"It looks terrific on you," I said.

She grinned. "Thanks. And believe me, I can hunt in this. It's a mini. Great range of motion. I am absolutely famished, so I intend to win tonight."

With that my own stomach rumbled. I had drunk another pint of type O negative from my refrigerator stash before I left the apartment. After my "donation" to Darius, the pint didn't leave me feeling sated. I should have drunk two, I guessed. And as my thoughts turned to Darius, I felt anxious about getting back home as early as I could. If I hadn't promised Benny I'd help her, I would make up some excuse to leave and be on my way back already. All I could think about was being with him.

No, experience had not been a good teacher. I had been avoiding the truth. Now I had to face facts. You don't get to choose whom you love. And I had blindly, wildly, unreservedly fallen in love with Darius. It was the kind of love that happens once in a lifetime. For me, in a very long lifetime, it had happened just twice. First, nearly two hundred years ago, I had felt this way about George Gordon, Lord Byron. Now, from the day we met, it had been Darius who commanded my heart.

It was unlikely I would ever feel this way again. Like Othello, I loved not wisely, but too well.

And love was a terrible paradox for me—for everyone who has ever loved, I suppose. Alone I had been an independent creature, proud of my ego, certain of myself, even when I didn't admire my behavior very much. But with this kind of love the self was submerged into another's being. At worst, this love was a voluntary servitude. At best—and by that I mean at its deepest, most powerful—love became eternal submission. The beloved's wishes meant more than one's own. The beloved's life was worth sacrificing one's own. Without the beloved's reciprocation nothing mattered. One fell into a hell of one's own making more agonizing than any other torment.

And one of the truisms about love was that women and men both felt as though they must bind themselves to their beloved, two as one. They willingly gave up their freedom. For their lover, they forsook all others, even family, even friends. Betrayed their king. Gave up their crown. Think Romeo and Juliet. Lancelot and Guinevere. Tristan and Isolde. King Edward and Wallis Simpson. Darius and me.

I had fought the inevitable long enough. I took a deep breath. Confession time.

"I have something to tell you," I announced.

The last time I said those very words, we were also all together in the backseat of a New York Yellow Cab. Then I had asked Benny and Audrey to be bridesmaids in my wedding—to St. Julien Fitzmaurice. I inwardly cringed at that, for while I had been very fond of Fitz, I had not been in love with him. What I was about to tell my friends would sound vain and fickle. Never mind. I plunged on.

"I'm back with Darius. At least, I think I am."

That bombshell meant nothing to Audrey; she had never met my ex. But it landed like an IED on Benny. Among the many slights and offenses she ascribed to him, Benny blamed Darius for vampire hunters exterminating our teammate Bubba Lee. I could tell she wasn't exactly jumping up and down with joy at my news.

"Since when?" she demanded.

"Last night," I replied.

Benny turned to Audrey with a jerk of her shoulder that eloquently stated her pique at me. "Now, you don't know him, Audrey, so let me tell you something. This here Darius, he's a snake in the grass. An ungrateful snake too, as if being an ordinary rattler, poisonous as can be, ain't hardly enough."

"You're kidding." Audrey poked her head around Benny's big Texas-style hair so I could see her. "Is that true?" she asked me.

I shrugged. "Not exactly."

Benny swiveled her head in my direction. She was spitting like a cat. "Don't you dare call me a liar. Let Audrey make up her own mind." She showed me her rigid back and faced the vampire librarian–turned–fashion model to make her pitch for Darius as a no-account, two-timing, double-crossing hound dog. I didn't like it much.

"Here's what happened," she said. "This Darius? He was a Navy SEAL who got into the intelligence end of things. And we was all after the same terrorists here in New York City. This wasn't all that long ago, either. Things got rough toward the end of the mission, a firefight out in New Jersey, and Darius, he got shot bad. Daphne . . . well, she had already gone gaga for him. I give it to you that he's good-looking and sexy as all get-out. But, honey, pretty is as pretty does, my mama always said.

"Daphne was right there when he took the bullet, and she saved his sorry life by giving him the kiss of death. She made him an immortal, and what did he do? Thank her? Uh-uh. He dumped her. He hated her for making him a vampire, and that's the truth."

She looked back at me again, her eyes snapping with anger. "Now, don't you go denying it either." She turned back to Audrey.

"Then he formed a rock band which he went and called—get this—Darius DC and the Vampire Project. Talk about having cojones. He hit the charts, made it big. None of us could believe it. Pretty soon he comes a-crawling back to Daphne. And she takes him back, o'course.

"So then he's getting all kinds of famous, and he asks Daphne here to go on tour with him. O'course she couldn't. She'd have to quit the Darkwings, and she weren't going to do that, now, were you, girlfriend?"

"No," I said sadly, "I couldn't do that." To tell the truth, I nearly agreed to go with Darius. Benny didn't know how close I had been to quitting. But some things you don't tell even your best friend.

Benny's strident voice was ringing in my ears by now. "So what does Mr. Big Rock Star do? He goes on tour anyway *with his ex-girlfriend*, that's what he does. But before he leaves—and listen to this, Audrey—"

Audrey *was* listening—with big eyes and rapt attention—to Benny's tirade. She was hearing pure, unadulterated, juicy gossip. She was eating it up, enjoying the story. I didn't exactly blame her. I slid lower and lower in the seat, feeling miserable, as Benny worked herself up for the grand finale.

"So this too-big-for-his-britches new vampire not only advertises who he is all over the place with Darius DC and the *Vampire* Project, he becomes a vampire vigilante and goes around the city biting drug dealers and such. He draws so much attention to his sorry self that vampire hunters by the dozens come here to New York, causing all kinds of problems."

Benny turned to me then with an I-told-you-so look on her face. "So he's back. And surprise, surprise, Miss Daphne Urban, so are the vampire hunters. Are you seeing a pattern here?"

I was. And Benny never knew the worst of it with Darius. He wasn't just a spy for some other agency. He had been a vampire hunter, and at one time he had been hunting me.

CHAPTER 9

"Whoso in ignorance draws near them and hears the Siren's voice, he nevermore returns . . . and all about them is a heap of bones of moldering men, and round the bones the skin is shriveling."

—Homer, *The Odyssey*, Book 12

A terrible misery settled over me. I'm not the only woman to have her best friend dis her current lover and much prefer an ex-boyfriend who was a great guy. But that didn't make Benny's oration any easier to listen to.

Benny had been crazy about Fitz. All my friends thought he was perfect for me—except me. He was a paragon of virtue. Maybe that was the problem. I have a weakness for bad boys, I suppose. But I had always seen the good in Darius. Benny didn't. Hell, nobody else did.

Okay, Daphne, my inner voice said. *You're right. The rest of the world is wrong.*

Damn straight, I answered myself. *And someday I'll prove it too.* I was getting pissed at my rational, reasonable doubts.

As we disembarked from the cab at the vampire club, I noticed Audrey looking at me hard, with pity, as if she were thinking what a weak, foolish creature I was. She should be thinking, *There but for the grace of God* . . . She'd find out the hard way. Most women did.

I held my chin up a bit higher as we entered the dimly lit interior of Lucifer's Laundromat. Cormac and Rogue already had a table, which was actually a Whirlpool dryer surrounded by high stools.

Audrey waved at them before taking my Bloomie's bags from me and heading for the bar. She looked like a million bucks. I glanced down at my old jeans and black T-shirt. I looked like a grunge rocker from Seattle.

Benny, still radiating righteous indignation, marched over to the male team members and announced, "Listen up, y'all. Daphne has hooked up with Darius again. Probably because of him, the vampire hunters are back in the city. Daphne was already attacked. And we're all going to get stakes in our hearts if'n we don't watch out."

I came up behind her, ready to give my side of the story.

Rogue, who had joined the team just weeks ago for our previous mission, didn't know about Darius any more than Audrey did. The world-worn biker sat at the table, his weight on his elbows. He picked up a shot glass filled with whiskey and dumped the contents down his throat. Then he picked up a beer bottle and chugged it. After he wiped his mouth on the back of his hand, he said, "Personally, I don't give a shit about who she's sleeping with. The poor schmuck has my sympathy if she has her claws in him. But what's he got to do with vampire hunters?"

"Nothing!" The word exploded from my mouth.

Benny countered, "Oh, yes, he does. He must have. He's back, and Daphne got attacked the other night. And Martin's missing. I think they got him. I think . . . I think . . . I'm afraid . . . he's dust." Her voice crumbled and she started making soft crying noises.

Aha! I suddenly understood Benny's hard-line attitude toward Darius.

"I liked Darius," Cormac said to no one in particular.

"Let's ask around about Martin," I suggested, touching her lightly on the arm. "Maybe he just left town."

The tears ran down her face. "I did that. I asked. He was supposed to lead his team last night. He never showed up. The hunters got him; I jist know they did."

Rogue rolled his eyes, tipped his bald head back, held the beer bottle above his mouth, and caught the last few drops on his tongue.

"Benny, calm down," I said. "Think about it. The vampire hunters haven't come after anybody but me. I'm sure he's all right. Did you try going to his apartment?"

Benny sniffed. "No. I . . . I felt foolish. What if . . . what if I did and he was with somebody, you know? He'd think I was chasing him. I jist couldn't."

My thoughts exactly, but I wasn't willing to voice them. Benny was upset with me as it was, and her rejection and hostility hurt more than I imagined they would. "All right. Tell you what. Let's go together over to Martin's. All of us."

I gave Rogue and Cormac a look that said I expected them to go along with this. "Then, if he's there"—I turned back to Benny—"he'll see right away it's all of us and it will take the pressure off you."

Audrey had rejoined us by this time. "What's this about going over to Martin's place?"

"It seems he's missing," I said. "I think we *all* should go."

Audrey looked over at the blue neon clock. "Sure. The race for the blood doesn't start for a couple more hours."

*   *   *

Ten minutes later the five of us stood shoulder-to-shoulder in the poorly lit, dank hallway on the sixth floor of a crappy walk-up tenement on East Fourth Street. A lot of Eastern European immigrants must have moved into the neighborhood. The place stank of boiled cabbage.

Rogue pounded on Martin's front door with his fist. "Martin! Hey, buddy! You there?"

No one answered. Instead a door opened at the far end of the hall. A tiny, white-haired woman wearing a babushka appeared. She was holding a butcher knife in one hand and a crucifix in the other. I knew what she was. I had seen her kind before.

"Get out of here! All of you. I call nine-one-one!" she said in her wavering crone's voice.

"It's okay, bubbie," Rogue said. "We're friends of his."

"You no friends. Get out!"

At that point I did what I had done before under similar circumstances. I smiled at the old lady widely enough to show my fangs. Then I hissed at her, drawing out my Ss and sounding exactly like what I was: a vampire. "Gypssssy, thisss isss not your businesssssss."

The butcher knife dropped from her hand to the floor. "Aaaiiiee! *Strega!*" she cried out, and shook her crucifix at me as she backed into her apartment. The door slammed shut. I heard the dead bolt slide into place.

Rogue pounded on Martin's door again. "Martin! Martin, buddy! You in there?"

I heard rustling from within. Locks were being opened. I heard the floor brace being moved. The door opened a crack. The security chain was on. Martin's white face appeared in the opening. "Huh?" He squinted. The man looked shit-faced drunk. "Whadda you want?"

Benny cried out. "Marty, thank the Lord. Are you okay?"

"Hol' on a min'it," Martin said, slurring his words. He closed the door to take off the chain. Then it opened again. "Come on in."

The five of us squeezed into his vestibule. Martin, unsteady on his feet and seemingly moving with some pain, led the way to a tiny living room that was so dark I could barely see the furniture.

"You wanna drink?" he offered. Clearly, from the half dozen empty bottles on the coffee table and the stench of stale booze in the air, he had already had one or two—or twenty.

Nobody said yes. Obviously we had interrupted one hell of a binge.

"Sorry to bother you. When you didn't show up at the club last night people got worried," Rogue said.

"You didn't answer your phone either," Benny added. "I called."

"Sorry 'bout that. I didn't feel like talking. Too freaked out." Martin rubbed his fingers into his eyes. "I don't usually drink this much. I didn't know what else to do 'bout the situation."

"What do you mean?" Benny said, taking it personally, I could tell.

"I nearly got staked. Last night on my way to the club."

Benny gave me an I-told-you-so look.

I ignored her reproach and asked Martin to tell us what happened.

The wiry, boyish vampire—he looked young, though he was probably pushing two hundred or so—sat down gingerly in a chair and put his face in his hands. "Closest I ever came to . . . you know." He looked up at us with bleary eyes and started to tell his story.

Martin said he had left his apartment at dusk, just as he did every night. His routine consisted of going to the Laundromat and hanging out until the nightly blood race. This evening was the same as all the rest. He lived only a few blocks from the club. As usual, he walked, taking his time, looking around for potential victims who might be foolish enough to be loitering in this neighborhood. He picked up the *Post* at a newspaper kiosk, since he preferred its sudoku to the *Times* crossword. It helped pass the time, he added wearily.

Passing time was something vampires did a lot of.

Martin had nearly reached the Laundromat—he was maybe a half block from it—when he noticed this big guy on the other side of Second Avenue, leaning back against a storefront, watching the street. The man had dressed all in black leather on this hot night, wrapped chains around one arm, and looked like the villain half of a WWF tag team.

Martin didn't pay him any special attention at first. Sure, the guy looked weird, but this was the East Village. Nine out of ten people looked weird.

All of a sudden the guy pushed himself upright, ran toward the street, jaywalked through the traffic as horns honked and brakes squealed, and started racing toward Martin. Martin reacted with sangfroid, unconcerned, even a little pleased. If the guy wanted a fight, no problem. The burly WWF wannabe was about to tangle with a vampire.

Then, in his peripheral vision, Martin spotted another leather-clad ugly dude coming down the block toward him from the other direction. Martin took a better look and saw a long, pointed wooden stake in the ugly dude's hand. Martin swung his eyes back toward the first guy. He was armed with a similar device.

Vampire hunters, holy shit! Time to get the hell out of here, he thought.

With escape cut off from the front and behind, Martin went the only way he could: into the nearest doorway. He felt panic and real fear for the first time in his vampire existence, and his heart was thudding in his chest.

Fortunately Martin, a native New Yorker, knew that particular tenement well. The first-floor hall served as a passageway that cut through the building and exited into a rear courtyard. A three-story colonial-era structure sat there, freestanding, decrepit, but still in use. A writer friend of Martin's had lived in its tiny first-floor flat a decade before.

The old building's fire escape ladder hung down within reach. Martin snagged it and swung himself up. He quickly climbed toward the roof of the old building, fast, but not fast enough.

As Martin pulled himself up the rusted iron rungs of the decaying ladder, one of the hunters took a swipe at him with the stake. It missed his heart. It buried itself in his cute little butt.

That was my characterization. Martin actually said, "The fucking piece of shit got me in the ass."

Martin reached the roof, kicked his closest pursuer in the teeth, transformed into bat form, and flew skyward. He came in the window of his apartment and had been holed up there ever since, afraid to venture out again.

"As soon as my butt's healed—by tomorrow, I guess— I'm going to get out of town. I'm afraid they're watching my building. I don't know how they found the Laundromat. I didn't even sleep today. I'm scared to close my eyes. I want to head to someplace safe. Maybe Portland. The West Coast, anyway."

That piece of news dropped on Benny like bird guano. Her mouth twisted downward, her face clearly reflecting her distress at the abrupt end to her dreams of snagging Martin.

Guess who she was going to blame? I jumped in with the first idea that popped into my head.

"Martin, let's not be hasty. We've got our full Darkwing team here. How about we go out and reconnoiter, see what we can do? Running's not the answer. These guys are going to get somebody else if they're not stopped. If they've targeted the Laundromat, we're going to lose a lot of New York's vampires."

I turned to the other Darkwings. "What are your feelings on this?"

"I say we get them before they get us," Rogue said.

Audrey hesitated. "I'm not that good. Fighting. Physical stuff, I mean."

Rogue said, "Time you got a taste for it. All you need is practice."

"I'm down for it," Cormac said.

"Good," Rogue responded. "If they're watching for Martin or the other club regulars, they're probably lurking around nearby. I say we split into two groups. Cormac, you take Audrey and Benny and cover the streets on the West Side, looking for any hunters on the streets. Daphne and I will hit the East Side."

Huh? I thought. Why did he want to team up with me? Maybe he needed a break from being the Oscar Madison half of the odd couple.

Meanwhile mixed emotions chased across Cormac's

face. No doubt he'd rather be paired up with Rogue, but he was being put in charge of a squad by his idol. He couldn't exactly argue.

Martin hobbled over to the window he used for his aerial exits and threw it open wide. The window led to a narrow air shaft where the air hung hot and fetid. Stinking garbage lay on the ground six stories down. We'd have use our wings and feet to clamber vertically up the bricks to the roof and then take flight.

Oh, that's going to be fun, I thought.

Preparing to transform, we all removed our clothes without hesitation or shame. All of us were focused on the transfiguration about to take place. Entering a fugue state, a place of no consciousness, the butterfly in the chrysalis about to break free, we would begin to change.

But the room was too small to hold us all in bat form, so the A-team of Benny, Audrey, and Cormac went first. Their energy whirled into a vortex that generated enough static to make my hair bristle. A kaleidoscope of colors danced on the walls. The three human forms disappeared within columns of light. Then the light died, the sound of rustling wings burst forth, and in a blast of wind and sound three bats appeared, larger than human and strangely, utterly beautiful.

All were sleek and pelted with fantastic fur that refracted light like hundreds of tiny prisms. Their faces remained recognizable except that their eyes were no longer human, but the huge orbs of the species. Audrey, lanky and gray with a prominent nose, best resembled Geoffroy's Rousette fruit bat. Cormac was clearly a large flying fox, and Benny, golden and glistening, took on the guise of an Asian yellow house bat.

Yet they were not bats at all. They were creatures of myth

and wonder, monsters to be feared, yet mesmerizing to any human who fell into their path and then, quaking in terror, felt their kiss and the flow of rich, red blood that followed.

Out the window each of them went, crawling batlike up the wall toward the black city sky.

Rogue and I changed then. For me it was a setting free of every emotion that I suppressed. With each violent transformation I became my inner self, my shadow self, the part of me I hated and yet the part of me that I suspected was the truest, the most real.

Euphoric with my power, reveling in my animal prowess, I nevertheless retained enough human reason to grab my backpack containing my gun and sling it over my head. A vampire's claws penetrate flesh, but bullets do it better.

I hopped onto the sill. I paused for a moment before I reached out to feel the rough bricks. I began the climb, now a fearsome thing ascending up the wall. Within moments I reached the roof. I spread my wings wide and, with a mightly thrust, left behind the bonds of earth and the asphalt rooftop.

Rogue's great black shape appeared behind me. With the distinctive flitting and swooping of the chiropteran, we stayed just above the rooftops, black forms against a black sky and therefore nearly invisible.

We headed downtown to the Bowery, continued as far as Canal Street, then doubled back. We reconnoitered the streets in Soho, then followed the traffic on Houston for a few blocks until we returned to Greenwich Village. We flew north above Sixth Avenue, made a sharp right at Eighth Street, circled around the strange black cube statue at Cooper Union, and kept going east toward the river.

We didn't see anybody suspicious until we reached Tompkins Square Park at Seventh Street and Avenue A.

A stand of towering American elm trees had survived Dutch elm disease in this unlikely refuge. Illuminated by the streetlights, they cast long shadows across the sidewalk. I hovered for a moment near them, cognizant of their majesty and rarity. And then I remembered the things that had happened in this small city park.

I circled the top of the Hare Krishna Tree. Beneath this elm in the summer of 1966, the beat poet Allen Ginsberg and the Swami Prabhupada chanted Hare Krishna and began a movement. After that, many people called the park sacred.

The junkies called it a place to score: heroin mostly, some meth, some coke. Then the homeless moved in.

Two decades later a bunch of gays started Wigstock, a daylong drag festival in the park, and in the 1990s the park was closed down for two years to get rid of the homeless and gentrify the place.

I had been an eyewitness to its colorful past. I had seen these strange and wondrous things unfold. I was among the girls in India-cotton dresses and boys in bell-bottoms because of my mother.

Mar-Mar had embraced the counterculture of the Village beginning with Kerouac and the beats in the 1950s. She found her stride and total acceptance during the Summer of Love. She developed a habit of smoking marijuana. She intoned poetry on the subways. She marched against the war, for free love, for poverty programs, and for equality. She formed a woman's group, the Night Birds.

She went to consciousness-raising meetings holding Mao's Little Red Book. She became a member of SDS and ran the streets with Kathy Boudin and Mark Rudd. She broke completely with the Weathermen over the use of violence before they started building bombs, but in other ways she tried to implement the revolutionary ideas she had held for at least five hundred years.

Through the 1970s she fought on, although the movement faded away. She considered Reaganomics a personal affront and redoubled her efforts to help the homeless, one of her deepest concerns.

On the night of August sixth, in 1988, she convinced me to come along with her to Tompkins Square Park. She and some other political activists were gathering to protest attempts to move out the homeless. I think she knew what was going to happen and wanted to "raise my consciousness." She was always doing shit like that to me.

Now, as I glanced down on the still, silent park below, I remembered the riot that broke out between the cops, the homeless, Mar-Mar, and some of her lefty friends—and me. Nightsticks knocked heads, tear gas went off, people screamed, everybody ran. The television cameras rolled. I saw myself on *NBC Nightly News* the next day: A cop had me by the hair and I was kicking him in the shins.

I got a little banged up, and forty-four other people were injured, some pretty seriously. Everybody screamed police brutality. A couple of cases went to court. Nobody got convicted. Nothing changed.

Right after that my mother gave up her Christopher Street apartment and moved to Scarsdale. I never quite figured out why, except that the incident broke her heart in a way. I think that was when she decided to shift tactics to change the world. She become a manipulator within the government instead of a protester against it.

I often wondered why the top intelligence bosses trusted

my mother to run their black ops. Who did they think they
were dealing with? Didn't they know Mar-Mar had been a
yippie? She once kept Abbie Hoffman's phone number on
her speed dial. I guess they did know—and didn't care. The
ends justified the means.

As I was woolgathering and not paying attention to anything on the ground, Rogue gave me a bat whistle.

He pointed down at Avenue B on the east side of the park.
I saw two large men, big as brick shithouses. They stood by
a sign that read, TO REPORT A PROBLEM, TO LEARN WHAT WE
DO, OR TO VOLUNTEER, CALL 1-800-555-PARX.

Before I knew it Rogue was diving straight at them. He
hit one vampire hunter with his feet and sent the bruiser
sprawling. Then Rogue landed and started hand-to-hand
combat with the other hunter.

I figured I'd better watch Rogue's back. I swooped down
on the guy who had gone ass-over-teakettle. The big lug had
gotten to his feet and pulled a stake from his bandolier. I
came somersaulting in from above and pulled the weapon
from his grasp with a tearing hiss. I landed, turned, and
flung it toward the Hare Krishna Tree, giving the instrument
of death over to karma and the gods.

Suddenly something hard and weighted hit me in the
head. Lights danced in my brain. The world went out of
focus. I refused to give in to the darkness. I shook it off and
spun around to see what had beaned me.

A third vampire hunter was emerging from under the
elms twenty feet away. He must have thrown a sock with a
roll of coins or a bar of soap inside.

Suddenly I had two hunters to deal with.

Rogue was busy slugging it out with his opponent. No
help was forthcoming from that quarter, and I was in trou-

ble. The first hunter had regained his bearings and lumbered toward me like a Sherman tank. The guy who came out from the shadows beneath the trees started closing in. I had to even the odds.

I did. I swung my backpack around and reached inside for my gun. With its laser guidance system I couldn't miss, though at this close range I could have used a snub-nose revolver and hit my target. I fired off two shots at my closest assailant. He went down without uttering a sound. I whipped around, steadied my hand, and shot the other vampire hunter, who had already turned to run. Too little, too late. The bullet hit him in the back of the head, and his skull exploded.

The noise got the attention of the last remaining vampire hunter. I couldn't shoot him, though. Rogue was in the way. Since his mama didn't raise no fool, Rogue twisted to the side, fell to the ground, and I squeezed off another two rounds. *Ping*—a bullet hit the vampire hunter's bandolier. *Pong* . . . it went through the guy's leather jacket somewhere in the vicinity of his heart. He sank to his knees and pitched forward.

My hand was shaking when I slipped the Beretta back in my Louis Vuitton. Rogue was standing now. He looked at the carnage around us, looked at me, and grinned.

"Nice work, Rambo," he said.

Afraid that the sounds of the gunshots would bring the cops, we took off skyward in great haste, leaving the dead hunters where they lay in a pool of blood. The dark red liquid radiated from beneath the bodies, flowed across the sidewalk, and dripped into the gutter.

I smelled it when I began to fly away. The odor filled my throat. It reminded me how much I needed some blood of my own—and soon.

Rogue must have been affected too. He flew close to me, his eyes looking crazy. "I've got something I got to do," he called out, then veered off.

I went in his general direction, not following him really, but heading back to Fourth Street. I had to return to Martin's open window to retrieve my clothes. Rogue was a block or so in front of me when I saw him fold his wings behind his back and go into a dive.

I flew faster, driven by curiosity and fear. I arrived just in time to watch what he did, and my heart beat wildly at the sight.

Four stories below me, a girl with long blond hair and pale white skin sat alone on the stoop of a run-down brownstone. She was smoking a cigarette, blowing the smoke out before her in lazy streams. A breeze wafted soft and warm, and the girl—she was perhaps seventeen—wore only shorts and a halter top. Maybe she wanted to escape her stuffy tenement rooms. Maybe she'd had a fight with her boyfriend or her mother. Whatever the cause, she was preoccupied with her thoughts. Foolishly she was not paying attention to the horror that was descending from above her.

And so the young girl did not see the evil coming down for her that night until it was too late.

A shadow passed over her. She looked up and jumped frantically to her feet. She backed up, her hands feeling behind her for the door. But there was no escape as the large, dark batlike creature landed before her. I saw terror suffuse her face. She opened her mouth to scream.

No scream came. I heard only a small sound, truncated, and silenced quickly as Rogue's hand shot out and grabbed her face, covering her mouth. His other hand encircled her arm, pulling her to him, pressing her against his unyielding body.

His victim struggled desperately, trying to push him away. He easily pinned her arms to her side and, letting go of her face, silenced her attempt to scream when his mouth came down on hers in a terrible kiss.

The blond-haired girl fought fiercely for a moment, trying to pull her head back. But suddenly she went completely still. Rogue let go of her then. Even though free of his touch, she stood unmoving, as if in a trance. She stared at the monster before her. The air became charged with a crackling sound. Then, in the ancient way, in the manner that had occurred uncountable times for innumerable years, the girl tipped back her head and showed her throat to him.

The ritual had begun. She was ready to become the vampire's bride. Docilely she obeyed when Rogue took his hand and turned her head to the side to allow him better access to her vein. His hand cupped her neck. She moaned. The vampire drew her toward him. She came willingly. He was ready to take what he came for: her blood.

I hovered above this scene of lust and hunger, both appalled and fascinated by what I was seeing. I couldn't look away.

Rogue's face lowered to the young girl's ghost white throat. I knew exactly when he bit her, when his sharp teeth pierced her smooth flesh, for she whimpered, her body trembling. Then she moaned, not in pain but in ecstasy. Suddenly, as she was overcome by her passions, the girl's legs gave way and her body went limp.

Rogue held her, preventing her fall. He dropped to his knees with her in his arms, his mouth still fastened to her throat. Once she rested on the stones of the landing he pulled her halter top down, revealing her perfect small breasts, and began to stroke them with one great, clawed hand. Then, his breathing quickening, he reached down and roughly ripped away first her shorts, then her panties.

I knew I should fly on, but instead, filled with shame but unable to go, I watched.

The vampire parted the girl's thighs as perhaps no man had ever done before. Never releasing her throat, he continued drinking deeply of her blood, and he moved his body over hers. Then, without hesitation, I saw the quick, hard way he took her. He was so large and she was quite a small creature, but he had no pity. He cruelly drove into her with great grunting thrusts. He was a beast. He had no gentleness. He was not human in his desire. He was a vampire.

The girl mewed beneath him for a moment, then sighed. He thrust faster, driving his member into her again and again. She opened her legs wider, and her thin arms embraced the monster that violated her. I could see it all. Finally the vampire's great body shook. The helpless girl's eyes snapped open. He had satisfied himself with her blood and her body.

Sated, Rogue released his victim. He stood up, blood dripping from his fangs. He left her lying naked on the steps, a discarded, ruined thing. But suddenly the girl stirred. She raised herself up as he moved away. Her arms reached out, her hands clutching at him, trying to pull him back.

I heard her say, "No, don't go. Stay. Stay with me," as humans will always say to the vampire lover who possesses them. They are in the vampire's thrall. They can't bear his absence. They are willing to die for their vampire lover.

But I was sure this cruel taking was over. Rogue shook the girl's hand from him and ignored her pleas to return to her. Silver tears on her cheeks caught the lamplight. Her blond hair fell like golden silk around her shoulders. Her white skin was bright against the dark steps where she lay.

I prepared to fly on. I veered off, beating my wings, setting my course for Martin's. I looked back to see if Rogue followed.

I was stunned at what I saw. Instead of leaving the girl, as he should have, he had gone back. He pushed her down. He leaped atop her like an animal. They writhed there on the stoop of the brownstone as he buried himself in her body, his animal lust driving his member into her again.

Seeing it tormented me. We are a terrible race. I tried to erase the image from my mind as I beat my wings hard and flew upward, anxious to be gone.

CHAPTER 10

*"I expect that Woman will be the last thing
civilized by Man."*

—George Meredith, *The Ordeal of Richard Feverel*

Lead from a position of strength. That's a lesson my
mother taught me.

I pushed all memories of the disturbing events of the
evening from my mind. I focused on the night yet to come.
I had to prepare myself to see Darius and get the truth from
him about why he had really come back.

And I had no intention of seeing him looking like a bass
player who had just stumbled out of a garage in Seattle with
Kurt Cobain. That was why, after returning to Martin's
apartment, telling him without elaboration that three hunters
were dead, and getting back into my street clothes, I had returned to Lucifer's Laundromat.

I needed my Bloomie's bags and I needed them now.

I retrieved my stuff from the bartender and headed for
the ladies' room. I stripped off my working clothes and put
on that killer halter dress by Mandalay. Its neckline plunged
to my diaphragm. It clung to me like a second skin. I put on
the matching shoes, unwrapped the exquisite rhinestone
clutch purse I had also purchased, and fished around
through the rubble in the bottom of my backpack. I found

my gun, the set of lock picks, some cash, and what I was looking for: my makeup kit. As the saying goes, Don't leave home without it.

I appraised myself in the mirror. My raven black hair fell straight and shimmering past my shoulders. My lips were glossed with cherry red. My skin resembled delicate white porcelain, but so pale it was almost translucent and I could see the light tracings of veins underneath. I was a hungry vampire and needed blood. On the plus side, my cornflower blue eyes popped in contrast.

I liked the effect. I looked kick-ass. I squared my shoulders, walked back out through the club feeling the stares following me, smiled at the attention, and got a cab.

I was armed and loaded for bear. Or Darius.

Darius was waiting for me in my apartment. Naked. Walking around my kitchen as if he owned the place. I felt a frisson of sexual excitement and a whole lot of annoyance. I wanted to announce, *No nookie tonight unless you start playing straight with me.*

I took a more diplomatic course. "I need blood," I said in lieu of hello.

Darius looked at me as if I were candy. He gave me a slow smile. "I'm here to serve you. Would you like a selection from column A or column B?"

"In the vegetable bin of the fridge. Any bag, any blood type." I sat down on the high stool next to the counter and crossed my legs. Darius took a long look. I had hoped he would.

I asked him to join me and requested he decant the blood into my Waterford wine glasses. He did. We clinked the glasses, and I said, *"Cin cin."* We drank. My mouth was filled with gore. I felt warmth and life returning to my flesh. By my taking the edge off my ravenous appetite—and Darius's—my plans might prove easier to carry out.

Darius reached over and clasped my fingers with his hand. He cradled them gently, stroking with his thumb. The fire of his touch traveled up my arm. I had a fragile enough hold on my self-control. I gently disengaged.

"I need to take Jade for a walk," I said with a smile. "Why don't you put some clothes on and join me? We need to talk."

Those are four words no man ever wants to hear. Darius raised a questioning eyebrow. "We do?"

"Are you surprised? I have a lot of questions. You have the answers, I think." I gazed into his eyes, green like lake water when the light filters through it, and filled with a sadness that his cocky manner belied.

I looked into them deep and long. Darius didn't hide anything from me there. His feelings were as naked as his body.

"I have only one question for you," he said, not breaking our eye contact.

"Which is?" I said.

"Do you still love me?"

A wave of sorrow passed over me. I had done so much since he had left, betraying my own heart as I did it. Yet I did not hesitate to say, "I never stopped loving you. Never. Not once. Not ever."

Darius reached over and pulled my head toward his, taking my lips in a kiss. When he pulled away, his head bowed and his eyes shut, he sighed, then looked up. "And I have never stopped loving you. Not once. Not ever."

"Well, now that we have that clear," I said, changing my

tone, "maybe we can stop acting like damned fools and get things straight between us."

Darius threw his head back and laughed. "Yeah, maybe we can."

Out on the street, Jade on a leash, my pet rat, Gunther, riding in my backpack—a fashion accessory that didn't go with the Mandalay dress, but the large white rodent didn't fit into the rhinestone clutch—I walked hand in hand with Darius.

The hour was late. Emotionally I was raw inside. The acts I had committed tonight, the acts I had seen tonight, I carefully compartmentalized in my mind. Eventually they would come slithering out from under the rocks of my mental landscape to haunt me. For now I had to do what I had to do.

I squeezed Darius's hand. "Why did you come back?" I said, focusing on the streetlight at the corner a few hundred feet ahead. It had just turned red.

"To see you," he said.

"Okay, I believe you. But, Darius, that's not the only reason." I paused, then said in a quiet, breathy voice, "That might not even be the compelling reason. Why did you leave Germany so suddenly? I need to know the truth."

I stopped moving then and positioned myself to face him. "Look at me. If we have any chance at all, if our love is possible despite the past, you need to tell me."

The sadness was back in his face. "I left Germany because I was given an assignment."

"Which was?"

"It's classified," he said.

"But ultimately it's why you're here. It led to your return. Didn't it?" I shook my head. His work, my work had come between us since the beginning. Darius had been in the navy when he was recruited by an alphabet agency in Washington, but not the same one that had recruited me.

Darius's boss didn't like my boss, J. J didn't like his boss, didn't like the rival agency, and especially didn't like Darius. He called him a loose cannon, and that was one of the nicer things he said.

Darius seemed to be carefully choosing his words when he answered. "In part, yes. The mission brought me back to the U.S. But I'm here, with you, because I couldn't stay away any longer, Daphne, and that's the truth."

"It's not the whole truth." I let out a deep sigh.

I felt Darius's body tense. His voice was tight. "It's all I can say. The rest of it is business. This is personal."

I dropped his hand and felt my anger rise. "The vampire hunters, Darius. They came back too. And that's not business. That's personal."

"If they are here, I didn't send them. I didn't bring them," he countered, his voice getting loud.

"They are here. I was attacked. Why did they show up at the same time you did? Why are they after me? Why are they after my friends?" My voice became a siren starting to rise.

He took my face between his fingers, which were not gentle, not kind. "Read my lips. I don't know."

Inside I was screaming. Outwardly I fought for control. I knocked his arm away, my ire building. "What's the connection then? What? You showed up. They showed up. It's no coincidence."

I saw the emotions chasing across his face. He didn't answer for a long moment. Finally he said, "I know that. I did know you were attacked. It scared me more than anything has scared me in a long time. I'm trying to find out what's going on."

"How did you know I was attacked?"

"Let's just say a little bird told me."

"Oh, that's cute, Darius. Who was the little bird? Your 'friend' Julie?" He was pushing all the wrong buttons, that was for sure.

"No. Not Julie. I still have contacts. In the church. I still hear things."

I gave him a long look, my anger simmering and about to explode. "So, do you know who they are?"

"Maybe."

I waited for more. Darius remained silent. I decided to try a different tack. "Do you know how many of them there are?"

His jaw worked. "You're not going to like this."

"How many, Darius?"

"Ninety. A hundred. Maybe more."

"A hundred! You have got to be kidding me. What the hell have you brought? A vampire hunter army?"

"I told you, I didn't bring them!"

"Whatever! Darius, what's going on?" I grabbed his arm hard and pulled him close to me. "Stop bullshitting me. Why are they here?"

Darius said nothing.

"Tell me, or so help me, I will walk away and I will not come back. I will *never* come back. Look into my eyes, Darius. I mean every word. You said you love me. Now fucking prove it. Tell me."

His face was like granite, hard and unmoving, when he answered. "I don't have any proof. What I've heard is that they're Opus Dei operatives. They're here to wipe out every vampire in New York."

I stood there frozen for a second, trying to take it in. Then the rage boiled up in me. My fingers dug into Darius's arm. My words struck hot sparks like flint on stone. "You get the message out. You get it back to them. This is war. And we vampires won't lose. I've killed five of them already. If I have to I'll kill every last one of them myself."

Darius just stared at me. Whatever he expected me to say or do, that wasn't it, I guess.

"And one more thing," I said. "If I find out you lied to me, if I find out you helped them or brought them or are one of them, no matter how much I love you, Darius—and I love you more than you will ever know—it won't save you. I won't be able to protect you. Don't fool yourself. If I don't have the courage to kill you myself, I know who will."

With those terrible, hurtful words, I understood something for the first time: I was my mother's daughter. I had learned her lessons well.

And I had spoken without thinking about the consequences. I didn't know what would happen after I said what I said. Once I stopped, I expected Darius to turn on his heel and leave. To my surprise he didn't. He looked at me with something I had never seen before in his eyes: respect.

He put his palm against my cheek, his fingers sliding into my hair. "If I ever betrayed you so, if I ever brought you harm, I would not deserve to exist. I swear to you that I am not one of them. Not anymore."

He leaned forward and kissed me as we stood on the sidewalk. His body was hard as it pressed against mine. I felt happy like this, touching him, close to him, but I couldn't let my passion blind me. I wanted to believe Darius. But the worm of doubt had burrowed deep, and it remained.

*   *   *

Mickey gave us a curt nod when we returned to the lobby. The doorman wasn't speaking to me tonight, his disapproval obvious.

"What did I do to piss him off?" Darius whispered as we got into the small elevator to ascend to the tenth floor.

"You came back," I said.

In that tight space, with Darius against me, my pheromones overcame me, getting the best of me at last. Despite everything that had transpired, despite my doubts and fears, I could not be this close to Darius and not want him. My body didn't listen to reason. It compelled me to reach over, open Darius's fly, and unbutton his jeans. He didn't stop me. He just watched me and smiled.

Both of us started to laugh then. He backed me against the elevator wall, hiked my new halter dress up to my waist, moved the crotch of my thong aside, and took me there in the elevator without preamble. He slid in quickly, thrust fast, and came before the elevator stopped on the tenth floor.

"You owe me one," I said as we stepped into the hall, adjusting my dress and my cheeks blushing rose.

"I'll give you a twofer." He winked. And later, until the night faded away and relinquished the darkness to the faint rosy glow of dawn, he did.

Before it was fully light out, Darius rolled over and got out of bed. He said he had to leave.

"Where are you going?" I asked. "Do you still have your apartment?"

"Nah, I gave it up when I left on tour." He pulled on his jeans and kept his back to me.

"So why not sleep here?"

"Next time," he said, sidestepping the question.

"So where are you going?"

"I have some business to take care of," he said, keeping his voice light.

The *Family Feud* buzzer sounded in my head. *Blaaat.* Wrong answer.

"Does the business have short curly hair and a nasty attitude when it comes to me?" I said, and sat up.

I saw his body stiffen. He didn't face me when he answered. "If you mean Julie, no. Why can't you get over it?"

"Because, Darius, she tried to kill me. And even after she tried to kill me, you took her to Europe with your band. A few weeks ago you left your band *with* Julie. What am I supposed to think?"

Darius came over and sat on the edge of the bed. He didn't say anything as he put on his shoes. I sat there, the sheet tangled around my waist, my breasts bare.

Finally he twisted around and looked at me. He took my hand and brought it to his lips. He bent down and kissed my breasts. He kissed my lips and filled my mouth with his tongue. I'd be a liar if I said it didn't feel good.

Then, pulling me close against him, my skin brushing against the roughness of his shirt, he hugged me. "You're supposed to think that I love you. Because I do. And I'm here with you, not Julie. She's just a member of my team."

That was true, so why did I say in a whisper, my lips close to his ear, "But you *fucked* her, Darius. So she's not just a team member"?

Darius dropped my hand and stood up. He gave me a long look before he spoke. When he did, his voice was anything but loving. "Daphne, when it comes to *fucking*, I don't think you're in any position to go around throwing stones at me."

He was right, of course. But when I slept with Fitz and had sex with Rogue, when I had descended into the den of debauchery and met the satyrs there, Darius and I had broken up. I had never cheated on him, not once. I had never even lusted in my heart. And I certainly didn't team up with anyone who had tried to kill him.

A wiser woman would have shut up and let bygones be bygones. But the thought of Darius with Julie hurt so much. And how did I know he wasn't going to her now? So I opened my mouth and asked, "Are you going to see her?"

"I told you, I have business to do. Leave it, Daphne. Now I have to go." He bent down and brushed his lips against mine. I wouldn't call it a kiss.

I watched him walk out of the bedroom. I heard the front door open. I heard it slam. Then the quietness took over and so did the ache inside me. And Darius had not told me if or when he was coming back.

CHAPTER 11

*"All things are poison and nothing is not a
poison; the dose alone makes the difference."*

—Paracelsus

Gilt, a chic bar with an adjoining restaurant at the New
York Palace Hotel, lived up to its name. Gold was
everywhere.

With a reservation for dinner at nine o'clock, Benny and
I showed up at the hotel around eight thirty, as soon as the
sunlight died down enough so we could venture forth from
our dens.

Being early, Benny and I sat for a while at a pie-plate-size
cocktail table near the well-known bar. The "gilt" referred to
in its name appeared on the gold-appointed walls in this section, the huge fresco in front of me, and the ornate ceiling,
where there was an abundance of shiny things. I guessed the
weird red geodesic dome at one end of the bar was an attempt to give a younger face to a rich old dame.

It didn't work.

We bided our time and talked about clothes. I played with
a glass of chardonnay but didn't drink it. Benny downed two
pinot grigios with gusto.

Finally we were ushered to our table at the rear of the
long, dark-wood-paneled restaurant. In Gilt, the restaurant

proper, the decor was opulent and aristocratic. Gold candle-sticks burned golden beeswax candles on each table. A single white lily stood in a golden bud vase. The tablecloth was fine linen. Crystal glasses tinkled. Voices rose no louder than a soft hush.

"Don't y'all just love it?" Benny said as the maître d' held her chair. She wore a little black dress by David Meister with a sweetheart neck and lots of cleavage. The maître d' took the time to admire the view as he got her seated.

It was, in fact, like dining at an Italian Renaissance palace, Hollywood-style. Don't get me wrong; it was very nicely done. No other patrons besides me had ever seen the real thing anyway.

Gilt also described the entrée prices, which were not for the fainthearted. But Benny and I weren't picking up the tab tonight. We had been assigned to act as backup for Audrey when she met the international cricket star Shalid Khan at nine fifteen.

That was one story, anyway. In reality, Benny and I "suggested" to Audrey that we would never speak to her again if we couldn't come along. We were dying to get in on this, the first real breakthrough in the case.

She didn't argue, bless her little Greek heart. She convinced J it was essential that she have backup. Cormac and Rogue were already booked: They went looking for the tire guy with the disappearing ketch out in Westchester. That left us.

Our drink order arrived promptly, a Pellegrino with a slice of lime for me and Benny's Pink Squirrel—a crème de noyaux concoction mixed with cream that wasn't pink at all, but a pale nutty color. I was looking at it with revulsion, thinking about how many calories it contained, when my partner gave me a swift kick in the ankle with her pointed shoe.

"Ouch!" I complained. "What?"

"Get a lookee. Lucky Audrey," she said, nodding toward the front of the room.

Mr. Khan was making an entrance. We had seen his picture. It didn't do him justice.

"Now, there is one fine-looking studmuffin," she said, great with wisdom.

I agreed. This guy was hot, hot, hot.

Shalid Khan wore Armani pants, a collarless shirt, Italian loafers without socks, and a Rolex watch. He was impeccably groomed. He carried himself like royalty. His light brown complexion made him seem as if he had a really good Florida tan. He could have just arrived from a polo match in Boca Raton.

Compared to Shalid's understated elegance, I felt overdressed. I had again put on my stunning Mandalay halter dress, new shoes, new bag. But my heart hadn't been into primping for this assignment. I felt too screwed up over the Darius situation. Some humongous security risk to the entire nation was taking place, and ninety-nine percent of my brain was occupied with my love life.

I pushed the piece of lime into the glass of Pellegrino with my index finger, licked the sourness left on my skin, and mentally beat myself up. I always thought recruiting vampires as the first line of defense against terror was a crappy idea. We're too self-centered and self-absorbed. I was proving myself right. How appropriate that I found myself in the Gilt Room. I would spell it G-U-I-L-T.

Meanwhile Benny openly stared at our quarry. I leaned

over and whispered, "Hide behind your menu. You're too obvious."

"Oh, never you mind," she said. "A man that gorgeous expects ladies to stare. Look around. Not a female in this here entire restaurant ain't swooning and fanning herself something fierce."

She was right. Every female in the room was gawking at Shalid Khan. The maître d' simpered and fawned shamelessly as he led the cricket star toward a table. As soon as Mr. Khan was seated, a waiter hurried over with a martini. Mr. Khan drank it down and signaled for another.

Evidently Mr. Khan wasn't a true believer: Islam forbids alcohol. None of the El Saud princes paid any attention to that taboo either. They leave the puritanism to extremist groups like the Wahhabis. More than ever I wondered how a person like Shalid Khan—wealthy, upper-class, and a celebrity—got himself into the middle of this.

Fashionably late, the hour nearing nine thirty, Audrey arrived. Compared to the exquisite design of her couture gown, my dress could have come off the rack in Filene's Basement. And in the same way the women had stared at Shalid, every man now ogled Audrey. The homely, bespectacled librarian had been reincarnated as a cross between Jackie O and Princess Di. She looked vulnerable, innocent, sexy, and filthy rich all at the same time.

Shalid got to his feet like a man in a dream. Audrey floated toward him. She reached out her hand. He brought it to his lips. Their eyes fixed on each other. It was kismet.

"Oh, shee-it," Benny said.

"Ditto," I said.

This meeting had already gone south. As was clear to one

and all, these two people had just had a storybook moment and fallen in love.

After that followed one of the longest dinners I ever endured. We kept surveillance on our team member and her quarry. We could have gone to any chick flick and watched the same plot unfolding.

Audrey ducked her head shyly. Shalid kept leaning over and whispering to her. They tentatively touched fingertips. He fed her a tidbit from his plate. She wiped a speck of food from his lips. He kissed her fingertips.

Their feet eventually interlocked beneath the fine linen tablecloth. They seemed to have forgotten the world existed. I wondered if they'd ever remember to get to business before they decided to go somewhere more private and tumble into each other's arms.

Finally neither Benny nor I could take it another minute. Benny went to the ladies' room and called Audrey on her cell phone. I watched Audrey's face—first horror that her cell phone was even ringing, followed by embarrassment about answering it. I didn't know what Benny said, but Audrey didn't say more than a word or two before snapping the flip phone shut.

Audrey leaned toward Shalid and began talking fast. I guessed she finally brought up the reason she was there in the first place. I could tell I was right because Shalid's face turned grave. His body went from languid to tense. He pulled out an envelope from his hip pocket and slid it across the table. Audrey took it and put it in her purse.

Then Shalid engaged in a lengthy soliloquy, his face earnest. I kicked myself that I didn't have a bug planted so we could hear. Some frigging spy I was.

Audrey and Shalid talked back and forth now. Benny

strolled back to our table, passing close by them. Suddenly Audrey stood. She looked over at me and made just the smallest movement of her head.

"Stay here and watch Shalid." I kept my voice low and spoke out of the corner of my mouth at Benny. "I'm going to meet Audrey in the ladies' room."

Audrey had been in front of the mirror reapplying lip gloss. She spotted me barreling into the washroom. She froze.

"What the hell do you think you're doing!" I yelled as I rushed past a wide-eyed attendant. Then, before I uttered another word, I pivoted, whipped a fifty-dollar bill out of my clutch purse, and told the elderly Hispanic woman to go out for a smoke.

With a murmured, *"Muchas gracias, señorita,"* and no protest, she left.

Then I put a finger to my mouth for silence as I peeked under each stall to make sure we were alone. We were. I straightened and took a good look at my fellow Darkwing.

Audrey's eyes shone. Her face glowed. She was a woman in love. How fucking terrific.

"I . . . I . . . " she stammered, and lifted up supplicating hands. "I don't know what happened."

"Audrey! You're on a mission. You're a secret agent. He's the enemy. For God's sake, girl, get a grip."

"But . . . but I was just a research librarian until a month ago! I'm not really a spy. I didn't expect . . . I didn't know." Her voice wobbled. Tears were imminent.

"Deep breath, deep breath," I counseled. "This kind of thing isn't so unusual," I said, thinking back to my own peccadilloes with Darius my first time out. "Maybe it's a good thing. Pillow talk and all that. But you have to get control of yourself. You look like a moonstruck cow."

"A cow?" I had offended her. She got huffy. "You know, I'm not like the other Darkwings. You, Daphne, were brought up in this world. Rogue's a criminal, and besides, he used to be in the CIA. Cormac's an actor. Benny . . . well, she has an aptitude. I don't think I was cut out to be a spy."

I put my arm around her shoulder and gave her a bracing hug. "You're just having a crisis of confidence. You're doing great," I said, lying through my teeth.

"No, I'm not. I've been 'compromised.' " Her face crumbled. She was heading for the waterworks again.

"Compromised? Absolutely not. Technically you haven't um . . . you know. You're doing superb. I mean that."

"You do? I figured I had totally messed up."

"No, really, you're acting like a real pro. What did you find out?" I asked.

"He gave me this envelope. It's got instructions or something in it. I didn't look. I'm supposed to deliver it to the 'right person' in the government." She handed it over; then she summed up the little she knew.

Shalid's uncle, an adviser to President Musharraf, called him into his office in Islamabad. The uncle told "Shally" that he needed him to handle a matter of grave importance and asked Shally to act as a courier to the United States. Since the cricket star traveled internationally with some frequency, his trip would raise no questions.

Shally swore to Audrey he didn't know anything more. He'd apologized for involving such a beautiful woman in something potentially dangerous. He'd suggested they leave the restaurant and go back to his room "to get to know each other better."

Oh, boy, I thought. What I said was, "And what do you want to do?" I already knew the answer, but I figured she wanted my approval.

"I think I should go with him and try to get more information, don't you?"

"Oh, yeah, sure. Definitely. Benny and I will take the envelope back to J," I said. *After we open it,* I thought. "Will you be okay, though?"

"Yes. I have to try, anyway. It's like Rogue said last night about the fighting part of this: It's time I learned. I need the practice, that's all."

"Good attitude. But remember, you haven't been compromised *yet.* Don't let it come to that, okay? Call Benny or me if you feel you can't handle things and need us to get you out of there." I might as well be spitting in the wind, but, as Darius pointed out, I lived in a glass house and couldn't throw stones.

Audrey nodded and then she smiled, her beautiful face radiant. "Shally, he's just an amazing man. Isn't he handsome?"

"Yes," I said. *And he's human, he's Muslim, and he's working with terrorists,* I thought, *and, girl, you are so screwed.* But I didn't voice any of that. She was too far gone. She wouldn't have listened to me anyway.

We watched Romeo and Juliet leave the restaurant; then Benny and I hurried out. We descended the wide curved stairway with its gold banisters and went as far as the Palace's lobby. A comfortable sofa in a relatively empty section of the huge space provided some privacy. We sat. I breathed openmouthed on the glued flap to try to get it open. That didn't work. It still stuck tight. I shrugged.

"Just tear it open," Benny encouraged. "We'll tell J we're sorry after we read it." My sentiments exactly—better to beg for forgiveness than to ask permission. I used a nail file as a letter opener. Printed on a single sheet of typing paper was this:

Praise to Allah, the Almighty, the Merciful, the Magnificent.

You idolatrous infidels, traitorous apostates, and turncoat deviants have violated the pure way of the Prophet. Now the splendor of the spearhead of jihad is aimed at your hearts.

We demand the swift and immediate return of our brother, the beloved of the Prophet, cleric Hassan Omar and the holy relic in his hands.

When that which is sacred is restored to us, that which the Great Satan prizes will be returned to you.

If the profane violation of the Prophet—may Allah bless him and greet him—and that of our brother cleric Omar does not cease, a fatwa issued by the gracious brother Abu Masab decrees that your death ship, your liberty, and every living thing around it shall be struck down by the swift lightning of the Almighty.

May God protect Hassan Omar and watch over him; may his religion, his book, and Sunna the Prophet aid him. We ask the Almighty to bless him, us, and all Muslims. With his divine aid, may our clear victory and Hassan Omar's release from suffering be at hand. We ask the Almighty to gather us as he sees fit for the glory of the next world and the prize of the hereafter.

—The Wahhabi Mujahedeen

"Now jist what do you get from that?" Benny asked.

"About as much as you did, I guess. Audrey's theory about kidnappings and exchanges was dead-on. From what I can figure out, the Wahhib Mujahedeen thinks we're holding the cleric Hassan Omar and some 'holy relic.' They want both back in exchange for the *Intrepid*. If they don't get them, they're issuing a fatwa, an order, to destroy not just the ship, but America."

"Do we have this here Omar?" Benny asked, reclining back against the plush cushions and staring up at a huge chandelier.

"Damned if I know. Maybe he's one of those 'persons of interest' who J said was in custody."

Benny contemplated the chandelier for a bit longer; then she sat up and took the letter into her perfectly manicured hands. She studied it for a few minutes. "What do you make of this 'relic' business?" she asked at last.

A strange uneasiness sent a shiver up my spine. "It's a guess, but maybe whoever took Omar took something else. I have a bad feeling about it. I'm afraid all hell is about to turn loose if we can't get this cleric and his relic back."

"I sure do agree with you. Just holding this here letter makes me real nervous," she said, handing it back to me. I folded it up and put it in the envelope.

She shook her head. "That stuff about 'every living thing around it shall be struck down by the swift lightning of the Almighty' makes me think they're planning some kind of missile strike or explosion unless they get what they want. It don't set easy with me. It makes me think the *Intrepid* might become their weapon to do it.

"It's got me all worked up. I want to do something—

besides just deliver this to our head man, I mean. Any ideas?" she asked.

I took my own long look at the chandelier. The light bouncing off the crystals mirrored the motion of my thoughts as I came at the situation from every angle I could think of. Finally I made up my mind. I stood and offered Benny my hand. "Come on, girlfriend. In my humble opinion it's time to go over J's head. Let's visit my mother."

"Sugar, you sure do know how to rile up that man. He's gonna be madder than a cut snake when he finds out."

I figured J was going to be pissed off when he found out about me and Darius. I might as well lump together all the bad news he was going to get. I pushed open the doors of the Palace Hotel and stepped into the warm city night.

I squared my shoulders, descended the stairs, and started down the long path that once belonged to the Villard Mansion, passed between the double fountains, crossed through the wrought-iron gates, and stepped out on Madison Avenue. With vampire hunters roaming the city and my heart in critical condition already, I really couldn't worry about J's perpetually bad temper.

I looked back over my shoulder. "You know, Benny, about J? I just don't give a shit."

When I phoned my mother, she offered to send her usual car service to take us up to Scarsdale. She asked me to hold for a minute while she contacted them. When she came back on the line, she said the service would pick us up at eleven. I didn't complain about the wait. It gave me time to run an errand.

The FedEx Kinko's on Forty-seventh Street and Avenue of the Americas, conveniently open twenty-four hours, was located only four blocks from the Palace. But two of those were avenue blocks. Neither Benny nor I had on walking shoes. We took a cab.

The fluorescent lights of the brightly lit store bothered my eyes, but I shouldered my way in, Benny right behind me. I was here to take out some insurance.

I had become a cautious person over the centuries. History had taught me some invaluable lessons. Government documents had a disturbing way of vanishing as if they had never existed. So as insurance, I not only made copies of Shalid Khan's letter for Benny and me, I slipped another copy in a FedEx envelope and addressed it to myself. Then I had the letter scanned and e-mailed to my home computer. I might be overdoing it, but I was short on trust and long on suspicion.

A few minutes before eleven, Benny and I were back on Madison Avenue in front of the New York Palace, waiting on the sidewalk for our ride as if we had never left.

St. Patrick's lay directly in front of us across the avenue. This view of the building, the largest Gothic-style church in America, was magnificent. The carved gray stone, stained-glass windows, and soaring arches proclaimed the glory of God, or at least the glory of the archdiocese of the city of New York. But I wasn't contemplating the architecture.

I was remembering that barely a month ago I was supposed to have my wedding there, me—a vampire bride in a cathedral—wearing an off-white ivory satin dress with a puddle train. Benny and Audrey would have been there too, holding calla lilies. Cormac had promised to show up in drag. And in one of the side chapels, I was supposed to have become Mrs. St. Julien Fitzmaurice.

The fact that my groom wanted a ceremony in a Roman

Catholic cathedral officiated by a monsignor should have been a red flag that the relationship was a marriage of heaven and hell and doomed from the start. Nevertheless I felt a pang as I looked at the building. At least a man had loved me enough to want to marry me and to spend eternity with me. That's an astonishing commitment. He was willing to make it. I wasn't.

Just as the church bells pealed the hour, a white Rolls-Royce pulled up. It sure wasn't most people's idea of a "regular car service," which at best employed a Lincoln Town Car. But it was Mar-Mar's. And it was our ride.

Benny looked happier than a pig in you-know-what when the chauffeur got out, walked around the car, and said, "Miss Urban? Miss Polycarp? Yes? Please get in," and he opened the door for us.

"Oh, don't pinch me, 'cause if I'm dreaming I don't want to wake up," Benny whispered as she slid across the glove leather of the backseat. "There ain't nothing like this back in the Miz'ora hills where I come from. Shee-it, in the holler where I was born, we thought we're living high on the hog if we had indoor plumbing."

I climbed in behind her, leaned back in the seat, and pulled out my cell phone to check my messages again. Nothing appeared in the window, not even a text message from Darius. It both pissed me off and hurt like hell at the same time.

My mother was waiting for us outside, standing in front of the door of her Scarsdale house. Although she had passed her thousandth birthday, she was pert, pretty, and appeared at the very most to be in her early twenties. Unless one noticed her eyes. My mother's eyes were ancient and wise. Sometimes they were terrifying.

Tonight Marozia Urban wore a floor-length diaphanous black gown with a high collar. It reflected no light. Around her neck on a heavy gold chain hung an amulet—a small vial carved of lapis lazuli, surrounded by an ornate filigree of finely worked metal. Its style was medieval. Its content was a drop of blood said to belong to Dracula himself.

Her attire attested to the vampire she truly was. I was surprised at her choice of clothes. She usually wore jeans and tie-dye T-shirts left over from her Dead-head days. And this was a weeknight at home. Something was going on.

My mother smiled without warmth at Benny, then stood on tiptoe to plant an air kiss by my cheek. Uncharacteristically reserved, almost grave in her demeanor, she appeared less than overjoyed to see me.

Once Benny and I were ushered into the living room, I saw that Mar-Mar was in the midst of a meeting. A dozen venerable vampires sat around a large folding table. All wore black. All had amulets similar to Mar-Mar's around their necks. A few bottles of imported Pellegrino water sat next to some tumblers. A laptop computer loaded with a PowerPoint presentation was projecting a map of the city of New York on a screen.

My mother introduced us. "Some of you have already met my daughter. For those of you who have not, this is Daphne. I believe at least one of you has met her companion, but for the rest of you, this lovely vampire is Benjamina Polycarp, a native of Branson, Missouri."

The six men and six women nodded at us. Nobody spoke. Everyone looked as sober as a judge. My mother turned to Benny and me. "We are having a council meeting." To the council she said, "Please excuse me for a few minutes, and do carry on with the issue on the table."

I didn't know all that much about this vampire governing body except that my mother, as usual, had her fingers in it. I had asked her about it once upon a time. She evaded my question, but I had figured out a few things on my own.

For one thing, the vampires who held seats on the Vampire Council were very old. I guessed that they could be the world's oldest existing vampires. As for what the council did, I wasn't sure. I did know they could decide who lived and died. My almost-bridegroom, St. Julien Fitzmaurice, had been marked for death by them after I had refused to make him a vampire like me. He ran from them still.

The council's role as a watchdog agency regarding vampire hunters, however, did come as news to me. But I wasn't surprised. I mentally filed the information.

Before we walked away, I tried to take a good look at their faces. I recognized Zoe, the old crone who Benny had met, the mother of the now-dust Louis from New Orleans. Other faces looked familiar, but I couldn't put names to them.

Little by little I intended to learn more about them. Knowledge was power, as they say. Today this select group of the world's oldest vampires were my allies. But tomorrow they could be enemies.

Mar-Mar led Benny and me into the kitchen and shut the door. She turned to me. "You said you had uncovered a code-red situation and it was urgent that you see me. Not your commanding officer, J. You had to see *me*. Now, what is it?"

Benny raised her eyebrows. Mar-Mar's daggers usually remained sheathed in front of company.

I was taken aback. Mar-Mar clearly was barely holding her anger in check. Something had really set her off.

I didn't waste time with words. I removed the envelope from my purse and handed it over. She noticed that it had been opened. Only then did I explain. "We obtained this tonight. Once we read it, we decided you should see it without delay."

Mar-Mar turned away from us and read the letter. When she was through, she carefully folded it, put it back in the envelope, then slipped the envelope into a pocket hidden in the folds of her gown.

I waited expectantly for her to discuss its contents with us. Benny's attention too was fixed on my mother, as she awaited her response. She spoke, but not of the letter. Instead she turned to another topic entirely.

"As you saw, I am in the middle of a council meeting. An emergency session. Both of you should know what is going on. Daphne, you were attacked by a vampire hunter earlier this week."

And she doesn't know the half of it, I thought.

"In the past few days there have been dozens of such attacks. We have lost a few members of our community who were surprised and overtaken. As of this evening we have verified that ten vampires have been exterminated. There may be more, but since vampires are loners and few have living relatives, the exact number is hard to validate.

"These attacks came as a surprise to me, and to the council. We thought we had largely reduced the possibility of the Church hunting us down because you, along with J and Cormac O'Reilly, retrieved the dossiers on New York's vampires from Opus Dei headquarters early in the spring."

Yeah, we sure did, I thought. It had almost killed the three of us. When I had received the orders to enter Opus Dei headquarters, I didn't understand why. The Darkwings were in the middle of an important mission: trying to keep a presidential candidate from being assassinated. All of a sudden we were ordered to break into the huge brick building that sat like a hulking mass on Thirty-fourth Street.

All my mother had told me at the time was that the Vatican had given Opus Dei boxes of historical information on the death of my father, Pope Urban VI. I wanted desperately to know what had happened to him.

We found the boxes easily, too easily. We tried to move them, only to discover they had been booby-trapped. In the harrowing moments that followed J had been injured. All of us had nearly died.

Later I discovered that my mother had known there was a considerable risk that I, her only daughter, could have been exterminated. I also found out that everything my mother had told me about the boxes was a lie.

The only historical document in the boxes we brought out of Opus Dei's headquarters was something called the Great Book, or *Liber Magnus*. Mostly the cartons were filled with files on vampires in every major city of the world. They held nothing about my father at all.

What bothered me the most was that my mother's lie had been unnecessary. I would have agreed to retrieve the vampire dossiers without hesitation. My anger surged at the memory as I brought my attention back to the present. My mother had continued speaking. I watched her mouth moving, wondering how many more lies I'd hear tonight.

"I fear that a duplicate of at least some of the New York files must have remained in the hands of Opus Dei," she said. "The files gave vampire names, home addresses, work addresses, and known associates. Now the vampire hunters have targeted specific vampires and attacked them at or near their homes. Some who worked were hit at their offices. Opus Dei's having duplicates of the files is the only explanation for such targeted attacks.

"The council has already voted on issuing an alert to as many local vampires as we can reach. The more difficult issues on the table are how to identify, locate, and rid ourselves of the menace."

So, it had been the crazies in Opus Dei who had sent the hunters after me and after us all. A tremendous feeling of relief washed over me. Darius's arriving at the same time as the hunters *had* been a coincidence. But I wanted to be sure.

"Are you saying that Darius della Chiesa had nothing to do with the vampire hunter invasion?" I asked.

My mother's lips pressed together in a line. She stared at me, her eyes hard; then she answered as if unwilling to say the words. "I would not conclude he had *nothing* to do with it. I have it on information and belief that he did, at one time, have a connection to these people. I do not know at this time if he still has such a connection."

Mar-Mar didn't exonerate Darius, but I knew that if she had any concrete evidence that he was involved, she'd use it to discredit him. Hope blossomed in my heart that Darius had told me the truth.

Yet why were my mother's eyes boring into me, angry and adamantine?

She spoke again. "But there is something you should be aware of, daughter of mine. The letter written by an extremist Islamic sect demands the return of a cleric, Hassan Omar."

I nodded.

"Do you know anything about this situation?" she asked me in an accusing voice, ignoring Benny completely. My palms began to sweat. Anxiety tightened the muscles in my chest. When I uttered the word *no* it was barely more than a croak.

"Well, my dear, here is what *I* know. Hassan Omar was abducted from the streets of Srinagar by two U.S. intelligence agents. One of those agents was Darius della Chiesa."

CHAPTER 12

*"What dire offense from amorous causes
   springs,
What mighty contests rise from trivial things."*

—Alexander Pope, "The Rape of the Lock"

The revelation hit me like an electroshock treatment. For the next few seconds I was so stunned, I did not realize Mar-Mar had continued speaking. Finally I gathered my shattered thoughts well enough to pay attention to what she was saying.

"The abduction was a rogue operation," Mar-Mar explained. "Black ops. Not sanctioned. Opportunistic. That in itself has become almost routine." She lifted one delicate shoulder dismissively.

"But sometimes these things blow up in our faces. Remember in the spring of 2007? Italian authorities filed charges against U.S. agents and their Italian operatives for kidnapping a member of the Muslim Brotherhood in Rome and taking him to Egypt.

"The incident became an intelligence and public relations disaster. This situation is much worse, capable of triggering a devastating act of terror on American soil."

My face showed that I didn't understand.

"Let me spell it out for you. Darius and his partner screwed up. Big-time. It wasn't whom they took. It was when they took him. They grabbed Omar on a holy day right after he had addressed a crowd of thousands in the huge quadrangle outside of the mosque of Hazratbal."

I looked at Benny. She shook her head. We were both missing something important, obviously.

My mother was growing impatient with what she evidently believed was exceptional ignorance on my part.

"You really don't know? I assumed that since you have been dealing with Islamic extremists . . ." She ran her fingers through her hair and sighed. I had disappointed her once again.

"Let me explain then. The mosque of Hazratbal is known throughout the world because it purportedly houses a hair from the head of the Prophet Muhammad. The single strand of hair is kept inside a crystal bottle, which is finely decorated with worked silver wire. The location of the bottle is proscribed by ancient ritual, inside a series of containers, like a Russian matroyshka doll.

"To get to it you must begin by passing four guards outside a cell, which is the first of four cells, each inside the other. Within the innermost cell is a cabinet. Inside the cabinet is a wooden box that holds a wooden box that holds another wooden box. In the smallest box lies the bottle, which is wrapped in three cloth bags.

"On Muslim holy days, one of the hereditary keepers of the hair takes the bottle out and attaches it to a chain that is locked around his waist. He goes forth to address the crowd outside and holds up the bottle, still on its chain, to display it to the believers who are waiting in the courtyard of the mosque.

"This act sets off pandemonium in the crowd. People faint, throw themselves on the ground wailing, break into tears. Are you following me now?"

I nodded. "Yes, I get it. The keeper was Hassan Omar, and when he was abducted the hair of the Prophet went with him."

"Exactly." Mar-Mar's eyes flashed. "Up until now the loss of the hair has been kept very quiet. If the Muslim world discovers the relic is gone, the mosque officials know their lives would be forfeit for allowing it to happen. Not only their own lives, either. Their wives and children, mothers and fathers, everyone in their family would be killed, torn apart if a mob got hold of them.

"Once news of this spread, a jihad would rise up against the West. It would be a jihad of terrifying proportions. Millions would die. Even the Wahhabis don't want that kind of grassroots uprising, mostly because it won't be under their control."

"So what's the problem?" I asked. "Why don't we just return Hassan Omar and the relic?"

Mar-Mar gave her head a small shake, her patience completely gone. "Of course we would return it if we could. But we can't. Your precious Darius took the bottle from the cleric Omar. Somehow, and we have yet to determine how, that bottle was lost. The hair is gone."

At that point all I could think was, *Oh, shit.*

Benny and I got back into the Rolls for the return trip to the city. We made ourselves comfortable in the plush interior. I leaned against the cushions to think things out. Benny, who had remained silent the entire time we were with Mar-Mar, reclined against the seat as well, closed her eyes, and suddenly started to talk. She said she was heartily sorry she had blamed Darius for the vampire hunters.

I accepted her apology.

Then she opened her eyes and gave me an I-told-you-so look. Her words snapping, she proceeded to tell me she surely had been right, however, that Mr. Darius della Chiesa didn't waltz back into my life because he was "a lovesick hound dog." He had an ulterior motive, the same way he always did. She crossed her arms across her chest, huffed, and fell silent again.

"So what's his motive?" I shot back. "He doesn't know the Darkwings are looking for the *Intrepid*. I doubt he knows the ship is missing. He certainly can't know that its disappearance is linked to his kidnapping of Hassan Omar. We didn't even know that until tonight. You and I can connect his screwup with what we're into, but that's not the reason he came back to see me."

Benny stared straight ahead. "I still say he's up to something."

"I love him, Benny."

"That don't make him any better than he is," she said, purposely not looking at me. She was quiet for a moment; then her voice softened. "And I'm afraid he's gonna put you in a world of hurt. Even if he don't mean to, he will. I swear, a black cloud hangs over that man's head."

I didn't say I agreed with her, but I had a deep uneasiness that Darius was going to put me in a world of hurt too.

Before we reached Manhattan, Cormac rang my cell phone. He asked Benny and me to meet Rogue and him downtown, all the way downtown, Whitehall Street, at the Staten Island

Ferry terminal. I asked why. Cormac told me they'd explain when we got there.

I rogered that and repeated it to Benny. She leaned forward to tell the driver our destination.

"Wonder why we're going to the ferry terminal?" she turned to me and asked.

"Sounds like we're going to Staten Island. They must have found something out there."

I resigned myself to the fact that I was going to be working all night. Whatever the future held with Darius would have to remain in the future, for now. I doubted he would have shown up tonight at my apartment anyway. Once Mar-Mar revealed the contents of the letter to her cronies in the upper circles of power, people would be getting in line to talk to Darius. I imagined I would be standing pretty much at the end.

The Rolls didn't arrive at the ferry terminal until nearly one thirty, just in time for us to spot Cormac and Rogue in front of the terminal waving urgently at us. Benny and I tumbled out of the Rolls and ran like madwomen, tipsy in our high heels. The four of us rushed into the terminal. The huge doors at the far end were open; the ramp was down. The fat orange ferry with its blue lettering wallowed in its slip as other passengers scurried in front of us, everybody in a hurry even at this hour of the night.

Halfway across the huge room an empty Utz Cheese Curls bag caught on my flimsy sandal. I danced around trying to free it, lost my balance, and started to fall. A strong arm grabbed me around the waist as Rogue caught me before I went down. Laughing now, we kept running up the ramp at double-time and clambered on board the *Alice Austen.*

The gate closed and, with a revving of the engines, the huge ship painted safety orange like a traffic cone—not white, like most of the world's ferries, but loud and bold like its city—pulled away from the ferry slip into New York Bay.

The water lay calm, black, and glittering with the reflections of thousands of lights as we began the twenty-five-minute ride to the St. George terminal in Staten Island.

Benny immediately asked Rogue what was going on, but it was hard to hear what he said over the drone of the motors. He moved close to her and whispered something in her ear.

She nodded, then moved to the high rail. None of us went inside. I enjoyed being out there in the darkness, silent, content to look at the lights of Manhattan's skyline slipping away as we journeyed into the night.

Waves slapped rhythmically against the hull of the ship. The air left damp kisses on my face. I smelled salt and sea.

We all stayed as we were, not speaking, looking at the view. Benny had never ridden the ferry before. She tipped back her head and looked, awestruck, her face transfixed with wonder.

She wasn't the only one. The beauty of this crossing kept me riveted in place, a lightness coursing through me, a swelling of emotion in my chest. I gazed behind us at Manhattan. The familiar skyline reminded me why I was doing this job—the real reason, not the threats the agency had used to coerce me. I longed to protect this place, this unique and special island. I would do it at any risk, at any cost.

My emotions broke completely when I saw the Statue of Liberty to the right of the ship. Floodlights at the base revealed her green gown, but the glow of the illuminated torch and crown looming high, a beacon of welcome, closed my throat with tears. *Give me your tired, your poor,* the Emma Lazarus poem began. *Even your vampires*, I mentally added.

The sight of the statue's lights once again brought back memories of Fitz. The first time we went out together he had brought me down to the Battery to point out Lady Liberty in the harbor. He wanted to explain to me what it meant to him. That night the fog had rolled in and we never saw her. It had been the gesture itself that told me everything about him.

As Whittier wrote, *For of all sad words of tongue and pen, the saddest are these: "It might have been."*

Before I could get too maudlin, a hand tapped me on the shoulder. Cormac motioned with his head that they were going inside. I left the deck and joined them.

The harsh glare of the interior lights stabbed hard at my eyes. I should have brought my sunglasses. Cream-colored plastic seats with yellow pads lined the walls. Benny went looking for a clean one to sit on.

She was wiping one off with a tissue from her purse when she saw a stoop-shouldered man with a *New York Post* under his arm about to sit down on a seat that she had already inspected. Being Southern and having never met a stranger, she turned to him and called out, "Hey, y'all, something spilled on that one."

The man paused, checked it out, and said, "It's dried up." Then he sat on the stain. "Doesn't matter anyway. I'm wearing black," he said.

I saw her give a little start. She put the tissue back in her purse and walked over to where I was standing. It was then that I noticed that both the male Darkwings were carrying gym bags over their shoulders. I didn't think they had been working out.

"Wazzup, guys?" I said, hand on hip and all attitude to mask how fucked-up I felt.

"We made some inroads," Rogue said.

"And some indents." Cormac smiled.

"Yeah." Rogue grinned, reached out, and draped a big arm around Benny's shoulders, pulling her closer into our circle to talk.

"The tire guy is now in federal custody," he said. "Turned out he was a member of a radical Brooklyn mosque, the one associated with the Blind Sheikh—"

I stole a look at Benny and made a mental note to contact Lieutenant Johnson.

"—and that made him more interesting to us. We found him at home, at supper. He wasn't happy to see us."

"No, he definitely wasn't," Cormac said.

"To make a long story short, he denied knowing anything about his ketch's now-you-see-it-now-you-don't behavior. But we convinced him to let us take a look around the garage of the tire store. For a place that just sold tires there were some mighty interesting steel cables and electronic equipment. We called J, and pretty soon some guys in black showed up. Bye-bye, tire guy."

"So why are we on the ferry going to Staten Island?" I asked.

"J said to investigate bigger boats, freighters, oil tankers, you know. A couple of longshoremen friends of mine picked up some information we need to check out." Rogue took out a toothpick from his shirt pocket and put it between his teeth.

"In Staten Island?" I reiterated.

"Not exactly, but close," Rogue said.

"Now, stop playing with us, you guys," Benny said.

"Fun's fun, but if'n you want to know what *we* found out, you have to go first."

"You found out something?" Cormac said, sounding disappointed. He hated to be upstaged.

"Yes, we surely did, but it's still your turn."

"Okay, here's the deal," Rogue said, motioning us even closer together and lowering his voice, although outside of the guy on the other side of the cabin reading the *New York Post* there wasn't another person in sight. "Rumor has it that a container ship anchored in the Arthur Kill near the Verrazano Bridge did a disappearing act last week: there one day, gone the next, back the next. The coast guard was alerted about something fishy and has detained the ship in port. They were supposed to investigate. They got sidelined by priorities: thirty tons of marijuana on a freighter from Panama.

"The container ship incident happened before the *Intrepid* disappeared. Nobody connected the dots. We need to take a look-see. Course, it may already be too late, but I guarantee that by the time the coast guard gets there, there won't be anything to find."

"So why are we going to Staten Island?" I asked for the third time.

"Now, Rambo, hold your horses. I'm getting to that. It's a shorter flight from the ferry terminal on Staten Island out to the ship than from Manhattan."

"Really?" I said. "And I'm supposed to strip down and leave a fifteen-hundred-dollar dress on the ferry? I don't think so."

"We already figured out you might not want to go skinny-dipping on the way home," Cormac said. "We're going to take our clothes along in the gym bags."

*   *   *

Unseen by anyone, we left the *Alice Austen* by air before it docked at the Staten Island terminal. Four vampires aloft, staying under the radar, we winged our way over the dark waters of the bay until we were within sight of the bridge. Beyond that, the 653-foot bulk of the ship *Belgium* sat gently rocking on the calm seas. Its deck was loaded high with containers. The flag flying from its smokestack, lit by a spotlight, showed an orange silhouette of an island and a green olive branch on a white field. The flag of Cyprus.

That didn't tell us much. Cyprus maintained the sixth-largest registry for commercial ships in the world. Detecting the owners wasn't our job anyway. We needed to find out why the ship had appeared to vanish. And we needed to do it by remaining as invisible as possible ourselves.

Benny had made it clear she did not intend to get even a wing tip wet. I seconded that. I'd had a taste of the filthy water in the bay a while back. I wasn't enthusiastic about repeating the experience. She and I planned to inspect above the waterline for signs of cables or electronic equipment.

Cormac and Rogue had decided to search the ship itself. These freighters carry a crew of twenty or twenty-five—not many, considering the size of the vessel. The hour was late. They should be asleep. With any luck the Darkwings wouldn't be spotted.

Within minutes of our arrival I wanted to chalk this excursion up to another case of best-laid plans going all to hell. First of all, Benny and I flew around the entire outside of the ship and didn't see diddly-squat. We spotted a number of places on the hull that looked as if the paint could have been scraped by a cable. We saw nothing more. If anything had been there, it had long since been removed.

We took a second look just to make sure. I didn't like being this close to the water; it was working on my nerves. I really was ready to call it quits. And something else was nagging at me, making me uneasy, but I couldn't figure out what.

Hardly ten minutes had passed before Benny and I concluded we weren't going to find anything helpful. It was a long way to come to find nothing. Hoping the men were having better luck inside the ship, we landed near the bow on the metal plates of the deck, trying not to scrape our claws against the hull. We didn't want to draw anybody's attention. I worried that there might be a crew member left on watch, or that the sound might carry to anyone below decks.

Benny and I figured we could at least snoop around the containers for transmitters, electronic generators, or some kind of cloaking device. Hell, I wasn't sure I'd know one if I fell over one. As it turned out, we weren't poking around the containers more than a minute when I heard a small sound. I grabbed Benny's arm. We froze.

We listened. It sounded like rustling. *Rats?* I thought.

It wasn't. Someone yelled, "Hey, up here!"

Benny and I looked in the direction of the voice. Cormac and Rogue had landed on top of the stack of containers above us.

"Come up here," Rogue yelled louder.

My heart almost stopped. *The idiot!* The crew was going to hear that big mouth. What did he think he was doing? I flew up there as fast as I could, Benny right behind me.

"Why are you yelling?" I hissed at him. "Are you nuts?" Before either man-bat had a chance to answer I looked at them both crouched up on top of the container. Something wasn't right. "What?"

Rogue turned his face toward the stern of the ship, with the pilothouse and crew quarters.

"Did you find evidence?" I asked as a shiver passed over me. "You were only in the ship a couple of minutes."

Rogue nodded his head affirmatively. "Yeah, we found something."

I stared at him. He didn't seem excited by his success. I looked at Cormac.

"What? What's going on?"

"They're dead," Cormac said.

"Who? What are you talking about?"

"The captain, the crew, even the captain's rat terrier. They've all been shot to death, every last one of them."

All I wanted to do was get off this ghost ship. I immediately figured out what had been bothering me: It was the smell of death, indistinct on the outside of the ship over the water, but there nonetheless.

Benny, who never flew without her handbag slung around her neck, reached inside for her cell phone. I had asked her to carry mine as well. She looked over at me. I nodded. She tossed it to me.

"Who are you going to call?" I queried as I reached out and caught my phone. "J?"

"I'm not calling nobody," she said. "I'm going in there to take pictures. *You* call the boss."

The Missouri girl had a lot of guts; I'll say that for her.

All of us flew to the stern with Benny, and everybody went into the ship except me. I'd seen enough dead bodies lately. I didn't see any advantage to viewing the carnage. I told them I'd wait out on deck.

I needed to think. It was pretty obvious that whoever was

behind capturing the *Intrepid* played hardball. They didn't leave witnesses or anything that could help us locate the missing ship. I was surprised Mr. Saud, the tire guy out in Hempstead, hadn't been eliminated. There had to be a reason. Maybe he was one of the key players. Or maybe it was just dumb luck that he was still alive when Cormac and Rogue found him.

It was a lucky break. Now he could be interrogated. I hope it helped.

Benny had told *me* to call J. She would rather face a murder scene than our handler. I made a face thinking about how pissed off he was going to be with me, but what could he really say? *He* was the one who suggested I go talk to my mother.

And since she was my mother, my bringing her the letter followed some logic. I had broken the chain of command in one way. In another way I had maintained the link between mother and daughter. A nice analogy, I thought, giving myself some credit for wit.

Then I had a sobering thought. I needed to watch my back. J would get even with me if he saw a way he could.

I hit the speed dial, number three. J's number appeared right after Mar-Mar's and Darius's. I hunched my shoulders against the gathering wind to shelter the phone so he could hear me better.

J picked up before the second ring. He sounded wide-awake. If he had been asleep tonight, my mother had probably gotten him out of bed right after Benny and I left Scarsdale.

I decided on a preemptive strike, talking fast. "J, listen— no, don't talk. I don't have much time. Four of us are out in the Arthur Kill on a ship. The *Belgium*. She's a container ship registered in Cyprus. We think she was used as a dress rehearsal for taking the *Intrepid*. But there's a problem. The crew's dead."

J told me in a flat voice that he'd get people on the scene and we should get the hell out of there.

I asked him if we needed to come into the office.

"No. Report in tomorrow." He hung up without saying good-bye.

Dawn broke through the darkness around five thirty this time of year. It was not even three a.m. when the four of us leaped off the container ship and flew back toward the ferry terminal. We swooped under the bridge and hugged the shore, staying low near the water.

A wind had blown in from the east, off the Atlantic. Wet and cool, it whipped across my face. The bay had developed a chop. I saw whitecaps below me.

I didn't think much during the flight. I never did. I turned myself over to instinct, flitting and diving, more animal than intelligent being. For me this was the best part of being a vampire—the ability to lift free of earth without effort, to soar, to fly under my own power in a way humans could only dream of doing.

Clouds had moved in with the wind. I couldn't see the stars. There was no moon. Darkness lay above me, darkness lay below me, but inside me I saw light. Sometimes it dimmed, sometimes I doubted it existed at all, but when I flew as I did now, I was sure it was there.

Once we were all back on the ferry, clothed, in human form, and en route to lower Manhattan, I asked the guys if they had plans for the rest of the night.

They were headed to Charlie's Harley Hangout on West Street, Rogue told me. He asked if Benny and I wanted to join them—if I thought I could behave and not get us kicked out on our asses.

I looked at Rogue. He sat back on a plastic seat, his arms behind his head. He wore a black T-shirt with the sleeves ripped out. It showed off his massive arms with their rock-hard biceps and triceps. He saw me watching and flexed his muscles. Then he winked, the arrogant bastard.

As was his habit, he held a toothpick between his teeth. He'd replace it with a cigarette as soon as we landed. He would strike anyone as a tough guy, a biker, maybe an ex-con, someone not to be messed with. But no one would take him for a vampire.

Yet he *was* a vampire, and bad to the bone. His lack of restraint, his brutality, and his immorality embodied the darkest parts of our race, all that I detested. I hadn't forgotten what he had done last night with the human girl.

And I hadn't forgotten what I had done in Tompkins Square Park either. Until now I had been successful in pushing the memories out of my mind. But they were there, like shadows lurking and waiting to torment me.

I knew right then that I didn't want to return to my empty apartment. I would sit around until I was tired enough to climb into my coffin. Meanwhile I'd do the crossword puzzle. I'd listen for a knock on the door. Finally I'd stand by the window, looking out at the night, hoping Darius would appear, a dark angel descending from the sky. But I knew that tonight he would never come.

So when Rogue asked me to go to Charlie's, I answered without hesitation. "I'm in."

"Me too," Benny said.

CHAPTER 13

"Not of those whom we care for most, do we easily suspect wickedness."

—Peter Abelard, *Historia Calamitatum* PORTA OCTAVA

For the rest of the trip back to Manhattan I stayed out on deck and watched the harbor lights. Benny remained inside the ferry, giving Cormac and Rogue a rundown on the letter delivered by Khan. She also planned to tell them about our visit to Mar-Mar's and the impending vampire hunter war. She might have told them about Audrey as well—or not. Rogue and Cormac had little interest in women's love lives.

Audrey's instant infatuation with Khan, a poleaxing of the first order, amused me. That kind of thing was not supposed to happen to *her*. When I'd confessed my preference for human men, she'd looked aghast. She'd *never* fall for a human. They were so inferior to vampires. It was just *too* gauche.

Another case of never say never.

But I had lived much longer than Audrey, over two hundred years longer. I'd had time to learn that one must not predict the workings of the heart, human or vampire. It's tempting the gods to have some fun at your expense.

Eros scored a direct hit with his arrow in the Gilt room. He must have been laughing his head off tonight.

A cloud of stale cigarette smoke lay so thick in Charlie's Harley Hangout that breathing didn't come easily. But the crowd had thinned out as the hours moved toward dawn. The blonde tending bar looked dead on her feet. The purple smudges under her eyes had faded to black. She managed a smile when I walked in and gave me a thumbs-up.

I was getting a reputation as a badass. I wondered if I wanted it.

Benny still wore her little black dress. I had on my Mandalay gown. Our fashionable attire was a poor fit for the testosterone-driven ambience created by the bar's oil-rig theme spiked with eau de Budweiser.

Over in one corner I spotted Cowboy Sam. He tipped his hat and gave me a smile that could easily turn into a promise. I tried not to encourage him. I gave him a noncommittal nod.

Rogue led our party to a table in the back of the room, paused to light a cigarette, then excused himself. Benny and I pulled out chairs and sat. Cormac offered to take our bar order. I wanted nothing stronger than mineral water. Benny asked for a light beer.

When Cormac came back, his hands full, he set a bottle of Guinness in front of me.

"Live it the fuck up," he said.

He put down a Coors for Benny, then two bottles of Bud, one for himself and one for Rogue. Monkey see, monkey do. Cormac was still seriously into hero worship.

Rogue returned to the table carrying a large brown box. He set it down next to my chair, took a minute to use his cigarette butt to light a fresh cancer stick, then said, "That's for you."

"What is it?" I asked, nudging it with my foot. My suspicions came into play immediately. I had played a really dirty trick on Rogue by handcuffing him to my bed. Maybe it was payback time.

"Open it," he said, taking a deep drag of his Camel and exhaling a long stream of smoke.

I reached down and pulled the box closer. It was heavy. I looked in. Something leather? I pulled it out.

I held up a classic black motorcycle jacket made of horsehide. From its cut and careful detailing, I knew it had been hand-sewn by a skilled craftsperson. I turned the jacket over. BLOODS CLUB had been painted in red across the back. A white skull and crossbones appeared beneath it. *Oh, goody, just my style.*

There was more in the box. I found a pair of black leather pants, and they *were* my style, along with a pair of heavy square-toed boots, Fryes, just like I favored. In my size too.

"What's this for?" I asked, baffled by the gift.

"A thank-you would be nice," Rogue said.

"Thank you. What's this for?" I repeated.

"You saved my ass last night. You fight like a club member. You don't take shit from nobody. Lady, you are a genuine ballbuster. But you've been going it alone too long. We all decided it's time you had some brothers."

I opened my mouth to speak. Words failed me. Unexpected tears tightened my throat. I had been going it alone since the sixteenth century. Being a vampire is its own kind of brotherhood, but at their core vampires are solitary and self-absorbed. We are not pack animals.

When I joined the Darkwings I had found a kind of family. United by purpose and danger, we vowed to stay together. I had already felt the loss of two of its members. But this—this bond of friendship, this band of brothers—was being given to me unasked. The reason? Because I was *wanted*.

Finally I managed to say, "And what does all this mean, exactly?"

Rogue sat down and drank half his beer before he answered. "It means you are now a club member. Any of us gets in trouble, you're there. You're in trouble, we're there. You need something, we take care of it. And you can ride with me."

"Ride with you? Riding bitch? Uh, thank you, but I don't—"

"Oh, for shit's sake. What are you thinking? You ride your own bike, not mine."

"But I don't have a bike," I said, stating the obvious.

Rogue put his fingers in his mouth and whistled. Sam the cowboy got up from his table and sauntered over, weaving his way through the mostly empty tables.

A truly adorable guy, Sam gave me a sweet smile, then said, "Yeah, Rogue?"

"Tell her," Rogue said.

Sam's eyes enjoyed me for moment, his smile a little wider. "Rogue said y'all were looking for a bike. I found one for you."

I regarded Rogue with astonishment. The man had lost his mind. "You think I'm going to buy a motorcycle?"

"Hell, no. I already bought it for you. You don't know your ass from your elbow when it comes to bikes. You can buy the next one yourself."

"The next one," I echoed.

I felt as if I had gone through the looking glass and stepped into an upside-down world. Any moment now the Red Queen was going to appear, screaming, "Off with her head."

Rogue glanced at Sam. "Where did you put it?"

"Out back," Sam replied.

Rogue turned his attention to me. "You can't ride wearing that thing you've got on. Why don't you go change." It was not a question; it was an order.

"Come on, Daphne," Benny said. "I'll go to the ladies' with you."

It was a goddamn conspiracy. I picked up my Guinness and drank it down. All of it. Then I stood, pushing the chair back from the table. "Okay, let's take a ride."

"Oh, my God. You look so hot," Benny said as she studied me wearing my motorcycle jacket, pants, and boots.

"I don't know about looking hot, but I feel as if I'm going to pass out. It's June, not January."

"Now, Daphne, don't you go complaining. You need to wear them clothes when you ride. You don't want be like those damned fools who go sixty miles an hour wearing shorts and flip-flops. They wipe out and you know what happens?"

"Do I want to know?"

"Their flesh turns right to hamburger meat. Ground round. The road surface strips the skin and muscle right off down to the bone," she told me.

"Thank you for that," I said. "I think I just changed my mind about going through with this insanity."

"Oh, don't be a silly duck. You aren't going to get hurt,

and besides, you're wearing protection. Those pants fit you like a second skin. That poor guy Sam is like to lose his mind. He's cute, ain't he?"

"Don't even go there. He is cute. But I'm not interested."

"Maybe you should be, girlfriend. Everybody I talked to says he's a nice guy."

"If he's so great, why is he in here alone all the time?"

"I hear he had a really bad breakup. You know how that goes. He sure is interested in you, though."

"Nice try, but I told you, I don't want to date him. Even if I weren't with Darius, Sam is not for me."

"And why not? You just said you thought he was cute."

"He's cute for a vampire alcoholic who spends his nights hanging out in a biker bar. Benny, I have nothing in common with a man like that," I said, folding my dress and picking up my kicky sandals.

Benny stretched out her hands and took them from me. "I'll get a sack to carry these things in. I'll take them on home. You go on out to see your bike."

I sighed. "Okay, I guess I'd better get it over with."

We left the ladies' room and I headed for the back door. Benny called to me: "Daphne?"

I stopped and looked back. "What?"

"Can I ask you something?"

"Sure, go ahead."

"Just what do you have in common with Darius?"

Whatever I was expecting, it wasn't what I got.

First off, the motorcycle looked powerful enough to fly. Second, it was red. And fancy. Lots of chrome. Western fringe hung down around the long seat, and black leather saddlebags with real silver conchos were on the rear wheels.

"It's a 1973 Harley-Davidson FL Electra Glide," Rogue said proudly. "A shovelhead with a batwing fairing. A big touring bike. Got an electric starter too. It'll be easier for you."

"I'll take your word for it," I said. I felt a little light-headed and was tingling all over. I hadn't expected to be excited. I didn't think I'd even care. Instead I was breathless. I couldn't wait to try it out.

But I would wait. Rogue was not going to let me operate it until he gave me instruction. "You'd wipe out before you even got down the block," he said. I thanked him for the vote of confidence.

"Has nothing to do with you. It's a powerful machine. You got to learn to handle it. If you weren't so tall I wouldn't even have let you try it. Benny, here, her legs wouldn't reach the ground on this machine."

By this time Benny had come out the back door and stood next to Cormac, waiting to see how I'd react.

"That's the truth," she said. "You know what I'm getting, Daph? A trike. Brand-new. It's being delivered tomorrow. Harley just started making them. They're for older people. And even if I don't look it, you know, I am a senior citizen."

Benny's laugh was a merry trill up and down the scale. In years and spirit she *was* over seventy. In body, which in her case was pretty spectacular, she was twenty.

"Anyways, Daph. For somebody small as I am . . . well, I'll handle a trike better. It will be a lot safer—for my first bike, I mean."

"But I should risk breaking my neck, right?" I voiced my suspicions that there were strings attached to Rogue's generosity.

"You're a vampire. Breaking your neck wouldn't kill

you," he said, getting on my bike and handing me a helmet from the handlebars.

"Yeah, but it would hurt like hell."

"Climb on. This time you're riding bitch, Rambo. Next time, after I make sure you know what you're doing, you can go solo."

I got behind Rogue. I put my hands on his broad shoulders. My crotch was tight against his butt, which I found uncomfortably intimate. He started the engine and pulled out of the little courtyard behind the bar.

From that point on I forgot Rogue was even there. The thrill of the ride swept me away. The liberation of speed, the heady rush of power, the sensual feel of the bike beneath me carried me toward euphoria. I never expected it. I never expected to love this. I certainly never expected me, a scion of European aristocracy, the daughter of a pope, a descendent of kings, to be bound to a group of outcast vampire biker "brothers" with a bond as powerful as blood.

Know thyself, Socrates said. What a laugh. I seemed to have no clue who I was. Again and again I surprised myself. Vain self-delusion, for a vampire, could be a very dangerous thing.

Since it was close to morning the ride was short. My regret at its ending was long. Rogue dropped me off in front of my building. I saw Mickey peeking at me from behind the glass lobby doors.

I pulled off my helmet, shook my hair loose, and looked at Rogue. "What should I do with the bike?" I asked.

He said he'd take my bike home with him for tonight.

"Home? Where is that?" I asked, realizing I didn't know where Rogue lived any more than I knew his real name.

"Newark, New Jersey," he said without hesitation.

"Do you have a garage?" I asked.

He threw back his head and laughed. "No. And I don't have no wife, kids, or dog either."

"Well, thank you for the information," I huffed.

"Rambo, you want to know something about me? You just ask. Now that you're a Blood, I got no secrets from you."

I was tempted to hand him a laundry list of questions, but I could see the sky getting light in the east. I settled for asking him where he was going to keep *my* bike. Would it be safe? He was living in Newark, not Short Hills.

"Don't you worry. I park my bikes in the living room, right next to the sixty-inch TV."

He wasn't being at all sarcastic. He meant every word.

We agreed we'd find some time tomorrow night for him to give me a lesson. Before I turned to go, I said I was concerned about his getting back to Newark before the sun rose.

Rogue laughed again, the sound rich and deep in his chest. "The sun won't catch me, Rambo. I'm not somebody you need to worry about." With a roar of the bike's engine he zoomed away, leaving me standing there, the helmet in my hands.

Immediately Mickey opened the lobby doors to let me in. I saw him staring at my leathers. I could see he was eaten up with curiosity about the way I looked, about the motorcycle, and about what I was doing with Rogue.

"I just got a birthday present." I smiled a secretive smile and headed toward the elevator. Before the doors shut I saw Mickey standing there, mulling that over, his mouth open.

I winked.

I had been wrong about a lot of things tonight. One of them was about Darius not showing up. I let myself into my apartment, preoccupied, thinking about Rogue racing the rosy fingers of dawn.

No dog came to greet me.

I looked around, my anxiety instantaneous. She had been stolen before. I hurried into the living room. Jade had climbed onto the sofa. One eye opened to acknowledge me. Her head was on Darius's lap. She was comfortable. She wasn't moving.

Darius had been waiting for me. He didn't look happy.

"What have you been doing?" he asked. He looked at me in my leathers. He noted the helmet in my hand. That must have given him a hint. He sounded majorly annoyed.

"Working," I answered.

"Nice work," he said.

"I didn't think you'd be here," I responded, my hands now on my hips, my stance wide. "Why didn't you call me? Why didn't you send me a text message? I would have tried to get home sooner if I had known you were coming over. I haven't heard from you since yesterday." I was feeling a little pissed off myself.

"I just got here a couple of minutes ago. I did plan on calling you. I couldn't."

"Why not? My cell phone was working. I know. I checked it often enough." My voice sounded shrill. I realized I was preparing to hear what I referred to as one of his bullshit excuses.

Darius gently dislodged Jade and rose from the sofa. He started toward me, his step slow. Fatigue made his shoulders sag. His face was pale and gray.

"I couldn't reach you because my phone was confiscated," he said.

"What are you talking about?" I asked.

"Your mother had me arrested. I thought she was going to have me staked."

CHAPTER 14

Bring me my bow of burning gold!
Bring me my arrows of desire!
Bring me my spear!
O clouds, unfold!
Bring me my chariot of fire!

—William Blake, "And Did Those Feet"

It was another *oh-shit* moment.

I dropped my helmet on the floor, rushed over to Darius, and put my arms around him. He held me tight, his cheek against my hair.

When would I get it through my thick skull that Darius was not my enemy? He was a man, doing all the stupid, screwed-up stuff men did. But he was my guy. He loved me. And when it came to our problems, I had to take at least equal responsibility for our rocky road.

My mother was a different story altogether.

I had known that my mother would move swiftly once she received the Khan letter. I never suspected, not once, while Benny and I were with her in Scarsdale, that events were already in motion.

She already knew about Darius's kidnapping of the cleric and the loss of the bottle *because* she had just interrogated

him. She knew Opus Dei had orchestrated the invasion of
the vampire hunters and not Darius *because* she had just interrogated him.

Was that the real reason she had agreed to see me? Did
she fear I somehow knew she had Darius and was coming to
confront her? I was her daughter. She knew I would get him
released. I would insist on it—or I would fight her.

I squeezed my eyes shut. My feelings writhed and
whirled. My thoughts went to dark places.

Should I ask what methods she had used to extract the information? Had she used me as leverage? Did I really want
to know?

And where had Darius been when we stood in my
mother's kitchen and she told us about the hair of the
Prophet? Confined in the basement beneath the floor where
I stood? Or was he in the Flatiron Building, in the agency's
secret offices there?

"Are you all right?" I said softly, hiding the anguish I felt
at that moment.

"Now I am," he said.

"Do you want to talk about it?"

"Later, maybe. Maybe never." He sighed. "Your mother,
she . . . Never mind. It's more important that you and I talk
about what's going on. I'm making some coffee."

We went into the kitchen. Jade's tail thumped expectantly. She had retired to her doggy bed. Now she got up to
greet me. I stroked her head for a moment and looked toward the window. A weak glow fought the darkness behind
the shades. It was too close to morning to walk her. I'd have
to ask Mickey to do me the favor.

I slipped onto a high stool next to the granite countertop
while Darius poured two cups of coffee. Steam rose from the

cup he handed to me. I felt chilled now, and wrapped my cold hands around the cup and sipped the liquid, glad to feel the heat.

Darius hadn't skimped on the Gevalia coffee beans. The brew was strong and bracing. With this much caffeine in me, I wouldn't be falling asleep anytime soon. He must have a lot he needed to discuss.

He pulled another stool close to mine. Its legs scraped the floor. He sat down, his eyes weary.

It was time all the cobwebs got brushed away. I needed truth. I needed answers. The first thing I asked Darius was, "Why did my mother let you go?"

"I don't know," he said, and kept eye contact when he answered. "I really don't. Your mother had been there—during the interrogation, I mean. She left for a while. When she came back she told my captors to release me. Maybe she believed me that I didn't know anything else. Maybe she figured I'd lead her to something or somebody if she let me go."

I thought about my mother's motives. I guessed she couldn't terminate Darius and get away with it, that was all. Since Darius was working for another U.S. agency, it would be a dicey act for my mother to kill him, especially if J knew she had Darius in custody.

J might be a son of a bitch, but he was a by-the-book son of a bitch. He'd turn Darius over to a military court; he wouldn't let him be assassinated. And J was one of the few humans or vampires who had the guts to stand up to my mother. After all, he had stood up to me—even when he believed I was about to bite him.

"I've got some other questions too," I said.

"I bet you have. Let me get the kidnapping out of the way first, okay?" Darius reached out and took my hand. "I need to make something clear. My coming to see you had nothing to do with that mission. *Nothing*. Let me tell you exactly what happened."

He told me his band had been outside Hamburg, playing in a hole-in-the wall to a rough crowd, when he received orders to leave Germany immediately to carry out a snatch. Julie received the same orders. It was black ops, of course. But very high priority.

The two of them went to Turkey, something I already knew, and met with some people. From there they took a military transport to Islamabad. From that point they traveled by jeep and on foot, moving only at night, until they could cross the border into the Indian Kashmir.

Darius said more than once that Hassan Omar was a key man in Al Qaeda. As a popular cleric, he also commanded tremendous power. Hundreds of thousands of Muslims followed him. A fanatic—the worst kind, blind to reason—he had financed suicide bombers against Israel for years.

Omar, although he was educated at Virginia Tech here in the United States, was extremely hostile to the West. His capture had been on U.S. intelligence's wish list since 9/11. No one could get to him. He kept himself carefully guarded.

Recently U.S. intelligence had caught a break. Omar denounced a more moderate faction of Sunnis. He insisted they adopt his extremist version of Wahhabism or he'd issue a fatwa against them. The moderate faction couldn't openly strike back against Omar. They hoped we could.

Then Darius said, "Julie and I were given a small window of opportunity in which to carry out the mission. A hell of a lot could go wrong. We knew that. We went for it. To tell the truth, Daphne, I didn't know if I'd get back. We were supposed to work at night, but I figured there was at best a fifty-

fifty chance I'd get caught in the open after dawn with no shelter. I didn't really give a shit."

He poured more coffee. He stared down into the cup. Then, for the next half hour, he told the rest of his story, what happened in Hazratbal and afterward. He seemed driven to talk. It was the first time he'd ever discussed his work with me. But he had to tell me his side of things, he said. I wondered what my mother's version would be.

Darius, Julie, and their escorts got to Srinagar, a small village near the mountains that rose up to become the Himalayas, shortly before dawn. He could see the white marble dome of the Hazratbal mosque and the black-glass surface of Dal Lake beyond it. One of the conspirators hid them in a storage area behind his home. He locked them in with a small radio, promising to come back at dusk. Darius tuned in to the weather forecast: temperatures in the region would reach 104 degrees Fahrenheit. A dust storm threatened the region from the north.

Darius's hiding place was close enough to the mosque that he could hear the men being called to prayers throughout the day. Other sounds filtered through the cement-block walls: water splashing, music playing, salesmen haggling, and children laughing. A fair had been set up nearby. It was a holy day on the Muslim calendar.

In the hidden room Darius had no air. He needed no light. He was a night creature now that I had transformed him into a vampire. He said he still missed the sun, even though its rays were now his enemy.

I noticed some lingering regret, or was it bitterness?

Exposed to the sun he still craved, he would soon be dust. The words of one betrayer to Hassan Omar would bring assailants through the door he watched, letting the light flood in and making that windowless room his tomb.

Julie was there too. In a native sari, her skin darkened, her hair covered with a scarf, she slept despite the stifling heat. She never showed fear, Darius said. Or conscience. She was no vampire, he added, but sometimes he wondered whether she were human.

As the hours passed Darius sat on the floor, watched the door, and thought. Once during the afternoon the door opened. Darius shrank back into the shadows. A servant had brought afternoon mint tea.

Meanwhile, in the mosque at Hazratbal, Hassan Omar went through the ritual of obtaining the hair of the Prophet. He locked its bottle around his waist, then went out on a flat walkway above the quadrangle where people had gathered below. Seven mosque officials accompanied him. Two armed guards carried AK-47s.

Omar addressed the crowd in the way he always did, but even as he spoke the wind started to pick up. The dust storm arrived in what has been called paradise on Earth with a howling vengeance.

Visibility quickly dropped to near zero in the open court-yard. Most people scattered even before officials cut short the viewing of the hair of the Prophet. Guards dispersed as many of the others as they could. They tried to convince worshipers to go back to their vehicles. Those who had walked or come by boat to the mosque took shelter inside the walls.

Normally, following the ceremony, Omar would have returned the relic to its cabinet immediately. But the dust storm had knocked out the electricity. The power failed.

Newly installed electric locks on the four chambers mal-functioned.

Omar decided that until the chambers could be secured, the bottle containing the hair should remain chained to his waist.

Darius's coconspirators didn't know that. They had assumed the relic was back in its cabinet when evening arrived, and they went ahead with their scheme.

As night fell, Julie, screaming in Hindi, caused a diversion outside the mosque. It involved a lot of noise and interaction with the guards. While they were checking out the woman complaining about a thief, a van pulled up nearby. Its driver fled the scene and escaped in another vehicle. Guards raced over and discovered the van was loaded with explosives. As they ran, its blast rocked the street.

A few blocks away a second van exploded. In the confusion that followed, Omar's guards went to secure the building. The conspirators inside the mosque knocked Omar out with chemicals. He was delivered, unconscious, blindfolded, and wrapped in a straitjacket, to Darius. At this point no one knew the cleric still had the relic on his person.

Darius discovered the bottle hours later, after searching Omar for weapons and documents. Darius couldn't get back into the Kashmir. And by this hour an alarm would have been raised about Hassan Omar's disappearance.

Knowing he couldn't personally return the relic to the allies in the mosque, Darius followed established protocol. After some coded exchanges with his handler, it was arranged that a courier—a longtime informant for the U.S.—would take a package containing the relic and slip back into the Kashmir. He would deliver it to the conspirators.

The courier, who was not told what the package contained, never arrived at Srinagar. Efforts were being made to discover what happened, but the bottle, as well as the courier, were missing.

Darius, waiting in Islamabad, still had custody of the cleric when he received orders to fly back to New York. He turned the cleric over to others. He didn't know where the man was being held. He didn't know whether he had been brought to the U.S. He doubted it. They never were.

Darius squeezed my hand. "That's the story. All of it. As far as I was concerned it was an intelligence operation. It had nothing to do with you. It had nothing to do with me coming to your apartment. I came to see you because being away from you was tearing me up inside."

He brought my hand to his lips and kissed it. Then he started talking again, his voice low, strained, filled with pain.

"I had resigned myself to your marrying Fitzmaurice. I've been a soldier all my adult life. I always figured I'd die young. I had girlfriends, sure. I never had a committed relationship. You seemed to need it. I didn't do such a great job giving it to you.

"I found out who Fitzmaurice was. Nobody had a bad word to say about him. I figured the right thing to do was step out of the picture. Give you a chance to be happy.

"But, damn it, Daphne, it killed me. If I had still been human I would have hung it up. I really didn't care anymore about anything. When I found out you didn't marry him, I can't lie to you, I was glad.

"Right then I started making arrangements to wrap up the band tour and get out of Germany. Before my orders came through for the mission I was putting in for a transfer back to the States. If they didn't go for it I was going to resign. I had to see for myself how you felt."

Despair had dictated his words. Hope came with confession. His face had more color now. His stare moved up and down my face. I hoped he saw what he was looking for.

"I have to be up-front with you. I can't promise much. I don't know what the hell is going to happen. We'll have to figure it out as we go along. But if you want me to love you for as long as I exist on this planet, I can give you that."

A seismic shift took place deep inside me. "I never asked you for anything else," I said, and leaned toward him.

His lips came down on mine. I felt the kiss all the way to my toes. I slipped off the stool and melted into his arms. I had nothing on under the leather jacket. His hands came up under it and stroked my back. I made a little sound in my throat, something between a purr and a moan.

I positioned myself between his legs and pressed into him, feeling him getting hard through his jeans. I knew what I wanted. I knew what he wanted. We were always good at the physical part of our relationship. Right now I'd settle for true love and great sex. We'd wrangle about the domestic details of our relationship some other time.

The city was quiet in the hushed moments between the end of night and the first stirrings of dawn. No traffic sounds rose up from the street. No sirens wailed. I glanced toward the window. A moth struggled against the glass, its wings moving as fast and fluttering as the beating of my heart.

In my bedroom, in the bed where I did not sleep but where I lay with Darius this morning, I cared about nothing but being with my lover. I cared about nothing but what his hands were doing to me as they pulled off my tight black pants and spread my legs.

His thumbs pressing into the white flesh of my thighs, Darius knelt down beside the bed. His fingers glided up my naked sides, leaving a trail of fire. Pausing at my breasts, their tips brushed my nipples with electric effect. I shut my eyes and reveled in the pleasure.

Now his soft lips began to nibble where his thumbs had pressed, kissing one inner thigh, then the other. Then he pressed his face into my nest of curls. His tongue was warm when it touched me, there at the dark, wet center of myself. His lips encircled the small, hard nub above my velvet shaft. He sucked and nibbled. I moaned.

I moaned again, then mewed, the sensations rapidly building in my belly. I pulled my knees up and back until my feet were flat on the sheets near my waist, giving Darius complete access to me. I wanted him to do whatever he wanted with me. To touch and probe, bite and suck. I offered myself completely.

He used his mouth in magic ways. My pleasure was a playground swing carrying me toward the heavens, then back to earth, each arc going higher. But soon, as much as his cunnilingus excited me, it was not enough. A stronger yearning drove my needs; a nameless yearning filled me.

I needed to join our bodies, fuse our flesh. I had to have the oneness of lovers, the loss of my own self in order to gain his.

"Come on top of me," I whispered, lifting his head with my hands.

"I want to make you come first," he said and refused me.

"No, please," I begged. "Go inside me," I pleaded.

Instead his lips came down on my nub again, making me groan partly in protest, partly in submission.

But he let us join—not as I expected, but just as completely. He shifted his body to one side of me, pressing one of my legs down. Then, his body inverted, his leg swung over me, until he knelt astride my head, his long, hard member poised above my face. I reached up and stroked its smooth length. Then I saw Darius look back and begin to lower himself until the smooth head of his shaft touched my lips.

I opened my mouth and took him deeply into it, enveloping him. My fingers encircled his base, and I sucked on his rod of love.

And then my body jumped. I felt something hard entering me below where his lips had been. It was not his member, which I greedily devoured, but his rough, thick hand. First he pushed his index finger in, then his middle finger with it; then he pulled them out and added his ring finger. Three firm, long fingers slowly worked their way into my body, forcing their entrance, stretching me wide.

I bucked and bore down. My weight forced the fingers in deeper. He pressed harder with his mouth at the same time as he slipped his pinkie around to join the others, and his hand, his whole hand, slid deeper, my slippery wetness allowing him to do what I didn't think could be done.

That engorged with him, I was struck with a lightning bolt of sensation that coursed from his hand through my entire body. I moaned, the sound issuing despite my full mouth. I sucked on him harder, and Darius matched my rhythms with his rocking hand.

We did this for what seemed like a very long time, together in the most intimate way, our boundaries gone.

Finally, though, I began to peak. Sensations gathered inside me, starting to lift me high. Wild and out of control, I wanted still more.

My velvet well pulsed around his fingers. My own hands grabbed hard on the cheeks of his ass.

I took my mouth from his hard rod. It was wet with my saliva. At that moment I pulled myself up with my arms and bore down with all my might, forcing his fingers deeper till they hit that place inside that sent me into a swoon.

"There," I whispered. "Press there." The G-spot. The tantric secret. "Oh, my God. More, more." I whimpered. "More, oh, my God. Yes. Yes."

The sensations were sweeping me toward distant realms. I was on the verge of orgasm. I was holding off, prolonging the pleasure, rhythmically moving against his hand. Then, without warning, Darius's other hand stroked across my ass, slipping under me. I felt a finger enter me from behind.

My eyes snapped open. He pressed from that direction, and a guttural groan came out of my throat. His member sought my lips again. I opened and swallowed him hard as waves of ecstasy began to rock me. My body shuddered.

Darius refused to release me. He held me with all his strength. The orgasm intensified. I could barely breathe. His fingers impaled me front and back, his mouth still fastened tight on my nub as his fingers probed.

He had me then. He had me forever. He had me body and spirit for his own.

A still greater orgasm rocked me from head to toe; my whole body shook; I gave up all control and let the feelings consume me as Darius consumed me with his lips, his tongue, his teeth, his hands. And then, only then, when my pleasure had passed and my body relaxed, did he himself start to shake.

In a warm flood he released his sperm. His fluids filled my throat. I drank them down.

I was completely in his power, holding my lover inside me, unwilling to let him release me. Tears sprang to my eyes, and, finally realizing I was sated as I never had been before, I became still.

Later, Darius had carried me from the bed into the living room, my face buried in his neck. With me on his lap he sat on the sofa and held me. We didn't speak, we just let all the hurts of the past fade away. I felt whole and content.

We made love again before we entered my secret room. We slept in each other's arms, on blankets on the floor next to my coffin. I didn't want to release my embrace of him. I couldn't bear to let him be out of my touch.

When we awoke at dusk I stretched the length of me next to him. "What do we do tonight?" I asked in a whisper.

He stroked my hair. "I have to go to talk with my people. I have to leave. So do you. But it doesn't matter. I'll be back. I'll always come back. I'm never leaving you again, Daphne. And when we're apart, I'll still be with you."

He kissed my eyelids. " 'Twice or thrice had I loved thee / Before I knew thy face or name / So in a voice, so in a shape-less flame / Angels affect us oft, and worshiped be.' John Donne wrote that, and you, my angel are," he said.

"And you are my sun, my moon, my guiding star," I replied.

Benny had asked me what I had in common with Darius. The answer was, my soul.

CHAPTER 15

"Sweetest love, I do not go
For weariness of thee."

— John Donne, "Song"

Duty demanded our parting, calling us both to the same work for different masters.

Darius washed, dressed, and started to leave, not revealing where he was going. He still kept his secrets, far too many of them. I stood in the kitchen doorway, leaning against the jamb, watching him as he headed for the front door. Before he left he turned and recited, " 'The world is too much with us, late and soon, Getting and spending, we lay waste our powers.' "

"Wordsworth," I said. "You are a man for pretty words."

"That I am," he said, and was gone.

Only then did I jump in the shower and wash away the traces of our loving.

The Darkwings had a briefing scheduled at eight thirty. Despite my remorse at arriving late the other day—which upon second thought had clearly been an overreaction—I called Benny and told her to meet me at Saks Fifth Avenue across from St. Patrick's in twenty minutes.

I called Audrey too. She didn't answer her cell phone. I hoped she was busy in a good way.

Benny and I decided we should get our stories straight before we saw J. And I needed to pick up some D & G Light Blue, my favorite summer fragrance. Some people might think that the middle of a national crisis wasn't the right time to go shopping. I believed in multitasking and taking advantage of opportunity. Saks was as good a place to meet as any.

Benny didn't mind. She liked Bulgari Blu and wanted another bottle. Wearing white linen pants beneath a navy blue linen blazer and in full makeup, as always, she blended in with Saks' clientele as she waited for me in the cosmetics department.

I didn't. Not that I wanted to. I had a thing for Neiman Marcus, especially the store in the Houston Galleria. To me, anything from Saks was dressing down. And I had a motorcycle lesson later, so I had opted for just denim—if Neiman Marcus's two-hundred-dollar jeans and D & G jacket costing the earth were "just denim."

"One thing about this here job of ours," my pal Benny said as she let one of the roaming salespeople spray the underside of her wrist with L, Gwen Stefani's debut line for L.A.M.B. "What do you think?" she said, thrusting her wrist beneath my nose.

"Nice. Floral. Some musk."

"And 'watery greens,'" the saleswoman said, hopefully aiming the atomizer in my direction.

What the hell are 'watery greens'? I thought. *Seaweed?* I shook my head in the negative. I liked a citrus base for myself.

Benny gave the woman a thank-you, but no sale. We walked on.

"As I was saying," she said, "about this job, I surely do like the paycheck. And the use of the apartment. I never could afford to live in Manhattan."

I didn't know the agency had provided Benny with a flat. I didn't disapprove; in fact, I thought it was a great idea. Cormac, in his tiny Greenwich Village space, might see things differently. But why shouldn't he get an apartment too? And what about Rogue, stuck out in New Jersey? I didn't think he was living in Newark because he liked the amenities. I put housing on my list of things to stick my nose into at some point.

I didn't need government funding. Like Audrey, who lived down in the Village, I owned my apartment, always had. In fact, through a dummy corporation, I owned the building. Money was not an issue with me for a lot of reasons. My mother's being one of the world's wealthiest women was one of them. She had endowed me with an inheritance stashed in a Swiss bank account long ago.

My interception of a multimillion-dollar cashier's check destined to buy blood diamonds was another. *Interception* is a euphemism for what I did. I stole it, pure and simple. And I didn't feel the least bit guilty about *that*.

Our purchases made, we left Saks by the Fifth Avenue exit, and I flagged down a cab. Once we were settled into the backseat, I said to Benny in low voice so the cabbie couldn't overhear us—not that he could hear much above the screaming announcer at the Yankees game—"You know, I've been thinking. We know what these guys want. It's not up to us to give it to them. So I think we have to focus on finding the ship."

"You think they're all dead? The crew of the *Intrepid*, I mean?" Her eyes looked distant. She curled a strand of blond hair around her finger.

"Forget what you saw on the *Belgium*. The terrorists need the *Intrepid*'s people for hostages. They'll be okay," I said with more certainty than I felt. In truth, I figured it could go either way. They could already be dead. "What are your ideas about our next move?" I asked her.

"Let's see," she said. "Audrey might have something to tell us. And maybe J got information out of that there tire fellow. Then we can go talk to the Looie again," she suggested.

I thought for a moment. "If you had to guess, where do you think the *Intrepid* is?"

"Right now, with what we know, I'd say it's within fifty miles of here."

"Why?"

"There ain't no advantage taking it farther. If the threat is to blow it up, what's the fun of blowing it up out in the ocean? Hell, nobody would even know it. Right?"

"Smart, very smart. So it's someplace nearby, but we can't see it. How are we going to find it?"

"Now, I ain't no fortune-teller, Daph. That's more your thing. I'm out of ideas."

I went back to thinking. I'd known a lot of Gypsies throughout my life, and not one of them was a real fortune-teller. They were sensitives, a lot of them. I mean they "sensed" things, seen and unseen. They had a talent for guessing. That was as far as it went.

We didn't need a fortune-teller. As Rogue had said more than once, the best way to get information was by getting ourselves a snitch.

"You know, Benny," I said. "I think we need to talk to that tire guy ourselves."

"I hope he can still talk. I don't want to think what the men in black have been doing to him," she said.

Or my mother, I silently added. And speaking of my mother, I realized I had some unfinished business with her. I had come close to cutting her out of my life more than once over the centuries when I thought she went too far. This thing with Darius, it was a deal breaker. She'd stepped over the line this time.

Rain was falling when we got out of the cab at the Flatiron Building. A brisk wind swept across the island from New Jersey. The leaves on the trees in Madison Square Park on the other side of Twenty-third Street moved in a crazy dance, stirring memories of forests long gone.

"Damn," Benny said. "I didn't even bring a scarf. I'm going to be all frizzed."

"I hope it's just a shower. Rogue promised to teach me to operate my bike before dawn."

"You didn't wear your leathers," Benny remarked.

"I'm wearing jeans and a denim jacket. I'm probably just going to be riding around a parking lot at five miles an hour. I'll risk it."

In the elevator I said to Benny, "Where do you suppose they are?"

"Who? The crew?"

"No, I mean J's people. The agency. They have to be in this building somewhere."

"Does it matter?" she asked, pulling out a lipstick and putting it on without a mirror. "Any on my teeth?" she asked, showing me her pearly whites and fangs.

"No, you're good. And yes, it matters. It's the kind of thing I want to know."

"We don't have time to snoop tonight. We're already fashionably late," she said.

"Not fashionably," I said, stepping out of the elevator. "Vampire late. Let humans worry about being on time."

J's manner was so frosty, the temperature in the conference room dropped ten degrees as soon as I stepped through the door.

"Madder than a junkyard dog," Benny said under her breath as we took our seats.

Cormac and Rogue were there, Audrey wasn't. Guilt darkened my mood. We'd left her alone with Khan. Could something have happened to her?

Benny noticed too. Before we could say anything, J spoke. "I can't contact Agent Greco. Do you know where she is?"

Benny jumped in, chattering. "Audrey? She rendez-voused with us in the ladies' up at that there hotel, you know, the Palace. The Khan person she met . . . well, he gave her the . . . the . . . well, ah . . . the letter, you know. She passed it off to us, but she wanted to keep surveillance on the guy. She had him talking real good and everything. She thought he might be going to meet somebody. She stayed behind at the hotel."

J's brows drew together. "You haven't heard from her since?"

J would be apoplectic about Audrey's getting involved with Khan. Any way you looked at it she had compromised herself. Benny and I had to protect her if we could.

"No, sir. But I'm sure she's jist fine. She's probably jist

sitting there at her computer, like she does. Forgot the time. She'll be along shortly." She turned to me with questioning eyes.

"That's right, ain't it, Daphne?" Benny added.

"Yes, exactly. She said she wasn't going to let Khan out of her sight."

J shuffled some papers. "She needs to learn to stay in cell phone contact," he said to himself. He looked up.

"We have to get started. I'll talk with her later about it, assuming she shows up. If not . . . " He looked around the room. "I have heard earlier tonight that there is an influx of vampire hunters into New York City. I understand that all of you may be targeted. I trust I don't have to tell you to be cautious."

My heart squeezed. I hadn't even considered that Audrey might have run into hunters. I just figured she was with Khan and currently occupied. They were in the stay-in-bed-a-week phase of their relationship.

But anxiety was gnawing at me. I thought about excusing myself from the meeting to head up to the Palace. If Audrey was there, great. If not, I needed some answers from Khan. I gave Benny a worried look.

I should have saved the angst. Just then the door from the hall banged open and Audrey rushed in. Her hair was tousled and her cheeks were pink. She looked as if she was wearing one of Khan's shirts and maybe his jeans too. It was written all over her: She had been well and thoroughly fucked. Recently. Like, right before she came to the meeting.

Been there, done that—I should know.

I also noticed that her color was high for a vampire who

didn't ever eat enough. But then, I thought, maybe she had dined on Khan last night. Or this morning.

"Sorry I'm late," she said in her high little voice. "My cell phone died. Just wouldn't hold a charge. I stopped by the Sprint store to get the battery replaced."

Yeah, right. This was a woman who had been charging her battery since we'd left her last night.

Audrey took the chair on the far side of Benny. I saw Benny lean close to her and give her a vicious pinch on the arm.

I could hear what Benny said too: "Y'all better call us next time. You like to have scared us half to death."

J wasn't deaf either. "We're relieved to see you, Agent Greco. Agent Polycarp is right. With the situation as volatile as it is right now, we need to stay in close contact."

"Of course," Audrey said, blushing deeply and ducking her head. "Won't happen again."

Immediately J got down to business. He reported that negotiations would soon be under way for the return of the *Intrepid*. Audrey would continue to act as the liaison on the matter. A formal reply was being prepared for her to take to Khan.

Her complexion went from pink to scarlet.

"How are they going to return the relic if it's lost and they don't have it? Fake it?" I asked.

J explained that experts were duplicating the bottle from museum artifacts. Maybe the hair that had originally been in the bottle was totally bogus, like the slivers of wood that supposedly came from the cross of Jesus, but it didn't matter. The hair that was returned had to match the period and the DNA likely to be found in the region. It might have to withstand the scrutiny of carbon dating. The replacement strand was being obtained from a mummified corpse from the Middle East, which had been found in storage at the Metropolitan Museum of Art.

"Now we come to what the rest of you need to be doing. Find the ship and find it fast," he said, echoing my thoughts exactly.

"But why?" Audrey asked. "As soon as the hair and Hassan Omar are returned, the ship will be returned."

The room went silent. She glanced around at the rest of us. "Why are you looking at me like that?"

Rogue shook his head. "Now, what do you think the odds are that the ship is coming back in one piece?"

"Why, excellent." Her voice rang out with confidence. "Shal—Mr. Khan told me that his uncle and the Pakistani government have guaranteed that the terrorists will turn over the ship and the crew unharmed. He was given assurances that they would act in good faith."

I didn't know what J was thinking. I hoped he chalked up her response to inexperience and naïveté. At any rate, he answered her without suspicion.

"Agent Greco, it may well be that Shalid Khan sincerely believes that. You seem positive that he does. But we are dealing with terrorists here. We can hope that the exchange goes off as promised, but we need to be prepared if it doesn't. Our priority will be to find the ship."

"But what if we do find the ship?" she asked. "What then?"

"Do you mean will the relic be returned? Of course. Hassan Omar as well. The State Department will apologize for the unfortunate mistake. Believe me, nobody wants this hot potato. It's an international crisis waiting to happen.

"Until the exchange actually takes place, you need to

convince Mr. Khan that he has our full cooperation. Gain his trust as much as you can. Can you handle that?"

"Of course," Audrey replied. "Mr. Khan is a reasonable man. I believe he has been completely open with me so far."

"Excellent," J said. "The official response to the terrorist demands is being prepared. Did Khan give you a way to reach him?"

"Naturally. I made of sure of that. He's waiting for my call."

"You've been staying right on track, Agent Greco. Make sure you stay in close contact with me. Otherwise, just continue what you were doing."

I restrained myself from rolling my eyes. Benny wasn't so diplomatic. The librarian had it bad, and that wasn't good.

I told J we wanted to speak to Mr. Saud, the tire guy. He raised an eyebrow and tried to tell us that whatever information Mr. Saud had would be relayed to us. He'd get a report for us.

Rogue stretched his long legs under the table, leaned back in his chair, and lazily fished a toothpick out of his shirt pocket. J should have figured out by now that all the signs were there that he was about to get some flak from the other alpha male in the room.

"Well, now," Rogue said, "I'm sure those experts at interrogation have done a bang-up job. But I'm with my friend Daphne on this. We need to talk to Mr. Saudi Arabia. Ourselves."

"I don't think your request is possible," J said, tight-lipped and hard-eyed. "I assure you Mr. Saud has answered all questions."

"He hasn't answered mine," Rogue replied.

Both Benny and Cormac jumped in, supporting Rogue

and me. Audrey kept stealing glances at her watch and stayed out of the discussion.

J looked around. "All right. I'll see what I can do."

"And we need to know what was found out about the *Belgium*," I added. "Do you have anything on that?"

J shuffled through his papers and pulled out a report as he talked. If any cloaking equipment had been on the ship, it had been removed. The forensics people said more than one assailant did the shootings using .50-caliber rifles. Probably an 82A1 semiautomatic. The U.S. Army used them. So did terrorists. They had the power to kill a man from a mile away. They'd been used at practically point-blank range on the ship. "Anything else?" he added.

"Yeah," Rogue said. "I'm not sure I buy that nothing was found on that ship. And I saw equipment in Mr. Saudi Arabia's tire store myself. So what's the truth? You know how they made the *Intrepid* disappear?"

Benny hopped in. "Really, we need to know, J, su—sir. It might help us find it, you know?"

J let out a deep breath. "Look, I'm no scientist. And I don't know what was found and what wasn't. And what I do know is top-secret. Anything I say at this point you never heard."

We all nodded.

"From what I understand, the *Intrepid* was probably made invisible by a process involving plasmons. Frankly I don't understand what the hell a plasmon is. It has something to do with the movement of light particles, or photons on the surface of an object. And theoretically, if something can excite those plasmons with a lot of energy, like a huge surge of electricity, they will cancel out the visible light or radiation coming off the object. At that point the thing—in this case, a ship—becomes invisible.

"That's what happens in theory. As far as we knew it happened only on *Star Trek* when the Romulan ship disappeared. Never in reality. If it's been done with the *Intrepid* it's a huge breakthrough in cloaking devices.

"And since this process requires a constant source of energy—and a great deal of it—there's a good chance the ship can't remain invisible for extended periods of time. Its generators, even if boosted somehow, can't sustain that kind of production. As the ship loses power, it will be visible more and more frequently."

"So somebody will spot it," Rogue said.

"Yes," J agreed. "And you need to find that somebody and get to the ship before the terrorists decide it's time to blow it to kingdom come."

With that, J turned to Audrey and handed her an envelope. "The formal response to take to Shalid Khan."

"Good. I've arranged to contact Mr. Khan at eleven," Audrey said, and was out of her chair before any of us.

"Just hold a minute, girlfriend," Benny said, rising herself and putting her hand on Audrey's arm. "We need to get our movements coordinated, if you know what I mean."

Audrey opened her mouth to speak. Closed it. Looked over at me with an anxious face. She obviously had something to say and couldn't say it in front of J. She was learning her ABCs of having a forbidden affair.

Welcome to the club, I thought. "You can give us an overview of your plans on our way, okay?" I suggested.

She nodded yes and looked relieved.

J said he'd be in contact, and the rest of us decamped.

Downstairs in the Flatiron's dark, silent lobby beyond the

bank of elevators, we held our own ad hoc meeting. Cormac and Rogue agreed with Benny's assessment that the *Intrepid* was relatively close to the city. Although Rogue felt talking with the tire guy might narrow the search, he and his best bud were heading back to the waterfront, seeing if any boaters or longshoremen had anything else for us. He would meet me at Charlie's at four a.m. unless we got rained out.

Benny walked over to the lobby doors to get better cell phone reception and put in a call to Lieutenant Johnson. As I watched her speaking into the phone and giving the lieutenant the hard sell in order to convince him to meet with us, I hoped that our *entente cordiale* with the New York police still held.

Meanwhile I pulled Audrey in the other direction. "Spill it. All of it."

I saw her chin lift ever so slightly, and she said in a fluty voice, "I like Shalid. A great deal. We spent the night and day together. Indoors, of course. I found it . . . I found it illuminating."

"I gather that. You're lit up like a lightbulb. My point is, are you able to handle the situation?"

She paused. Her mouth trembled. Her voice wobbled. "I don't know what I am going to do. Naturally he doesn't suspect I'm a vampire. He thinks I'm an international model who is working undercover for the U.S. government. He has expressed regret that I'm not Pakistani and I'm not a Muslim."

"That's the least of his worries," I muttered, shaking my head.

"I told him I'd consider converting," she said.

"That's thinking with a clear head! Why would you say

something like that!" The words flew out of my mouth before I could stop them.

"So we could keep seeing each other. It's important to him."

"Audrey, Audrey, Audrey," I moaned. "You're a spy and he's your informant. If you sleep with him, the point is to get secrets out of him. And that's a best-case scenario. At worst you're sleeping with a terrorist. But the real issue is, in case it slipped your mind, you now being an international model and all, you're a vampire. Religion aside, how long do you really think you can keep seeing him?"

"I don't know. But I can't give him up. I can't. I've never . . . I've never felt this way before."

"Oh, my God," I groaned. "It's like a bad movie."

Benny came over in time to hear what Audrey said. "Girlfriend! Y'all need to get hold of yourself, y'hear? You ain't in love with him. You're just a little starstruck. And it's the danger. Whooee. That will supercharge any sex, you know. The excitement has gone to your head. You need to get back with your own kind and get some perspective."

Audrey sniffed and wiped a tear away with her fingers. "You mean go back to a vampire club?"

"No! I mean find some librarians, and find them right quick."

Audrey actually agreed with Benny, which shocked the hell out of me. Nobody could have talked me out of being crazy about Darius when he was still a human and I was a runaway train headed for a major wreck. Back then I had derailed big-time.

Audrey was a more sensible woman.

As it turned out there was an American Society for

Indexing convention going on in Manhattan. Audrey had signed up months ago.

"It's a librarian thing," she told us. She checked her watch. She confessed she had an appointment for a manicure and wash and set. She said she'd cancel it and go over to the Marriott East Side to the ASI welcome reception instead. She could hang out there for a couple of hours before she went to see Khan at eleven.

Being among all those indexers, a staid and intellectual group, she explained, should bring her back to reality if anything could. "They have a workshop on taxonomy that really interests me too," she added, looking dreamy.

I glanced over at Benny. She widened her eyes and mouthed back, *Whatever.*

Lieutenant Johnson had taken his grumpy pills. He drove across Twenty-third Street and picked us up in front of the Flatiron Building. The rain had stopped, but the wind still blew. I felt chilled despite its being summer. We climbed in the backseat of the unmarked police car, as usual a white Chevy.

Johnson barely looked at us. I could see the tension in his shoulders. His hands gripped the steering wheel as if he were strangling it to death. His discomfort at having two creatures such as us behind him must have been enormous.

He started heading east, then turned north on Park Avenue going uptown. Finally he spoke. No hellos. No how-are-yous. "You have something for me?" he said.

"Yes," I said. "We're still worried about an attack coming in via ship or boat. Did you hear about the murders on the container ship out in Arthur Kill?"

He slammed on the brakes, causing the Chevy to skid

slightly on the still-wet pavement. Benny and I had to brace ourselves to keep from catapulting into the front seat. We were lucky we didn't get rear-ended. He twisted the wheel sharply, pulled out of the lane, and parked in a bus stop. A stormy face turned in our direction. "What ship? What murders?"

Whoops. The feds must have hushed it up. But we had a deal. Benny told the lieutenant all. She showed him the pictures she took on her cell phone. He wanted copies. He also wanted to bring down the wrath of God on the feds. As far as he was concerned, this crime happened in New York City. It was a New York case. Another black mark went into his scorekeeping book.

Johnson did hold his anger in check. I gave that to him. We were just the messengers. I wouldn't want to be around when he turned it loose.

And now he owed us one.

"To change the subject," I said, "your people ever get names for those two guys killed in the subway a couple of days ago?"

Johnson's eyes narrowed. He had just picked me up at the Flatiron Building. The men were killed in the subway tunnel between the Broadway stations at Broadway and Twenty-third and Twenty-eighth streets. The engineer said he might have seen a woman running through the tunnels. The lieutenant put two and two together to come up with bingo.

"You want to tell me what that was all about?"

"I might. Answer me first."

"Yeah, we got them ID'd. Two ex-military. Special ops. Dishonorable discharges, both of them. Seem to have disappeared from sight after they left the service. Until they turned into fish chum under a subway train. You want names?"

"If it wouldn't be too much trouble," I said sweetly.

"All right. I'll get them for you. So what's the story?" he said.

I picked my words carefully. I didn't want to outright lie if I didn't have to. I didn't want to tell the truth, either. "They're working for the other side. We've had attacks on our team. They cornered me on the platform. I got lucky. They didn't."

He said something that sounded like, "Umf." I'm not sure he was happy I didn't get squashed too. It would have been one headache cured.

I might have had a snotty remark for him, but I felt my cell phone vibrating in my jean jacket pocket. I pulled it out. The caller ID indicated J was calling.

"I have to take this," I said.

J's voice was urgent. "You've got hunters following you."

"How do you know?" I asked.

I heard a muffled curse and a muttered word. "Surveillance spotted them."

On us? I thought, and remembered the young man on the street smoking a cigarette the other night.

J went on talking fast. "You, all of you, were tagged by a group of men—vampire hunters, we're sure of it—as you were going out of the building. I spoke to Rogue and O'Reilly. I can't get to Greco. A squad is after her. Do you know where she is?"

"Yeah," I said. "At a librarian thing up at the Marriott East Side."

"How close are you now?"

"Ten blocks or so," I said.

"Get there." He hung up.

CHAPTER 16

"Tell love it is but lust;
Tell time it is but motion;
Tell flesh it is but dust."

—Sir Walter Raleigh, "The Lie"

"Can you lose a tail?" I asked Lieutenant Johnson. "We have company."

He glanced in the rearview mirror. "Silver Taurus?"

"Could be," I said.

He took off down a one-way street the wrong way.

"We need to get up to Forty-ninth and Lex," I said. "The Marriott."

Johnson cut in front of a cab and floored it, jolting us back against the cushions.

"I'll call for backup." He grabbed his handheld from somewhere on the floor.

New York cops busting vampire hunters? I looked at Benny with a question on my face.

She shrugged. "Why not?"

Johnson wove in and out of traffic. On his way through a red light on Lexington, he asked, "The Marriott?"

"Our partner's at a librarian something-or-other there. We need to get to her."

"Right," he said.

"No, honest. She is."

Johnson pulled up in front of the impressive neoclassical fa-
cade of the Marriott East Side. "The Taurus turned off two
blocks back," he said as a white-gloved doorman opened the
car door to let Benny and me out.

"I'll sit here and watch the entrance," Johnson said.
"Couple of uniforms are on their way."

"Thanks," I said as I slid across the seat. I turned back toward him for a moment. "Keep watch for some big guys. In
black leather. Possibly carrying chains."

"Nice," he said, and rolled his eyes. "Armed?"

"Oh, yeah," I said as I got out of the car and started after
Benny. She was sashaying toward the lobby doors, bellmen
rushing to let her in.

Once inside Benny pasted on a big smile, unbuttoned her
jacket to show the impressive cleavage visible above her red
silk cami, and, with swaying walk, approached the concierge.
I hung back, my body rigid with tension, and kept looking
around nervously as we crossed the lobby.

Benny reached the concierge's tall mahogany desk,
where he sat as if in a pulpit. "Well, hi, there," she said in a
slow drawl filled with the South, as if she had all the time in
the world. My nerves ratcheted up a few notches. "My
friend and I, we're supposed to be attending that conference
you're having. You know, with all the librarians."

I watched with admiration. I had not yet met any man
who could or would deny Benny anything. The concierge,
his hair neat and his beige suit immaculate, did his best not
to stare at her chest. He failed.

"Librarians?" he asked, and tore his eyes from Benny to

look at his computer screen. "No librarians, but we have an American Society for Indexing cocktail reception tonight. Could that be it?"

"Why, it surely is," she purred, "And you found it quicker than two shakes of a lamb's tail. Now, where did y'all say it was?"

"In the Fountain Room. Sixteenth floor. The elevators are over there," he said, and pointed.

"You are just the sweetest," Benny said, and melted him with a look filled with promises. Then she walked casually away from his desk.

It was all I could do not to break into a trot. I had to resist the urge. We needed to keep a low profile. I hoped we could grab Audrey and get her out of there before anything happened. Vampire hunters wrapped in chains and carrying wooden stakes couldn't just waltz in the front door, so we might get lucky. But what if they found a back entrance? Anxiety crept over me like a nasty night crawler.

A portable sign sitting by the elevator said, ASI COCKTAIL RECEPTION. FOUNTAIN ROOM AND TERRACE. 8:00 TO 11:00. FLOOR 16. I turned it around to face the wall so any vampire hunter getting this far wouldn't see it. A futile gesture, but I did it anyway.

I tapped my foot impatiently during the elevator's climb upward.

"That ain't going to make it go any faster," Benny said.

We scooted out on the sixteenth floor, walking fast, following the signs to the Fountain Room and terrace. We pushed through double doors into a large, crowded room that appeared even larger and more crowded because of the mirrored walls.

I checked the premises. There had to be three hundred

guests or more. Most of them were women. Most wore glasses. Some carried books. Others opted for a food plate in one hand and a wineglass in the other. They looked gentle and scholarly, for the most part.

Laughter erupted from various parts of the room. I didn't hear any screams. That was a good thing.

We started politely shouldering our way through the guests. We avoided the buffet table, where the crowd was thickest. Near one of the mirrored walls we passed a slim young Asian man setting up a software demonstration at a folding table. I paused.

"Do you know Audrey Greco?" I asked.

He smiled a serene, Buddha-like smile. "Audrey? Oh, yes."

"Have you seen her?" I pressed.

"Out on the terrace, near the fountain. She was there a few minutes ago."

"Thanks," I called to him as I tapped Benny on the shoulder and pointed toward the open terrace doors. The hairs on the back of my neck started to prickle. It wasn't a good sign. "Hurry," I said to Benny.

I spotted Audrey's dark hair and white face as she stood talking with a group of women. She glanced up and saw us, her face puzzled.

I reached her side first. "Audrey, trouble's coming. You have to leave," I said with urgency.

Audrey got very still. Her fingers tightened around her wineglass. "Is it Shally?"

A friendly-faced woman with tortoiseshell glasses and long black hair framing her face like a Madonna's veil stepped closer, concerned and protective. "Is there something wrong?"

"Yes," I said, reaching around her to grab Audrey's arm.

"Maybe we can help." Another woman with blue steel in her voice moved forward. She had neat gray hair held back by a headband, and a thin face that brought to mind New England. Behind her rimless eyeglasses her glittering eyes demanded attention—or silence.

"I don't think so—" A tremendous crash from the Fountain Room interrupted me, followed by another and another. Our heads swiveled in that direction.

Coming in low and at a run, like a military assault team, four vampire hunters charged into the crowd. They were swinging their chains in front of them, attempting to clear a path through the densely packed room. Tables and chairs fell helter-skelter to the floor.

Masked, dressed in black, and bulky with muscle, the intruders attempted to shock and scare the guests as much as to clear them out of their way. Meanwhile their heads moved from side to side, surveying the room, as they tried to locate Benny, Audrey, and me, and coming inexorably in our direction.

Instead of scattering like frightened doves and giving the vampire hunters access to the terrace where we stood, the indexers closed rank. With practiced precision they swarmed like killer bees toward the assailants. Those nearest to the hunters grabbed chairs and held them like Clyde Beatty, stopping the chains' arcs with the rungs. Others took chairs and shoved them into the hunters' path to slow them down, all the while deftly ducking the blows aimed their way.

The sweet software guy let out a karate yell and went into a Bruce Lee fighting stance. Like a whirling dervish he twisted his body and landed punishing blows on the leading hunter with his fists and feet.

The crowd closed in as the big hunter feinted backward, trying to fend off the wild attack. A chair hit the big brute from behind at the same time the software guy executed a flying kick. His Nike smacked into the hunter's thick Adam's apple, propelling the invader into a mirrored wall.

The glass shattered. The hunter went down and didn't get up.

But the other hunters advanced.

Rushing forward and screaming like a banshee, a large, substantial woman in a powder blue pantsuit picked up a huge three-ring binder from a table and hurled it into the face of the hunter in the lead.

"You go, Carolyn!" somebody yelled. Everybody else got the idea immediately. Hundreds of books flew through the air like guided missiles.

Meanwhile a middle-aged man with a Ted Koppel shock of brown hair falling over his forehead picked up a wine bottle from the bar and thwacked a vampire hunter from behind. The hunter wobbled but stayed upright. Ted Koppel reached for a second bottle while he yelled to another man, "Hit him with the pinot, Richard!"

Richard did. The knackered vampire went down.

Outnumbered, outmanned, and outwomanned, the two remaining vampire hunters stopped their forward movement. It was a major tactical error. Pepper spray appeared in the hands of a dozen women, who surged forward and blitzed them at close range.

I had been poised, ready to rush into the fight, but the woman with the steely voice had immediately grasped my wrist, holding me back.

"No. We can handle them," she said, brooking no argument. She spoke in a brisk tone to the woman with the black hair. "Cheryl, we need to get Audrey to safety. Can you get her and her friends out?"

"Sure, Deborah," Cheryl said, and motioned us toward a side door. We didn't hesitate.

The four of us ran down a long corridor that led to a service elevator. We could hear the melee behind us continuing. Once we were in the elevator, safely descending, I turned to our guide and said, "Thank you."

"You looked a little surprised at what happened up there," the woman called Cheryl replied in a soft, melodic voice.

"Your friends were very impressive," I said.

"Yes, yes, I'd have to say we were."

"I never in all my born days thought librarians could fight like that," Benny said, running fingers through her hair.

"Oh, not all indexers are librarians." Cheryl laughed. "That's a common misperception. Only some are, but all indexers are extremely organized. Our job is to construct pathways to information. We have a habit of looking for patterns.

"Let me explain. We realized shortly after nine-eleven that any large gathering was vulnerable. And the more innocent the participants, the more tempting the target.

"The society immediately called for a discussion about procedures to follow if we were attacked by terrorists. Many of us took self-defense classes. We also created a SIG, that's a special-interest group—and its members came up with a broad-based defensive plan. The indexers who are librarians have been carrying out drills at their workplaces to stop a terror attack on our nation's libraries."

She gave us a broad smile. "I am proud to say we have proven it works."

I felt I had to say something. "If those men had automatic weapons, you'd all be dead."

Cheryl gave me what I took as a pitying look.

"We're not fools. I assure you we are not. In the first place, our security chair, Richard, served in Vietnam. The years may have passed, but his courage has not diminished. Second . . ."

She opened the Guatemalan striped cloth bag she carried by a woven band over her shoulder. I could see the interior. A long-barreled, menacing-looking Luger rested inside.

She closed the bag quickly. "About thirty of us carry. Quite of few of us compete in international marksmen competitions. You met Deborah, another of our security team. Colleen, the tall woman by the door where you entered, was actually coordinating the members' response to the invasion.

"Had the assailants been armed, plan B would have been put into operation. We would prefer not to use our weapons in such a crowded area, but I am quite certain that if those men had had weapons, instead of heading for a jail cell they'd be going to the morgue."

Chastened, I apologized for underestimating the indexers and for my prejudices. I fell silent as the floor indicator light above the doors blinked from number to number during the rest of our descent. I realized something important: The indexers had been prepared. We Darkwings escaped because we were lucky. And luck had a way of running out.

When we reached the main floor we followed Cheryl through another narrow hallway back to the lobby. A dozen uniformed police officers were charging toward the other bank of elevators.

"Is there another exit besides Lexington?" I asked Cheryl.

"Take the Forty-ninth Street one." She pointed. We headed for it, hoping no other hunters were lurking about in the side street.

"What now?" Benny asked when we were back out in the night.

"I'm going to the Palace," Audrey said, a little whiter than her high rose of earlier tonight but otherwise calm. "I'm supposed to give Shally the communiqué."

"It's only a block," I said. "We'll walk you over."

"I'm going to try to call Cormac," Benny said as we started toward Madison Avenue, keeping to the shadows. I periodically glanced behind us and kept a close watch on any cars that traveled down the mostly empty street.

Our footsteps made a lonesome tapping on the sidewalk. A damp wind blew in from the East River. It lifted up scraps of paper and sent them scampering down the sidewalk. It brushed by the buildings, moaning as if expressing some secret grief.

I had an increasing sensation that something was dreadfully wrong. I saw Benny talking into her cell. I watched her anxiously as she flipped the phone closed.

"They're fine," she assured me. "The other bikers came piling out of Charlie's and beat the crap out of the two vampire hunters who had followed them. Cormac says what was left of them is floating out to the Atlantic with the tide."

"Anything else?" I asked, twisting around and looking behind me again.

"Yes. Rogue wants us to meet. To come down to Charlie's. He says we have to do something about the current situation. And he heard something interesting."

"What?"

"Reports have been coming in about a ghost ship on Long Island Sound."

I slipped my hand through the crook of Audrey's bare, braceleted arm as we approached Madison Avenue. Her flesh was cold. I whispered to her, "Benny and I can wait for you in the lobby while you deliver the letter."

She gave her head a small shake and kept walking, not looking at me. "I'll try to catch up with you later."

I didn't argue. She was old enough to make her own mistakes. "All right," I said, glancing at her profile and catching a flash of tears. "I hope you know what you're doing."

"I hope so too," she said.

"You look awfully pale," I added. Her high color earlier must have been a postcoital flush. "Have you been getting enough blood?"

She shook her head no, not speaking.

"Please at least eat a rare steak or anything tartare. Tell Khan you need to order a steak from room service."   •

She didn't acknowledge me. We reached the corner of the hotel's block, kitty-corner from St. Patrick's across the broad avenue. I pulled Audrey to a stop and turned her around to face me. Benny watched us as if wondering what was going on.

Audrey looked like a hurt deer. Her arms felt thin and fragile under my hands. "Listen to me," I said as if speaking to a child. "If you get too hungry you won't be able to stop yourself. You will bite him. Do you understand that?"

Audrey's white face turned ashy gray. She stared at the ground and nodded yes.

"Well, hell's bells," Benny cut in. "It ain't the worst thing she can do. He won't even remember it afterward. Why not have your cake and eat it too?"

Audrey started to protest. I shot Benny a disapproving look but thought about what she'd just said. I kept my hold on Audrey's arm with one hand and used the fingers of the other to tip up her chin. I brushed some loose strands of hair back from her face.

"Audrey, sweetie. It's not love. Not this quick. It's infatuation. Benny's right. Hold on to your heart and drink your fill of him."

Color flamed into Audrey's cheeks. She stared into my eyes with fire in hers. She jerked her arm violently away from my hand and spit out her words: "Who are *you* to tell me how I feel? I don't care what either of you think. I know I love Shalid. I loved him the minute I saw him. I'd rather die than turn him into one of us."

"Well, sugar, you just may do that." Benny's voice was sad.

Benny and I saw Audrey safely into the New York Palace. We stood out near the fountain while she climbed the stairs to the glittering brass of the front doors. The former mansion was a veritable fortress. No vampire hunters could by stealth or force get past the security of its gated entrance and well-monitored courtyard.

As soon as Audrey entered the lobby, a slim, dark man walked quickly to her. She turned toward him. His arms stretched out to her and took her in his embrace. Shalid had been watching the doors and waiting for her return.

Retreating to the street Benny and I hailed a cab. We were headed downtown to West Street when her cell phone rang. She looked at it.

"It's the Looie," she said, surprised.

She answered the call. She listened for a moment, then

told him we were all fine, thank you. Then she listened some more. She said, "Uh-huh," a few times, and finally asked, "Are you certain?" Then she clicked off.

"What's up?" I asked.

"The Looie says the police took all four of the vampire hunters into custody. Two of them needed to go to a hospital. Nobody else was hurt."

"That's good news," I said.

"But there's something else. Some kids found a body washed up on the beach at Breezy Point. The man had been shot in the head, execution style. Dead a couple of days. The Looie says they just identified him."

I raised my eyebrows. "And?"

"It's a naval officer. He was assigned to the U.S.S. *Intrepid*."

CHAPTER 17

"Can life be a blessing,
Or worth the possessing,
Can life be a blessing if love were away?"

—John Dryden, "Troilus and Cressida"

Benny pulled out a hand mirror and makeup kit from her purse to begin repairs. I slunk down in the seat. My hair could use brushing, I supposed, but at present I had no interest in my appearance.

Our battered chariot carried us through late-night Manhattan's half-empty streets. It jolted us along the uneven pavement, stopped suddenly at traffic lights, jerked forward across the intersections.

Inside the cab the air held the odors of rides past. Grime and greasy fingerprints covered the partition between us and the driver, who was a bony man. Sour of expression, as if embittered by some private insults, he muttered curses as he drove.

Uncomfortable, uneasy, I felt foreboding grip me again. I could find no specific source for my anxiety, except it focused, if on anything, on Darius. Like a startled flock of starlings my thoughts flew in all directions, only to circle back and light upon him again.

Death had ventured close tonight. It had come in chains and leather. Now, having found the love I had looked for, I had a reason to hold tight to life, a purpose for fighting for my existence. But I knew somehow that the fear that wrapped around my bones was not for myself. It was for Darius.

An ice-cold bottle of beer awaited Benny. A Guinness ready for me sat on the table near the back wall of Charlie's. The hopeful eyes of Cowboy Sam watched me walk across the room. He touched his Stetson with his fingertips as I passed by.

Just the other day this hole-in-the-wall bar seemed dingy and unfriendly. Now the stale smells and the room crowded with vampire bikers lifted my spirits. It had become a downscale version of Cheers for me and my pals, the Bloods Club crew.

Cormac stood and gave Benny air kisses next to her cheeks. He wouldn't dare try that with me, so he settled for a wave executed from the wrist up, like Queen Elizabeth's as she passed through a crowd. This perfectly mimicked move came from a vampire in a biker jacket. I gave him a look that said I thought he was an idiot.

I sat in front of my Guinness. I stared at it a moment before lifting it up and chugging it down. It wasn't the smartest of decisions. Alcohol lowers my inhibitions. I needed to keep a tight rein on my desires, especially in a testosterone-drenched atmosphere like Charlie's. My dark passions tend to get loose at inopportune times.

I finished the bottle and gave a ladylike burp. I smiled and felt okay again. I thought for a moment. I think I felt good.

Rogue had watched me drink the Guinness. His face betrayed nothing of his thoughts. When I was through, he sent Cormac for a second round and began talking. He wanted to tell Benny and me about the "ghost ship" spotted off the North Shore of Long Island.

"It even made the local paper." Rogue pulled a news article ripped out of the *Village Beacon* from the breast pocket of his T-shirt. He handed it across the table. I held it between Benny and me. The light was dim in the bar, but we could see well enough to read the brief report.

FLYING DUTCHMAN MYSTERY

Port Jefferson, NY. Two striped-bass fishermen reported yesterday that a large ship appeared, then suddenly vanished on the waters of Long Island Sound about a mile from Port Jefferson.

The two men, Alex Norton and Joe Rosenbaum, were fishing off the bow of the charter boat *May's Lark* at the time of the sighting.

According to Norton and Rosenbaum, an aircraft carrier suddenly appeared about a quarter mile in the distance from their charter boat.

"I know it was an old aircraft carrier," Norton said. "My dad showed me pictures of his ship hundreds of times." Norton's father served on an *Essex*-class aircraft carrier in World War II.

The men said they watched the ship a few minutes; then a mist or a cloud covered it and the ship appeared to vanish. The day was sunny and clear, with no fog on the sound.

Norton and Rosenbaum said they are convinced it was a ghost ship.

The U.S. Navy currently has twelve aircraft carriers in service. A naval spokesperson said none of their ships operate on the sound.

Rogue reached over and retrieved the newspaper clipping. "That wasn't the only sighting, just the only one to make it into the papers. People I spoke to at a couple of marinas told me the 'ghost ship' has been appearing all week. Everybody's talking about it. It will be sitting out in the water for a few minutes, then disappear.

"Most of the sightings were in the sound. But a dog walker saw it off Block Island, and a few reports came in from the Hamptons, which means the ship was out in the Atlantic.

"Just like J said, the cloaking device used on the ship must be having trouble with its power source. At least, that's what I think," he added.

I felt a surge of hope that we could find the ship. "Benny got it right. The *Intrepid* didn't go far," I said, and she smiled.

Cormac returned to the table with the beers. He set them down and pulled up a chair for himself.

Rogue continued. "I've heard the military's sending lots of air surveillance over the sound too. The air force must be looking for the ship. I guess we assume they haven't found it."

I thought for a moment, my eyes fastened on the Guinness label. "Do you think they're going to blow up the ship out on the North Shore? It's a wealthy area. Million-dollar homes. A strike at the rich, something like that?"

Benny answered, shaking her head. "I don't think that's

it. A ship that size couldn't get close enough to shore to do any damage."

"So if we were the terrorists and we were planning to blow up the *Intrepid*, where would we do it?" I asked, and looked around the table at the faces of the Darkwings.

Cormac broke his silence. "For maximum effect? For drama? Why not go for the biggest splash? Bring the ship back into New York Harbor. It's only a couple of hours away. They can ram it right into the Battery or bring it in at the World Trade Center site, then go kaboom."

The possibility struck me as being sick enough to be their plan. "I think you got it, my friend," I said. I suddenly felt like I needed a drink. I chugged down the second bottle of Guinness.

Rogue lit up a Camel. He took a deep drag and blew the smoke above our heads. Everybody smoked at Charlie's. Rules did not apply. Vampires didn't get cancer. In any case, nobody could pay a city official enough to want to come in here.

"Here's what I think," he offered. "Benny gives J a buzz. Tells him where the ship is and that we think the ship will be moved. Tells him to make sure the military keeps a close watch on Arthur Kill and any other channel into the upper New York Bay. If the cloaking device is failing, they should see the ship. If she's still invisible but she's moving, they should spot her wake. And, Benny, make sure he keeps us in the loop."

"If they spot the ship, then what?" Benny asked.

"The military will scramble some B-52s. Bomb it."

"You think they'll do that? Some of the crew might still be alive," Benny said, standing up and pulling out her cell phone.

"Yeah," Rogue said, grinding out his butt in an ashtray. "I think they'll do that."

I sat there thinking dark thoughts while Benny walked out toward the back of the bar to make the phone call. Rogue broke into my woolgathering by saying we should have our driving lesson in a couple of minutes.

"Are we done for the night?" I asked. "It's still pretty early."

"We're not done. We're a long ways from done, but you need to know how to operate your bike."

He told us why when Benny came back.

Rogue said what I had been mulling over since the vampire hunter invasion at the Marriott East Side. We had been playing defense with the vampire hunters. To quote the old sports truism, "The best defense is a good offense."

"You mean," I said, "we need to go after them."

"Yes and no. From what I can tell they're operating in squads of two to four men. We don't know how many squads there are or where they're based. Best guess is in Opus Dei's headquarters."

"I agree," I said. "The headquarters is also a residential facility. It's the logical site. But we can't make an assault on the building. It's too well fortified and too public for us to do it without being caught."

"Agreed," Rogue said. "But if we try to go after them one at a time, they still keep the element of surprise. I figure we have to draw them out. Get them to come after a large group of us with all they've got. I have a plan in mind."

He laid it out to us. He intended to move fast on it before any more of our kind got killed. Boiled down to its bare essentials, Rogue wanted a decisive battle between us and them, one that the vampires intended to win. The risk was, we could lose and most of New York's vampires would perish at one time.

We had the rest of tonight to get everything in place for the showdown. After my lesson Rogue said we'd head to Lucifer's Laundromat to bring that bunch into our D-day mission.

But he had something for me to do: I needed to run our scheme past my mother.

Oh, goody.

Benny came back inside the bar. She said she had told J about the *Intrepid*. She added that for J, he sounded excited by the report.

That task done, we all headed to a nearby parking lot. On the sidewalk, out in the dark, Benny was bouncing all over the place with excitement. Rogue told her that her trike had arrived. She was like a kid on Christmas morning.

Sam had come along, but I kept my distance from the laconic, good-looking Texan. He offered to show Benny how to drive her new Harley. Once we got to the parking lot she started whooping. She ran over and got on. She probably shouldn't have worn those white linen pants, but she didn't seem to care.

Soon her head and Sam's were close together. Then he was sitting behind her on the bike. I heard her giggling, clearly enjoying his attention.

I glanced over at them and smiled. I had the feeling that her crush on Martin was about to become a fading memory. And Sam had a more willing companion in Benny than he did in me. There could be a happy ending in the making with those two. I crossed my fingers.

As for myself, I had a lot of fun with Rogue. He showed me the basics of keeping my shovelhead upright and not making a damned fool of myself. Now that I was in the club, he kept his hands to himself and treated me like a sister. Crude and uncouth as he was, I even started to like him a little.

I felt a twinge of regret. I had drunk the Guinness. I had hormones in overdrive. Rogue was the epitome of the male animal. I knew that sex was not love. Men—nearly every single last one of them, human and vampire both—routinely separated the two concepts. Women usually mistook sex and love for the same thing.

I liked to think I knew the difference. At least at the moment, the alcohol in my blood and my inhibitions forgotten, I figured sex, no love involved, might be an okay thing to do.

But the fates were looking out for me, and I didn't fall into sin. I didn't even stumble. So why didn't I feel better about it?

Because I was a vampire, that's why.

The rudiments of operating my Harley learned, I was ready for my maiden voyage. Sam and Benny, Rogue, Cormac, and I took off, engines roaring, through the deserted streets of the city around three a.m. We headed crosstown toward Second Avenue near St. Marks on the Bowery. That was Audrey's usual hangout. Tonight she was otherwise occupied, but Rogue needed to incorporate the Lucifer's Laundromat vampires into his battle plan.

The ride made me euphoric. My blood was high when we parked out front, the club's big neon sign drenching us all in its red glow. Rogue paid the bouncer at the door an extra fifty to watch the bikes. We went inside.

I soon found out our timing was either very good or very bad, depending on one's predilection for debauchery.

The competing blood sports teams, the Chasers and the Racers, had just returned. They had gone out on their nightly hunt right after midnight. Fortunately, no vampire hunters pursued them tonight as they searched the streets of the East Village, the Bowery, Little Italy, Chinatown, and Soho for victims.

According to the rules of their competition, the team that brought back the most humans—young and good-looking for the most part—won the race. The winning team got to dine on the blood of the captives in the opulent feeding rooms that had been created beneath the street-level club. If hunting was good, the winners invited the losers to join them. If only a few captives were found, the losers were just that—hungry losers.

Tonight the Racers had won, but both teams had a good night. Almost thirty pretty women and handsome young men had been brought to the feeding room. They offered no resistance. Mesmerized as they were by the vampires, and in the throes of a forgetfulness that would erase their memories, by tomorrow this awful captivity would be for them, at worst, a bad dream.

They would, of course, discover two small puncture wounds on their throats. They would wonder how they got them. They would feel a little weak, hungover; their heads would pound, and they would try to figure out where they had been and how they had gotten so drunk. They would never know.

No harm, no foul. Few of these captives were ever bitten twice. The vampires considered this herding of innocent civilians to be harmless fun and a necessary source of fresh blood. I considered the game to be exploitive and wrong. At least, I did when I was sober.

Flushed with excitement from my first solo ride, I came into the vampire club with the others. I joined them at the bar for a quick drink. In this case it was a Jameson, straight up, no ice. I ordered it from habit and with a certain irony, since it was Fitz's drink of choice.

I poured it down my throat and asked for another. The whiskey's heat coursed through my veins. I scented blood in the air. A hunger deep within me began to rage. I told myself to be strong and to wait until I returned to my apartment. The blood-bank pouches in my refrigerator would sate me.

Then Rogue called everyone in the club together. Although most members were anxious to get below and begin their orgy, two dozen vampires gathered close to us and listened attentively to Rogue's idea.

He told them it would be dangerous. He told them why we had to do it.

To a vampire, they agreed.

The captain of the Chasers, the once-terrified Martin, was still limping a little from his stake in the butt. He had avoided looking at Benny since the moment we walked in the door. But this handsome vampire, the one she had mooned over for weeks, was already a thing of the past for her. Sam's arm lay around her shoulders. She was contented as a cat.

Along with pretty red-haired Gerry, captain of the Racers, Martin invited us to join the teams in the lounge below for the feast.

Quickly accepting the dinner invite, Benny, Sam, and Cormac headed for the stairs. Gerry looked meaningfully at Rogue. She'd had sex with him before and she obviously wanted him again.

He shook his head. "I can't stay. I have a date," he told her.

I looked at him with surprised eyes. "A date?" I asked.

He gave me an insouciant wink. "Yeah, a date. That pretty little girl with the long blond hair, the one on the stoop over by Tompkins Square Park—"

I stiffened. My face froze.

"Now, Daphne, don't go all schoolmarmish on me. She liked me. She liked what I did. I liked her. She'll be one of our kind by morning. That's the way of the vampire."

It was. There was nothing I could say to him.

What I did say was yes to Martin's invitation. I should have refused, but I was hungrier now, fairly fainting from lack of blood. The Jameson made my head spin. In the dim recesses of my rational mind, I told myself that in the refurbished space below the club, elegantly appointed and designed for one purpose, was the vampire life I had fought against. It was the addiction I fought every day. That night I am ashamed to say, I didn't hesitate.

I went with Martin down the stairs.

Once we reached the subterranean rooms I heard groans of delight and moans of ecstasy. I saw naked bodies tangled together in twos and threes and fours. The orgy had begun.

I picked out a young man with long wavy hair. His jeans fit him like a second skin. His shirt was off. He had six-pack abs. He was around twenty-five years old, with soft brown eyes and a fashionable day's growth of beard.

I walked over and smiled at him. He smiled back, although his eyes had a faraway look. He saw me but he didn't see me. I took his hand. I led him to a wide divan and laid him down, silken covers beneath us. He tipped back his throat and turned his head. I felt my fangs grow long.

The skin of his throat tasted clean and fresh. His blood was salty and rich. He made a lovely meal.

To my relief, no remorse followed. I didn't take him sexually, although he was willing. I just drank his blood. I left him to join the others if he wished.

I walked back up the stairs, my dignity untarnished, my vows to Darius unbroken. I felt powerful and strong.

In fact, I felt strong enough to make the call I dreaded: to Mar-Mar.

CHAPTER 18

"I have been here before,
But when or how I cannot tell."

—Dante Gabriel Rossetti, "Sudden Light"

Outside the vampire club, beneath the red glow of the neon sign, I called my mother on my cell. She answered on the first ring, sounding rushed, as she always did.

I laid out Rogue's plan to stop the vampire hunters. We needed Mar-Mar's approval. For one thing, she was our boss. For another, she had been a major force in the vampire community for centuries—here in New York and in the entire world.

My mother asked a few questions while I spoke. She seemed to listen carefully to what I said. When I asked her what she thought, she didn't speak for a moment, then replied that she thought the plan had merit.

She realized immediately that we needed her to leak the information to Opus Dei. Those in the Church who were directing the vampire hunters had to fall for the trap that Rogue had concocted. They needed to believe they had uncovered a secret meeting of New York's vampires. It would take place at Strawberry Fields in Central Park tomorrow night at midnight. The witching hour. The hour of their deaths, or ours. My mother's carefully maintained network of informants and double agents could deliver the message; of that I had no doubt.

Just then my cell beeped. I saw that I had a text message waiting. It had to be Darius. My heart lurched with joy. I asked my mother to hold a moment. I accessed the message. It read simply: SOS J 23.

I deciphered the text message from Darius right away. SOS—the classic distress signal. J equaled J, my boss; 23—Twenty-third Street. In other words, Darius had been grabbed by J and was being held in the Flatiron Building.

I hurriedly got my mother back on the line.

"Where's Darius, Mother? What have you done with him?" I screamed into the phone, then leaned against the building, distraught. My body sagged against the wall.

She denied everything, of course. She said she didn't have Darius. I supposed she thought she wasn't lying. It was a technicality; J did. He had to be following her orders. She was his boss too.

"Why have you taken him, Mother, why?" I cried out, caught between rage and tears.

She was silent for a moment; then she spoke: "You don't have to approve of me. You don't have to like me. But you have to understand that I am your mother. I do have your best interests at heart."

I became cold and brittle like ice. Fear gripped me deep and hard. She would kill Darius as casually as she would swat a fly if she thought she could get away with it. And she would do it believing it was for my own good.

"If you harm him," I said, my voice hard and heavy as rock, "I will no longer be your daughter."

After I ended the phone call, I cursed myself silently. My reflex reaction to confront my mother had given away that I had learned of the abduction. My threat to cut her out of my life might stop her from proceeding with whatever she had in mind. Or she might accelerate her plans, for she knew I would save Darius if I could.

Time had become my enemy. I had to move quickly. I could not transform out here on the street. Even in the depth of night, people walked around the East Village. A half dozen could see me right now.

I had no alternative. I hurried to my motorcycle. The Harley would carry me to Twenty-third Street nearly as fast as flying. I prayed I wouldn't wipe out as I opened the accelerator and raced through the streets at an unsafe speed.

I stayed upright, ran every light, hit eighty miles an hour on the avenue. I reached the Flatiron Building in minutes. I jumped off the bike. I took a chain and padlock from one saddlebag and hurriedly fastened the bike to a no-parking sign. The late hour and lack of passersby in this commercial neighborhood would be the greater theft deterrent, but I wouldn't make it easy for anyone to take the bike.

I ran to the lobby doors. My hands pushed against the glass and met resistance. The building was locked.

I slunk back into the shadows. I didn't dare alert the guard. He might recognize me from the previous night. He would never let me in a second time. Worse, he might call the police. I couldn't afford the time to explain what I was doing or contact Lieutenant Johnson to vouch for me.

I had no other option. I'd have to transform.

I ducked into the nearby subway stairs, hurriedly removed my clothes, and let the change begin. Energy swept me up into a vortex of light. Reason drained away. Animal instinct took over. A moment later I sprang forth as the beast I am beneath my human skin.

Moving awkwardly, my hands now claws, I managed to stash my clothes in the other Harley saddlebag, then leaped up into the air, flapping my great black wings, rising along the stone walls of the building.

The Darkwings' phony offices were on the third floor. J and his people would need to move quickly from one place to another. Chances were they had a private connection between the floors to give them fast access to the dummy facility without using the public elevator or stairs. I guessed that J's real office was either a floor above or below. I looked for lighted windows on the second and fourth floors.

All windows on the second floor were dark and blank like blind eyes.

On the fourth floor several were illuminated. I cautiously approached the closest one. I peered in and saw an empty room. I flew to another and quickly drew back. A young woman sat at a computer monitor, typing on a keyboard. I moved on, my nerves winding ever tighter. I peered into another window, then another. Finally I approached the light emanating from the office occupying the apex of the old building, which was shaped like a wedge of cheese.

I thought this window a too-obvious choice, since it sat directly above J's Darkwing office, the one I had been in frequently on the third floor. I felt little hope that I would find Darius there. But even before I reached the window I heard a moan.

I flew to the fifth floor, and, clinging upside down to the wall, I walked down the rough stones to the fourth so I could look in the top of the window.

Darius sat on a chair, his hands handcuffed, ropes wound around his body. Two men in suits flanked him. One held a wooden stake in his hand. Guarded in this way and securely bound, Darius could neither transform nor escape.

I saw J standing to one side of the room, speaking words I could not hear. Darius did not respond, his head hanging toward his chest. I didn't know if he was conscious. Blood had trickled down from his mouth and stained his shirt.

Then he stirred, his face raising a little. Something subtle in his expression changed. I thought he might somehow have realized I was there.

I had seen enough. In a fluid motion I swung my huge bat body around and kicked through the windowpane with my feet. Glass shattered and fell to the sidewalk below. I landed on the floor, my wings arched, my fangs showing, my claws extended.

I ignored J and tore the stake from the hands of the startled man who held it. I clubbed him with a vicious blow, and he went down. Urine darkened the pants of the other man. He trembled, then ran from the room before I could grab him.

J stayed where he had been standing, not attempting to move.

"Release him," I hissed.

"I told you not to trust him," J said. "You didn't listen. Now he has betrayed you."

I looked at Darius. He shook his head and said, "No."

J laughed. "So why, Mr. della Chiesa, Mr. Darius of the Church, were you in Murray Hill at Thirty-fourth Street and Lexington Avenue?"

I knew the address immediately, same as J did. We both almost died in that building. "Opus Dei headquarters?" I asked.

J focused his blue marble eyes on me and said, "We've

had a tail on him since we released him the other night. We picked him up coming out of the building a short while ago."

"Is this true?" I asked Darius, my voice a growl, the blood beginning to pound in my skull.

"No," he said in a voice barely above a whisper. "It isn't what it looks like. I swear." His mouth was bloodied, his lips barely able to move.

"So why were you there?" I asked him.

Darius shook his head. "Not to betray you."

J laughed a cold, hard laugh. "So, who did you betray? Which vampires were you sending to their death?"

I shot J a furious look. "Shut up. You hated us too. Maybe you still do." I looked at Darius, bound and beaten. "Darius . . ."

His words came hard through his swollen mouth. "I did not betray you. Or anyone. Believe me."

"Or believe me," J said, amused. "He's lied before. He's lying now. I know it. Your mother knows it. Only you don't know it, Agent Urban."

"I'm telling you the truth," Darius said.

I heard yelling, then footsteps outside the room. The alarm would be spread by now. More men were coming. I had to choose.

"Release him, J."

J picked up a key off his desk and threw it to me. I caught it and quickly undid the handcuffs, then tore the rope from Darius's body.

"This way," I said, and hurried back to the window. I turned and took Darius in my arms, holding him tight against my body as I threw myself through the broken glass and into the empty air. Pulled down by Darius's weight, we dropped like a stone. I spread my great wings wide, arched them, and slowed the fall. Then, pulling hard to counteract gravity and flapping my bat wings with all my strength, I lowered us safely to the ground.

No one had stolen the Harley. I transformed in an instant, a monster one second, a woman naked, standing on the sidewalk, the next.

I grabbed the key to the padlock from its hiding place under the seat. I didn't take the time to dress but jumped on the bike.

"Get behind me," I said.

Darius did. I hit the starter. The engine caught. I gunned it. The bike responded like a racehorse out of the starting gate. We went hell-bent for leather across Fifth Avenue, careened onto Twenty-third Street, and raced away.

"I knew you would find me. And I knew you were there," Darius said hoarsely in my ear.

"How did you know I was there?" I called back to him, not turning my head.

"I smelled your perfume," he said. "The one you always wear."

After zigzagging through the cross streets until I felt confident we weren't being pursued, I pulled the Harley over to the curb, grabbed my clothes, ran into a doorway, and quickly dressed. I didn't need New York's finest spotting me riding au naturel and pulling me over for indecent exposure.

When we reached my building, Darius pushed my Harley into the lobby. I figured I'd do what Rogue did, at least for now, and keep my bike in the living room.

Once we were inside Mickey took off his hat and scratched his head. "Now, where do you think you're going with that?" he asked.

"I'm going to keep it upstairs until I can rent a spot in a garage," I said.

"Won't fit in the elevator."

I looked at the elevator standing open. I looked at my bike. "You're right. Now what?"

"You go on up. I'll take it around the side of the building and bring it up the service elevator."

Darius's mouth was swollen; his cheek was turning purple. But he said clearly enough, "Hold on. This machine must weigh six hundred pounds. I'll help. Daphne, go on up; we'll be there in a couple of minutes."

Mickey started muttering, "I ain't that old, God damn it."

I cut in. "Mickey, I just got this motorcycle. I'd feel better if you both went. That way you can make sure Darius doesn't scratch it up on me."

His hurt feelings salved, Mickey nodded as if that were a good idea. He took a good long look at Darius. "You need some ice for your face?" I heard him ask.

I stepped into the lobby elevator and pressed the button. The door slid closed. A moment later I reached my apartment, went in, and took off my jacket. Suddenly my adrenaline drained away. Fatigue washed over me. I felt like a balloon after the air went out of it. I'd be glad to sit down and relax for a while. I promised Jade her dinner and walked back to the front door, figuring Mickey and Darius should be getting off the service elevator any minute.

I waited. I waited. I poked my head out into the hall. I waited another minute. Then I walked down the hall to the service elevator. I was beginning to feel uneasy. I was standing in front of the closed elevators doors when I heard the sharp crack of gunshots, the sound traveling up the elevator shaft from a floor somewhere below.

I threw myself through the door to the fire stairs next to the elevator. Taking the steps two and three at a time, I ran down the ten flights as fast as I could. Halfway down I heard another round of gunshots. At the ground floor I was about to go crashing out the door when caution stopped me.

I crouched down and slowly slid the door open just a crack. I was about five feet from Mickey and Darius. They were stooped down behind my bike, their backs to the elevator door. Mickey had his gun out, the one he had been carrying in his pants. He was steadying it on the seat of my bike.

"Hey," I called in a whisper. Darius looked over and gestured for me to stay down. Beyond the bike I could see a rivulet of blood spreading across the floor, and two feet, toes pointing toward the ceiling.

"I hit 'em both," Mickey turned his head and said to me. "One of them got away. That Orangeman"—he motioned with his head toward the feet on the floor—"he ain't going nowhere."

"I think it's safe," Darius said, and slowly stood, checking things out. Then he nodded. "Yeah, this one's dead. The other guy's gone. There's blood on the door where he pushed through it. You hit him, all right."

Mickey stood up, his hands on his creaking knees, the gun with its long barrel still in his hand. "I'm old, God damn it, but I still know how to shoot."

He looked over at me. "Ferking Brits were laying for us. Ran at us with clubs as we were coming in the back door."

Darius nodded. "The hunters must have been watching the building."

"You going to call the cops, Mickey?" I asked.

"You want me to, Miss Urban?" he asked.

"Not particularly, but what are we going to do with him?" I looked toward the dead vampire hunter on the floor.

"Garbage truck comes tomorrow morning. If your boyfriend will give me a hand, we'll make sure this piece of trash is in it."

I went back upstairs. I didn't want to know how they planned to handle the body's disposal. I tried not to think too much about it either.

About an hour later Darius knocked on the door. I opened it, and he pushed my bike into the apartment and set it on the side of the foyer.

"I need a shower," he said. His clothes looked wet and stiff. He looked down at them. " 'Yet who would have thought the old man to have had so much blood in him?' Speaking of 'Out, damned spot,' can I throw my clothes in the washer?" he added.

"Give them to me," I said. He peeled off his bloody jeans and shirt. I gently took them from him as he walked toward the bathroom. I watched his naked body as he moved. I couldn't help myself.

A few minutes later he came out of the bathroom with a white towel around his waist and another in his hands. He began rubbing it over his head, drying off his short hair.

With his arms raised I could see the defined muscles of his chest. A line of blond hair, darkened by the water, extended downward along his belly. He looked like the Greeks' Apollo, carved from stone.

"Hope it's okay that I skipped the pink bathrobe tonight," he said with a grin.

He could have said anything and I would have smiled

back at him. But I knew I had to get serious. Despite how I enjoyed looking at him, we needed to talk. I told him that.

He nodded. I led the way into the living room and sat on the sofa.

"Tell me what's going on," I said. "I need to know. Why were you at Opus Dei?"

"You still don't trust me, do you?" he asked.

"How can you say that?" I replied, instantly annoyed. "If I didn't trust you, you wouldn't be here now."

But in truth there was a small part of me that didn't trust him, a part of me that wanted so desperately to trust him, but still doubted.

"But I need to know. My mother doesn't trust you. J doesn't trust you. I think you owe me an explanation. What were you doing there?"

He sat down on the arm of the chair next to where I sat. "I can't tell you," he said soberly. "And it wouldn't help you to know. It has nothing to do with you or any vampire. You need to take my word for it."

I gave him a hard look. "Nobody else takes your word for it. How can I?"

"Because I don't love anybody else," he said. "I don't care what they think."

"Not caring what they think nearly got you killed to-night," I said, my voice rising. I stood up and walked in front of him. "If you do love me, stop the secrets, Darius. They might destroy you, but they're sure to destroy us."

My chest got tight, my voice strained. I pulled my hair back from my face with my fingers. He was impossible. I was losing my control and was heading toward an argument.

"Don't you get it?" I said, too loud. "Don't you get what I did tonight? I defied my commanding officer tonight. I defied my mother. I basically fucked myself every which way to Sunday. You owe me the truth."

Instead of yelling back, Darius put his arm around my waist and drew me down on his lap. He sighed and put his hand behind my neck and brought my face to his until we were inches apart. I felt his breath on my skin. His jaw was tight, the muscles twitching. Sadness filled his eyes. "Okay, you need the truth. Here's the truth. I was at Opus Dei tonight. I went to see someone there. I had to talk to him. I needed to know if he had brought the hunters. If he did, I was going to try to get him to call them off."

"I don't understand," I said, more questions tumbling into my brain. "Who was this person? Why would he listen to you?"

Darius's eyes searched my face. He seemed to struggle with himself before he answered. "The person is the prelature of Opus Dei. His name is Thomas. Brother Thomas of the Cross. But he used to be Tommy della Chiesa. He's my brother."

"Whoa. Holy shit," I said. No wonder my mother didn't want me with Darius. He must have gone to their headquarters before. She must know that. No wonder she didn't trust him.

"Yeah. That's about what I figured you'd say."

I grasped Darius's shoulders. "So what happened? What did he say?"

Darius broke eye contact and looked away when he answered me. "Nothing. He said nothing. I didn't see him. He wasn't there. I had just left the building when J and two other guys grabbed me from behind. I got lucky, in a way. If they had been vampire hunters I'd be dead now.

"They threw me in the backseat of a car. One of the men

asked J where to drive. He said, 'To the Flatiron Building.' I got off that text message to you before they searched me and took my phone. You know the rest."

"So why didn't you tell them why you went there? They think you're still a vampire hunter. They believe you're working with Opus Dei."

"And if I did tell them, what then? It would probably confirm their suspicions. They'd figure I'd been feeding information about other vampires to my brother.

"If they did believe that I wasn't betraying anyone, it would be worse. They'd use me against Thomas. Blackmail him by threatening to expose that his own brother is a vampire. It would give them access to the order."

He shook his head. "I wouldn't blame them. It would be a tremendous break, give them incredible leverage."

Then his grip tightened on my neck. He turned my head toward his. He held my face between his hands. His eyes were burning with intensity. "Daphne, you can't ever tell them. Tell anyone. Thomas is my brother. He loves me. He doesn't know I'm a vampire. It would kill him if he found out what I was."

I wouldn't tell. I wouldn't betray him. I told him so. I had made my choice tonight. I chose Darius over my own mother. I didn't have to prove anything to him after that.

Arm in arm we went into the bedroom and to bed. Before dawn crept into the world we made love in the dark, our movements long and slow. I felt naughty and mischievous. I told him I had an idea, that we should work our way, one by one, through the sixty-four positions of *The Kama Sutra.*

He laughed and called me a wild woman. But there is a position in *The Kama Sutra* called the Deep One, a means of total penetration. And so in that ancient pose, my legs drawn up against my chest, my feet across his shoulders, he moved his body over me and lowered his shaft into me.

Then I cried out, the sound coming from deep within my belly, low and animal, as I received him. And together, endlessly rocking, we joined more completely than we had ever joined before.

Later, the light of the day blocked by the heavy curtains, I lay in his arms, relaxed, content, almost happy for a while. Too soon, however, troubled thoughts began to overtake me.

Not long ago, on the eve of our wedding, Fitz had had to run for his life because of my mother. He was somewhere far away now, unable to come home, always watching the shadows because of her. And Mar-Mar had *liked* Fitz. His only crime was that I hadn't transformed him into a vampire. I hadn't made him one of us, and with him knowing all he knew about me and my friends, my mother considered him too dangerous to us to live.

But my mother *hated* Darius. Although he was a vampire, although he was one of us, his change had been a bitter one. He had become filled with self-hatred. He loathed the monster my bite had created. He had lost his identity as a man and become the very thing he hated. In his pain and anger, acting out, taking chances, he had led the vampire hunters to himself—and to me.

My mother had never forgiven him for that. She probably never would. But I loved this man. I was so tired of fighting her. I wanted to live my own life without her interference. Would she ever let me go?

A whimper escaped my lips before I could stop it.

"What's wrong, my love?" Darius asked, and stroked my cheek.

I reached up and took his hand, my fingers tightening around it. "My mother will not let this go. Our being together. What are we going to do?"

"I don't know. Take it a step at a time. Try to talk to her. Fight her if we have to. I won't let her drive us apart. I'll never let her do that," he said, and kissed my forehead.

They were the right words to say. But I knew with a sinking feeling, because I had heard it before, never to say never, because never was a very long time.

CHAPTER 19

"Of arms and the man I sing."

—Virgil, *The Aeneid*

Day slipped away into the gray mantle of dusk. I had spent the hours of light in my beloved's arms, and I did not want the sweet interlude to end. Spooned against Darius and contented as we lay amid the tangled sheets, I said, "Recite something to me."

Darius had told me once, during the weeks when we first met, that he had been taken captive by the Chinese when he was a Navy SEAL. He kept his sanity during the long months in prison by committing verse to memory. I didn't know if the story was true. I hoped it was; he did know lots of poems.

And I? I had been smitten by poets many times. Tormented creative geniuses were a weakness for me. Pretty words captured my heart time after time. Darius himself had used them to win me.

He trailed his fingers lazily down my bare back, soothing me with long fingers. He lifted my hair and kissed my neck. I tingled where his lips lingered.

"I learned some new poems in Germany," he murmured as he kissed me. "Touring with a band is tedious. Days traveling on uncomfortable buses. Nights spent in seedy hotels.

I had time on my hands. Tended to think too much. Here's something by William Morris. It made me think of you," he said, and rolled over on his back, stared at the ceiling, and began to speak:

> *Upon the day thou weariest of me,*
> *I wish that thou mayst somewhat think of this,*
> *And twixt thy new-found kisses, and the bliss*
> *Of something sweeter than thine old delight,*
> *Remember thee a little of this night*
> *Of marvels, and this starlit, silent place,*
> *And these two lovers standing face to face.*

When he had finished I swung my legs off the edge of the bed. My feet hit the wooden floor with a small smack. I stood, my stiff back toward my lover. "I think I shall shower," I said.

"What's wrong?" he asked. "You didn't like it? I thought the rhyming was brilliant."

I looked back over my shoulder at Darius, his face innocent of malice.

The poem he chose revealed too clearly that he had been thinking of me with Fitz when he memorized it. His anger was there in the lines. He wasn't as gracious about my leaving him as he had earlier implied.

"It was very nice," I said.

"But?" he asked.

"But? Nothing. Nothing to do with the poem. Something else," I lied. "What are your plans tonight?" I asked.

"My plans?" He propped himself up on his elbow as he remained lying carelessly on the bed. He looked down at his fingernails. "Besides staying at least a few steps ahead of the grim reaper, not any. I heard that the return of Hassan Omar and the relic are in the works. I'm out of it now. It's up to the State Department, I suppose. Anyway, it's over with for me." He raised his eyes to my face. "What are you going to do?"

I realized I had a decision to make, one that could determine the fates of many. I hadn't told Darius about Rogue's plan. I stood there and looked at him, wondering whether to listen to my believing heart or the niggling doubt in my head. Which was the better judge? I wish I knew.

I let out a deep breath. *In for a penny, in for a pound.* I walked back to the bed. I sat down on the edge and told Darius everything. I told him that a large gathering of vampires, primarily from Lucifer's Laundromat but others too, would meet in Central Park at midnight. They would be decoys, sitting ducks as it were, to entice the ninety or more vampire hunters that Darius said were in New York to attack.

But the vampires acting as a Judas goat would be ready, armed, and prepared to fight. More important, they would be in constant contact with Rogue and a squadron of us, also heavily armed. Upon the Central Park group's signal, we would join the battle, flanking the attackers from behind in a classic pincer maneuver.

The success of the operation would come down to precise timing—and completing the action quickly, before the police arrived to interrupt the vampire war going on within the city limits.

"We don't have to kill all of them," I explained. "But we do have to decimate their numbers enough so that Opus Dei sends the survivors back to whatever dark hole they came from."

Darius listened. I couldn't read his face.

"Count me in," he said.

*   *   *

The night came down on the city like black velvet, too warm
for the season, causing thousands of air conditioners to be
turned up to high. People lined up in front of ice-cream
stores. Policemen rode around in their squad cars sweating
beer into their shirts.

In the shower stall I let the cool water run over my body.
I was humming as I slathered liquid soap over my flesh. I
thought about a lot of things as I washed. Darius would
spend the early hours with me. We could talk some more.
Make love again, of course.

I didn't know if the Darkwings had a briefing tonight. J
didn't call. I would not have gone in any event. I didn't know
what I would say to him. I didn't know if I wanted to see him
again. I had cast my lot with Darius, not J.

I had nearly quit the Darkwings before. I was at that point
again. Perhaps I needed to rethink my career as a spy. Or
perhaps not. I liked what I did. Months earlier Darius had
encouraged me to leave my mother's group and join his
agency. He'd asked me to go to Germany with him, as a secret agent as well as his lover.

His request had put me at a fork in the road of life.
Before, I had taken the other path, and now, ironically, it had
led me back to the same junction.

Fate was giving me all the signs. This time maybe I
should pay some attention to them.

I emerged from the shower to find that Darius had retrieved his shirt and jeans from the clothes dryer in the
kitchen. He was already dressed. My brow furrowed.

"Are you going out?" I asked.

"Yes," he said, picking up his cell phone and wallet from
the bedside table and putting them in his back pocket.

"I thought you said you didn't have plans?" My voice was skeptical and suspicious.

"I didn't when you asked before. Now I do," he said, turning around and looking at me.

He must have called someone while I was in the shower, I thought. "So where are you going?"

"Don't worry," he said. "I'll meet you later. You said ten to twelve. At Seventy-second and Broadway?"

"That's where I'm meeting Rogue. I thought we'd be going there together." Anxiety began to gnaw at me like a hungry rodent.

"I have to take care of something first. Don't look so worried. I'll be there; I promise." He crossed the room and put his arms around me.

I was like ice in his arms. My mind was racing, matching my accelerating heart. "Don't you think you should have something—some blood, I mean—before you go?"

He leered and nuzzled my neck. "Are you offering me a meal?"

I pulled away from his kiss and pushed out of his arms.

"Hey, I was just kidding. I know you meant the blood-bank stuff. Thanks for the offer, but I'll take care of it later."

"You'll need all your strength for tonight," I said, not knowing what he meant by, *I'll take care of it later,* but questions were getting me nowhere.

He smiled at me. "You worry about me too much. I promise you I'll meet you on time. I promise you I won't be fainting with hunger. If anything, if you want to know the truth, I'm concerned about your going tonight. It will get rough. Somebody, maybe a lot of somebodies, will die. I don't want you to be one of them."

I lifted my chin. "I won't be. I know how to fight. You of all people should know that."

"You are one badass mama. I know that. There's still a risk. Being a selfish person, I don't want to lose you. I just got you back."

"Was it a contest?" I said, my words brittle.

"What are you talking about?" he asked.

"Getting me back? Was it a game for you?"

He rolled his eyes up at the ceiling. "God grant me patience," he muttered under his breath. Then his eyes came back to me. "Daphne Urban, you are one of the world's most trying women. Can't you accept the fact that I love you? I love you with all my heart. I want you to be safe. I don't want you breaking heads and maybe getting your own busted. I want us to have a life together, an eternity together, if you will.

"Oh, hell," he said, and took a step toward me, stretched out his hand, and grabbed my arm. He pulled me next to him, my bare breasts pressed against him.

"You're going to make me a crazy man; you really are. I wanted to find a better time to ask this, but I'd better do it now—Daphne, will you marry me?"

I whooped. I threw myself in his arms. I wrapped my naked legs around his waist and covered his face in kisses. "Yes," I said, "Yes, I'll marry you." No hesitation, no doubts.

Then he told me that he had been going out to buy me a ring. I felt like an idiot. A suspicious, irrational idiot—for about a nanosecond.

Although my outward reaction was uninhibited, inwardly I was deeply shaken. Twice within a short amount of time, within the same banner year, two men had asked me to wed them. For four hundred years I had affairs, liaisons, and long dry spells. No marriage. No engagements. A vampire bride is not a highly sought-after mate.

Why had that changed since I joined the Darkwings? Had something in me changed?

"So it's a yes," he said with a broad smile. "In that case, I think we have to make it official," he said, and unbuttoned his jeans and dropped them to the floor, exposing his upright member.

It was clear what "making it official" meant.

We never made it to the bedroom. We sank down together on the carpet. Without foreplay Darius entered me, a quick, hard taking. And since there were other *Kama Sutra* positions we had yet to try—sixty-three more, to be exact—I moved beneath Darius so that we could begin with the Mill Vanes, which required self-control of the man and strength from me.

After a few minutes in that pose, as the passion soared in us both, I shifted again and we moved into the Mirror of Pleasing, which allows no touching with the hands or face. But the tantalizing distance between us made me grow desperate with wanting to hold him. I pulled back and asked him to squat on his haunches. In a sitting position, I slid down onto him, taking him within me. Then, wrapping my arms around his shoulders, I met his lips with mine in an unending kiss. In this variant of the Medusa I was soon gasping, the stars whirling around me as I climaxed. Darius followed with an orgasm of his own.

I had been sated. I had been well and royally fucked three different ways. But somehow it was not what celebrating an engagement perhaps should be. My feelings must have been evident, for Darius, his body slick with sweat in the hot night, kissed me again.

"Didn't I please you?" he asked.

"Yes—" I began.

"It's getting late," he said, cutting me off. "I'll come up with something special for the next time. And that's a promise." He gave me a playful slap on the butt, got up, and went into the bathroom. I heard the water running while he washed up.

I should have been happier than I was, I thought.

Well, hello! I admonished myself. One reason I wasn't happier was that Darius was still going out. And not taking me with him.

After he left, stopping to kiss me as he headed out the front door, I told Jade I'd take her for a walk. She danced around with doggy joy when she saw the leash. Gunther squeaked in his cage, wanting to go too.

"Sorry, little guy," I said. "It's too hot for a rat in a pocket tonight."

In fact, all I had on was running shorts and a cotton cami, a pair of flip-flops on my feet. The humidity had created air you could wear outside; the temperature hovered in the high eighties, even after dark.

Mickey tipped his hat when Jade and I stepped off the elevator into the lobby.

"Are you okay?" I asked.

"Fit as a fiddle. Most action I've seen in forty years," he said with a smile.

"Thank you for what you did," I said.

"No need for that," he said, blushing, and changed the subject. "Saw your young man go out a little while ago." His previous rancor at Darius was absent. Getting attacked by killers and then disposing of a dead body must be a male bonding experience.

"Yes, he went out," I responded, feeling annoyed now that Mickey brought up the issue again. "By the way, Mick, can you give me some help getting my bike downstairs around eleven?"

"Just ring me when you're ready, Miss Urban," he said.

Time on my hands and nothing to occupy my mind made me fret and stew. I had little to do from now, a little after nine, until eleven thirty, when I would take my Harley downstairs and ride the few blocks over to Broadway. I planned to clean my guns, for I was taking two, then get together what I would wear for battle. Other than that, I faced idleness.

For a while after Darius left I sat at the breakfast counter with a mug of coffee, turning the pages of the *New York Times,* just as I had done hundreds of evenings before. Nothing kept my attention. Instead I worried that I had compromised our operation. Perhaps I shouldn't have told Darius. Right now he could be talking with his brother, figuring out a counterattack that would get all the vampires killed.

I hated myself for even fantasizing about that. If that were true, it would mean Darius's marriage proposal was a sham as well, a spur-of-the-moment deception to dupe me into believing in him. Had I been blinded by my passion? Where did his loyalties really lie?

These thoughts, born in my teeming brain, made me feel small and miserable. I *had* to trust Darius. I loved him. Also, he was the one who had told me about the vampire hunter army in the first place. And I didn't believe he could fake the lovemaking that fused us body and soul. He would have to be a heartless bastard to do something like that, to play me that way.

It was my mother's influence making me think he could

be so devious. She could be; I knew that. If I believed even half of what the history books reported on Marozia, it was clear she was a treacherous, ambitious, ruthless woman. Yes, she was my mother. That didn't change the facts.

She had poisoned my mind against the man I loved.

My cell phone rang then, and with relief, seeing it was Benny, I answered it.

She told me right up front that she was not alone. She lowered her voice, giggled, and said she'd been playing Ride 'Em, Cowboy since yesterday. But anyway, she didn't call to brag, she said. She called to tell me that she had talked to Audrey and she was sorely worried.

"I called her and left her a message, you know, about our plans for tonight. She called me back. Now, maybe I shouldn't have—my mama always said never to come between a woman and a man—but, you know, I just have to say what's on my mind.

"I told her that I thought maybe that there Khan fellow wasn't quite as good as she thought.

"I told her about that poor officer from the *Intrepid*, shot the way he was. And that those terrorists may have killed everybody, far as we knew, and we were a mite worried about them really returning the ship without some shenanigans and all. And maybe, since she was a spy, she should try to find out what the terrorists were really planning to do with the *Intrepid*."

Evidently Audrey didn't take Benny's news very well. She said she was sure Khan didn't know anything about any killings. He believed with all his heart that the Wahhabi group was acting in good faith. His uncle had assured him it was so. And Benny was deeply worried because Audrey's voice sounded hollow and weak, as if she hadn't eaten.

"She surely hasn't bitten him. I can tell you that, girlfriend," Benny said.

I asked Benny if Audrey intended to come to Central Park tonight, either with our group or the Laundromat crew. She said no. After realizing Audrey was in a weakened state, Benny had told her to stick with Khan—to find out information. She asked me if we should run an intervention, or do something to make sure Audrey got some blood in her.

I thought for a moment and decided I had time to take some blood from my refrigerator stash over to her. I said to Benny, "I think she needs to tell Khan she has anemia from dieting for her modeling career. He'd buy that. Call Audrey back and tell her I'm bringing some over."

"Sugar," she said, "that is absolute-y posultooty brilliant. I'll get on it right now."

I felt relieved that Benny didn't ask what I had been doing. And I didn't tell her. Although she was my best friend, I didn't tell her about Darius being abducted. I didn't tell her about Mickey and Darius and the vampire hunters. I didn't tell her about Darius popping the question. I didn't tell her he'd be coming along with us tonight. I curiously didn't mention Darius at all.

I changed quickly into close-fitting white silk pants, a white cami, and a long embroidered Indian-silk Sandy Starkman jacket. I slipped my feet into Stuart Weitzman mules. The overall effect carried a hint of India or Pakistan. I put on jewelry too—enough diamonds on my wrists, neck, and earlobes to need a police escort. In places like the Palace money talks, and I wouldn't have to say anything at all. The doorman would rush over all smiles, and the desk would call up to Khan's room to announce me.

*   *   *

Audrey was standing in the doorway waiting for me when I stepped out of the elevator. She wore a white terry-cloth robe, and her face was just as white. Her hand trembled on the doorjamb, the quaking traveling up her arm. I thought she looked ready to collapse.

When Audrey brought me into the suite, Khan was on the phone. He glanced up at me and waved but kept talking into the receiver.

Good, I thought. *I can get this blood into her without any long explanations.* "Let's go into the bathroom," I told Audrey.

She nodded and led me into a large, opulent one, all white tile and marble. The red bag of blood looked like a wound when I pulled it out of my backpack and laid it down on the sink. I reached for a glass with a paper doily covering its top.

"No," Audrey said as she sank down on the closed toilet seat as if her legs wouldn't hold her up anymore. "Just open it, please."

I did and handed it over. She poured it down her throat. I prepared a second, holding back the urge to lecture her on the need to take care of herself. She drank the second pint more slowly while I disposed of the empty plastic blood bag in the trash. I was sure the cleaning staff had found stranger items tossed away than that.

When Audrey was finished she stood and went to the sink. She ran the cold water and splashed it on her face. Her cheeks were pink now; the trembling in her limbs had disappeared.

"Let me introduce you to Shally," she said, glancing up and catching my eyes in the mirror.

"Who does he think I am?" I asked.

"A spy," she said.

Between Cormac's blabbing to most of New York's vampire community during our last mission and Audrey's revelation to Khan, I might as well walk around with a sign saying, *Hi, I'm Daphne. I'm a spy.* Didn't anybody—besides Darius—know how to keep a secret anymore?

Audrey opened the bathroom door. Khan was off the phone and looking worried. She introduced us as he walked over and stuck out his hand to take mine in both of his, holding it as he said, "Thank you. Thank you for bringing her transfusion. I didn't know about her hemophilia. I have been desperately worried. She should have told me."

I disengaged my hand. "I'm sure she would have when she got to know you better," I said.

Audrey came close to Khan and he put his arm around her, drawing her close. He kissed her temple. "Are you feeling better?" he asked.

She looked at him with doe eyes. They seemed to forget I existed. "Yes. Much," she murmured, lost in his gaze.

I cleared my throat. "Well, I'd better get going," I said.

Khan snapped out of his trance. "Wait. I know, um, that you are, um, working with the American government. If you don't mind, I need to ask you a few questions."

I stiffened a little. "You can ask. I don't know if I can answer you," I said.

"Of course. I understand. Can we all sit down, please?" Khan said. He had on a short-sleeved pullover, and I could see that his arms were muscular. He wore khakis. His feet were bare. When he smiled, as he did now, his teeth were very white. His manner was charming. He was an elegant man.

I perched on the edge of a chair. He and Audrey sat close together on the couch.

"Audrey told me a body had been found," he said. "A mate aboard the *Intrepid*."

I nodded.

"I have called my uncle in Islamabad. Please understand, I had been assured that as long as the Americans agreed to a peaceful exchange, no one would be hurt. The way it was put to me, my help in the matter would help prevent bloodshed, prevent a major jihad from taking place."

"I don't think anyone, not even your uncle, could guarantee that, Mr. Khan," I said.

"I am beginning to fear you are right," Khan said. He looked up at me as he hugged Audrey closer to him. Their emotions for each other were so strong I could sense them. I could almost see them.

Khan took Audrey's hand in his as he said to me in an earnest voice, "I am not an extremist. I am a Muslim, and like most Muslims I am a peaceful man. I have never hurt anyone. I don't share the beliefs of the Wahhabis. I find them abhorrent. And I don't hate America. It is a great country.

"Now I feel as if my honor is on the line here. I cannot condone a terrorist act. I cannot be part of it." He looked at Audrey, reassuring her as much as he was speaking to me.

I looked at the two of them. It made me sad. Their love couldn't have a happy ending, no matter what happened.

"I'm afraid, Mr. Khan, that you are caught up in this thing," I said. "I hope it doesn't end in bloodshed. If you are serious about preventing it, I can only encourage you to let us know—let Audrey know—if you hear of anything that might help us find the ship. Now I really have to go," I said, standing.

Khan jumped up. "Of course. Of course. I will do everything I can. I swear to you."

Only he wasn't speaking to me. He was speaking to Audrey. I let myself out of the hotel suite, leaving them wrapped in each other's arms, afraid for them both.

At eleven thirty I buzzed Mickey. He came to the apartment to help me get my Harley downstairs and out into the street. His rheumy eyes narrowed when he saw what I was wearing. Gone were the Stuart Weitzman mules. Gone was the teeny little cami.

On this hot night I wore my leather biker jacket—with a Kevlar vest underneath. My Beretta Tomcat Laser Grip was in a shoulder holster. I had on the Frye boots, with a knife inside one and a small .22 strapped to my ankle in the other.

"Not that it's any of my business," the old Irishman said, "but you look like you're going to war."

"Something like that," I said as we pushed the bike out into the hall.

We rolled it carefully to the service elevator. "More Orangemen, like the other night?" he asked.

"Yes," I said.

Mickey was quiet until we got in the service elevator and the doors closed. "Where's the boyfriend? He going too?"

"He's going to meet me. And yeah, he's going too."

Mickey said nothing after that until we got to the first floor. "He watching your back?"

"You'd have to ask him," I said as we got the bike out on the street. I stood there and strapped on my helmet.

Mickey shook his head in disapproval. "Don't sound like you have much of a plan."

"Don't worry, Mick. I have friends." I got on my Harley

Electra Glide. It felt good beneath me. I felt good on it. I hit the starter and the engine roared. I gave Mickey a salute and zoomed off down the block toward Broadway, toward whatever waited for me there.

CHAPTER 20

"And we go,
And we drop like the fruits of the tree,
Even we,
Even so."

— George Meredith, "Dirge in Woods"

I heard the Harleys before I reached them. I bet even Mickey could have heard them, since my apartment building was only two blocks away. Filling up the curb lane on Broadway, stretching from corner to corner, a hundred vampires revved up their motorcycles. To casual bystanders they appeared to be outlaw bikers, human, of course, like a new production of *The Wild One*, with Rogue playing the Marlon Brando role.

The ground vibrated with the thumping of the engines. The noise alone would constitute a nuisance. I figured somebody would call the cops. We didn't have much time to get the hell out of there.

I rode up next to Rogue, who was at the head of the pack with Cormac, Audrey, and Cowboy Sam. I kept scanning the group for Darius. So far he was a no-show, and my misgivings were growing.

Rogue nodded hello to me but kept speaking to someone

on his cell phone. I figured it was the Laundromat's Martin or Gerry over at the park. The two and a half acres of Strawberry Fields stretched from Seventy-first to Seventy-fourth streets. We were only a few blocks away. All we needed was the signal that the vampire hunters were making their move.

Cormac pushed his bike up next to mine. "Everything's set. Your mother even has ambulances and medics standing by."

"What for? We get hit with a stake or a bullet, no medic can stop a vampire from turning into dust."

"Not for any of us. Must be she wants to interrogate the vampire hunters who get wounded."

Rogue kept his gloved hand raised in the air, visible to all under the streetlights. A minute passed. Then two. I kept watching for Darius, checking out the long line of bikes, two and three deep, that ran the length of the block.

All the bikers looked antsy, impatient to get to the fight. It crossed my mind that if Darius had informed Opus Dei of our plan, maybe the vampire hunters wouldn't show. My heart began to sink, rapidly turning to stone.

Then I saw a lone rider coming down Broadway. Hope leaped up inside me. The bike came closer. The rider wore no helmet, no jacket either, just a T-shirt with the sleeves ripped out. His blond hair streamed back behind him.

Rogue saw me staring and, turning his head away from the phone, asked, "Who's that?"

"My guy," I said.

He laughed. "Rambo, it figures."

"Why?"

"He's riding a customized panhead chopper, probably a classic Vaughs and Hardy."

I gave him a blank stare.

He snorted at my ignorance. "*Easy Rider*. You picked yourself a wild one, all right."

Darius reached us, spitting asphalt as he did a controlled skid to line himself up with me. Big grin on his face. "Hey, sweetheart. Told you I'd get here in time."

"I didn't know you had a bike," I said. *Or that you had a lot of experience riding one.*

"I didn't. Where did you think I was tonight? I had shopping to do. A ring," he said, and winked, "and proper transportation to deliver it."

"Oh," I said in a brilliant retort.

At that moment Rogue's hand dropped. He gunned his engine. The rest of the bikers followed his lead. The rumbling grew, thudding like the beating of a great heart, stirring my blood. Like a single living thing, the dark mass of bikes and riders pulled out into the street.

Careening around the corner of Broadway, a hundred motorcycles on the move created a din that echoed off the buildings and filled the air with a raucous noise. Our armada charged across Seventy-second Street. The dark entrance to the park lay ahead, framed by stone pillars, shadowed by trees, and dimly lit, like the great, gaping maw to hell.

Once we were inside the park's walls, Rogue's bike jumped the curb, leading the way off the street and onto the grass, racing toward the vampires under attack and fighting for their very existence.

Suddenly, straight ahead, I could see them, most fighting hand-to-hand with the huge vampire hunter brutes who had come from the direction of the West Side and seemed to be advancing in waves. Not ninety. Not one hundred. At least three hundred of them, moving forward like army ants, stoked to kill their ancient enemy.

We were outnumbered easily two to one.

Acting according to plan, we resisted the urge to ride directly into the fray. Instead, like the gadfly Jeb Stuart encircling McClellan's huge army with his doughty band of rebs, we looped around behind the hunters, making a noose we hoped to hang them with.

Then, after we got into position, our fight began. I drove my Harley a few yards toward the foe before halting it on the grass. Parking it was going to be tricky.

I had rehearsed everything in my head. I had to be thoroughly prepared if I wanted to get out of this and see tomorrow. I had brought a metal plate in my saddlebags. I twisted around and got it, put in beneath the bike, and pushed the kickstand down with my foot.

Success. The kickstand landed on the metal, not on the soft surface. I couldn't let the bike fall over, or I was going to be totally screwed. Even I couldn't pick up six hundred pounds alone.

Now I jumped off quickly. I left on my helmet. I pulled my gun from my shoulder holster, and, using the bike for cover, I aimed the Tomcat at the fighting mass before me.

The red laser picked out my targets. I pulled the trigger. *Crack. Crack. Crack.* One after another the brutes went down.

I had no intention of being a hero; I just wanted to eliminate as many of the vicious killers as I could. I stayed back from the hand-to-hand combat as the Laundromat teams fought for their lives. My role was as a sniper, and my gun was a better weapon than my fists.

Darius had no such restraint. He rode past me toward the

thick of the fighting. My heart longed to call him back. But my head knew this was what he had been trained to do. As a SEAL, Darius had been one of America's elite soldiers, battle-hardened and without fear.

I saw him jump off the bike, pull a combat knife from his belt, and run toward a vampire on the ground in dire trouble, a stake descending toward his heart. Then the fog of war moved in. I saw Darius no more.

After that I thought of nothing but my mission. I kept firing, carefully, deliberately, letting my laser beam find the enemy one by one.

In the sky above me the vampires designated to transform and carry out an aerial attack swooped and plummeted toward the vampire hunters. The air vibrated with their clicks and high-pitched whistles, like fighter planes in a dive. I heard screams. I smelled blood. Not daring to take the time to look up, my mind devoid of conscious thought, I fired on.

Then I got a crawling sensation up my spine, a tingling at the base of my neck; the hairs on my arms stood up. I heard a noise coming close behind me. I swiveled in time to see one of the dark thugs advancing, a stake in his hand. I fired at point-blank range. I fired again directly into his face, which disappeared in an explosion of blood and brains.

Then I was struck from the side, bowled over, a body on top of me. My gun flew out of my hand. I tried to push the monster off of me, his bulk squeezing the breath out of me. I saw the sharpened stake in his hand. I gripped his wrist with both of mine, shoving backward with all my strength.

My arms shook with the effort. My back was pressed to the ground. My opponent had the advantage. I saw the ending of everything coming toward me in the ice-pick tip of that sharpened wood.

Then suddenly the vampire hunter arched backward with a terrible cry. I saw a hole in his forehead turn to black and blood before he writhed and hit the ground. I sprang to my feet and looked around for my rescuer.

With a start I saw an old man standing behind me.

"Mickey!" I cried out, and in that second the old man, his long-barreled gun extended in his outstretched hand, crumpled to the ground. I ran to him. I could see the blood spreading on his shirt. "Mickey!" I screamed, and knelt beside him, getting my arm under his neck. "Mickey! How did you get here?"

He opened his eyes and looked at me, a smile on his lips. His voice was weak, but I could hear what he said. "Easy to follow you. All that noise. Somebody had to watch your back." Then he slumped in my arms.

"Medic!" I screamed. "Medic! Over here!" A young man came running with a medicine case. "He's one of ours, but a human," I cried out.

The medic felt Mickey's neck for a pulse. He nodded at me. "He's alive. We'll get him out of here." I nodded, and the breath I had been holding came out of me in a whoosh.

I whirled around and frantically searched the ground with my eyes. Then I saw my gun, which still lay on the grass, and scrambled for it. I picked it up, regained my position behind my bike, and started firing again—until I heard the sound of sirens wailing through the streets of the city.

While it seemed as if we had been fighting for a very long time, it had probably been just minutes. Now we needed to get out of there before the cops arrived. Vampires didn't have the option of getting arrested. By the time day dawned they would be unprotected and die.

Vampires and vampire hunters both began to scatter. I

mounted my bike. I went to hit the starter. Then I stopped. Not twenty feet in front of me a vampire hunter on the run stopped too. Smaller than the others, though dressed the same, the hunter looked at me with hate-filled eyes.

I recognized her at once. It was not a face I'd forget. She had tried to kill me before. And I had seen her with Darius. In his band. In his arms. It was Julie, his lead singer—his fellow spy and formerly his lover.

I raised my Beretta Tomcat. The laser beam hit her dead center between the breasts, the surest target I could find.

"Daphne, no!" A hand grasped mine and pointed the gun toward the ground. Julie shot me a look, anguished but filled with loathing, and ran.

"Let her go," Darius said.

I turned my head to look at him. My voice was filled with fury. "Why did you stop me? She's one of *them*."

He shook his head. "I couldn't. You have to understand. I couldn't let you do it. No matter what she is."

But I didn't understand. I didn't understand at all.

The sirens wailed closer. We had to run. I stared at Darius. I felt angry and confused.

"Later," he said, and took off running.

I tried to put what had just happened out of my mind. I needed to get my ass out of this place. I pushed forward to release the kickstand of my bike, hit the starter, and raced toward the winding road that would lead me to Fifth Avenue on the west side of the park.

Within a minute I had the park exit at Seventy-second Street in sight. I slowed down, fearing there would be traffic on the busy avenue even this late at night. That caution probably saved my life.

As I entered the intersection a white Chevy cut me off. I hit the brakes, skidded, lost control, and toppled, the bike sliding out from under me. I rolled across the asphalt, pulling my arms in close to my body, grateful for my leathers. I came to a halt when my face collided with a pair of black, permanent-shine, regulation police department shoes.

It hurt like hell. I lifted my head and looked up. The bright light of a flashlight struck me in the face. I winced.

A familiar voice, pissed off more than usual, said, "Miss Urban. I should have known."

"Evening, Lieutenant," I said. "You mind if I stand?"

I got to one knee, my legs wobbling, my body swaying. The lieutenant put his hand under my arm. He helped me get on my feet. I felt light-headed. I pulled off my helmet and gritted my teeth. I tried to steady the spinning world.

"Miss Urban," the world-weary police detective said in a world-weary voice. "I hear we have maybe fifteen dead bodies in the middle of Central Park. May I ask you something?"

"Uh-huh," I answered, all the while thinking, *Only fifteen? There have to be at least a hundred hunters down. So that's what the ambulances were for. My mother planned all along to remove the dead before the cops arrived.*

"Do you think you could tell me"—Lieutenant Johnson said sweetly. I winced. I could see it coming—"WHAT THE FUCK IS GOING ON?"

"It's sort of a long story," I said.

"Why don't you get in the back of my car and tell me." It was an order, not a request.

"But my bike . . ." I protested, looking at my beautiful red Harley Electra lying against a tree, its front wheel mangled.

"I'll get a uniform to pick it up. But don't expect to get it back. It's evidence."

"Ah, shit, Lieutenant," I began to say, intending to argue with him, when my cell phone vibrated in my pocket.

"I'd better get this," I said, holding up a finger.

It was Benny on the phone, her voice high and excited. "The *Intrepid* is on the move. It's been spotted sailing toward New York Harbor, a couple of miles before the Verrazano. And, sugar? J says those stupid diplomats think the terrorists are jist a-bringing it back. The air force ain't going to bomb it."

"Ah, shit," I said again.

"Get downtown to the ferry terminal, will you, girlfriend? We have a ship to stop."

I turned to Lieutenant Johnson and gave him an insouciant grin. "Hey, Looie, guess what? I need a ride."

CHAPTER 21

"And I will come again, my luve,
Tho' it were ten thousand mile."

—Robert Burns, "A Red, Red Rose"

Say what you want about Johnson. He's got no personality, but the man knows his shit.

I told him about the *Intrepid*. He was a little peeved I hadn't told him the whole story to begin with. I figured that out when he crushed another Coke can with his hand while I was talking. But he totally agreed with me when I laid out my reasons for believing the ship was not just being returned—it was rigged to explode once it was inside New York Harbor.

I also told him what I thought might stop it.

He reached over to the floor by the passenger seat and grabbed the unmarked car's red police light, leaned out the driver's window, and stuck it on the roof. He flipped on the siren, put the accelerator to the floor, and headed for Whitehall Street.

He grabbed the handheld radio, muttering to himself all the while, "I bet those sons of bitches are going after the Statue of Liberty. Sons of bitches!" After that the lieutenant talked a mile a minute into the radio as he drove all the way downtown like a man being chased by the devil.

"I know everybody's up at Central Park," I heard him bellowing into the handheld. Hell, half of New York could have heard him. "Unless you want another goddamn nine-eleven, get every first responder out of there and down to the Staten Island Ferry. And move both the ferries to the terminal."

Whomever he was screaming at put him through to the chief. In a calmer voice Johnson told his boss what had to happen. In a minute he and the chief were patched through to the mayor and the head of the Port Authority. Next I heard the governor's voice on the line.

Everybody asked a lot of questions. Johnson gave them answers they didn't want to hear but had to know. Finally the mayor and governor gave the okay. Both men knew Washington had already nixed force and wouldn't go along with this. They were taking full responsibility for a tricky maneuver that could literally blow up in their faces.

Johnson left out the part about us Darkwings. That was okay. If everything went according to plan, nobody would ever see us—besides the terrorists, that is. That was a very big *if*, but I didn't let on that I had any doubts we could pull this off.

A wall of blue uniforms and firemen in full gear blocked Whitehall Street. Johnson stuck his head out the window and yelled his way down the street to get us to the ferry terminal.

Rogue, Cormac, Benny, Sam, and, to my surprise, Audrey and Khan stood in front of the terminal building waiting for me to get there. The *Alice Austen* sat in the ferry slip. Her sister ship, the *John A. Noble*, wallowed close by in the harbor. I jumped out of Johnson's car and raced over. As soon as I got close I could hear a furious argument raging. Audrey was begging Khan to stay behind. He was having none of it.

I went directly over to Rogue. I added my two cents to the controversy, telling him that Khan's going was crazy. And if he went, the man was going to get the shock of his life when we transformed into giant bats.

Rogue shrugged. "Khan agrees it's a double cross. Audrey said he got a call from somebody spilling the beans. He feels his honor has been lost. Let the man do what he's got to do," Rogue said to me, then yelled, "Time to move!" He grabbed Audrey's arm and said, "Let it go, Audrey. He's coming along."

Audrey turned toward him for the briefest of moments, her beautiful face full of grief. Then we all ran through the terminal and up the ramp to the waiting ferry.

Except for the captain and his first mate, we were the only passengers. The mate pulled the ramp up behind us, and even before he shut the gates the ferry was moving away from the dock, its horns blaring.

As soon as we cleared the slip, the *John A. Noble* pulled into our space fast, hitting the dock hard. Looking back over the rail, I saw the first responders start up the gangplank.

The *Alice Austen* turned toward the Verrazano-Narrows Bridge to intercept the *Intrepid*. With the engine opened as wide as it could go, our ferry sailed forth. We couldn't wait for her sister ship. It would take a good ten minutes to get the *Noble* boarded, and we didn't have that much time.

Even traveling at maximum speed, maybe twenty knots, the ferry seemed to lumber along like a great swimming bear. It took twenty long minutes to get to the Verrazano. I paced the rails, my anxiety mounting. I knew we had to stop the *Intrepid* while she was still out in the channel, just in case she blew.

Finally the high, graceful span of the Verrazano appeared in front of us. There, huge and impressive, the great old warship, completely visible, was steaming directly under it. All the Darkwings came up to the leading edge of the *Alice Austen*, not exactly the bow, since the bow and stern depended on which direction the ship was traveling. Ferries never turned around.

Audrey came striding over, still wearing one of Khan's shirts and his jeans, just as she was the other night. She looked grim. I reached out and gave her a hug.

She said Khan was up in the pilothouse with the captain.

I couldn't imagine what was going through her mind. No matter what happened, even if Khan got out of this alive, he'd see her turn into a vampire bat. She and Khan were through.

With the *Intrepid* in sight, it was now or never. The Darkwings transformed, all of us, all at once. Hopping up on the rail and balancing over the dark water, we took off into the pellucid air. Silently five great vampire bats soared upward and headed toward the huge, looming ship, invisible once we were airborne. We were black shapes against a black night.

Meanwhile the *Alice Austen* set her course, head-on, right into the *Intrepid*'s path. It was going to take a lot of courage to put the ferry on a collision course with the great World War II, steel-plated vessel. We hoped the terrific impact of the two ships hitting would slow or stop the *Intrepid*'s forward movement—and distract the terrorists from seeing us land.

But the ferry was only 207 feet long, less than a third the

size of the battleship. In all probability the *Intrepid* would roll right over her, crushing in the ferry's sides and sending her to the bottom, sinking her fast.

The ferry captain, his mate, and Khan knew that. They were told to abandon ship as soon as the deadly course was set. But jumping into the water and getting out of danger's way would be perilous in itself.

In my heart I knew none of them would make it. I also suspected they all knew that too. I bet they would stay on board until the ships collided, even though it would cost them their lives.

Meanwhile the five of us reached the aircraft carrier. With the element of surprise on our side, we had to keep the terrorists from detonating the bombs we were sure were there. And we wanted to kill them all, if we could.

We didn't know if any of the American crew was alive. We didn't know who was piloting the ship. We believed the terrorists were.

It didn't matter much. Whatever the situation, we had to do the job.

The bridge and control tower rose up pale and ghostly from the starboard side of the ship. With Rogue in the lead, he, Cormac, and Audrey flew toward it just as the *Intrepid* hit the *Alice Austen*.

The noise of the impact deafened me. Metal tore apart with a horrendous scream. The big ship shuddered, shook, and reared up, its bow in the air. It came down on the ferry, driving the orange ship under the water. The *Intrepid* dipped down, bounced up . . . and stopped dead in the water, caught on the ferry's roof.

I looked below me on the flight deck of the carrier. I could see four men running toward a large mound, like many crates piled high, in the middle of the wide, flat space. Explosives, I thought. Nothing high-tech. Maybe dynamite. Maybe nitro. They bombed the World Trade Center in 1993 with a urea-nitrate-fertilizer bomb.

I whistled to Sam and Benny. They spotted the running men too. We folded our wings back and dove toward them.

I hit the nearest man at full speed in the neck with my clawed foot, decapitating him. His head rolled down the flight deck while his body dropped like a stone.

Benny used her shoulder to ram into another, shoving him forward until she pushed him off the edge of the ship into the Arthur Kill. Sam threw himself onto another of the terrorists, slamming his body to the deck. I saw the cowboy disembowel him with one terrible clawed swipe.

The final terrorist was no problem to any of us. Seeing what happened to his comrades, he ran to the side of the ship and threw himself into the water.

I took a quick look at the boxes. I saw the wire and a detonator. I didn't touch it. I'd leave it for the bomb squad. For now it was harmless.

Then the three of us leaped skyward again and flew to the bridge. We landed in front of a room of silence. A half dozen bodies lay on the floor. Nothing living stirred.

Our three team members came around the corner of the bridge, signaling us to go. We didn't take time to search further. We heard the horn blasts of the *John A. Noble* as she came alongside. In minutes New York's real heroes would be climbing on board.

So far I was pretty sure nobody had spotted us. We didn't tarry. We took flight off the bridge on the side away from the approaching ferry. We aimed for a white sliver of crescent moon, and then set our course by the yellow glow of Liberty's torch.

Just as the first rays of dawn sent fingers of light into the sky, I landed on the ledge of a window in my apartment, the same one Darius had entered days before. I tumbled through the curtains, fell onto the floor, and let myself transform.

After the change, naked, my arms and legs trembling from exhaustion, I lay there breathing hard. Finally I pulled myself to my knees, then stood. I was whole; I was safe; I was home.

Pulling my tangled hair back from my face, I smiled and greeted my dog and white rat. I made my way with tired feet into the kitchen. Jade's water bowl was full; a few remnants of beef lay in her food bowl.

Then I saw the ring box on the granite countertop. Next to the box sat a folded piece of paper with my name printed on it.

I picked it up, my hand shaking. I opened it and read:

Sweetheart—

I know you're pissed. I hope you don't throw the ring in the trash. I hope you decide to wear it.

I have to leave town for a while. It will give you a chance to think. It seems that my boss believes that your boss's boss wants to kill me. I believe he's right.

I'm giving them a chance to straighten it out between the three of them and stay out of harm's way until they do.

I have something to live for now—something I want with all my heart.

Please forgive my stubborn loyalties and foolish choices.

There is only you. Now and forever.

I'll call when I can. Wait for me.

Remember what Bobby B. wrote—

"And fare thee weel, my only luve!

And fare thee weel awhile!

And I will come again, my luve,

Tho' it were ten thousand mile."

D.

EPILOGUE

The vampire hunter war brought some irrevocable changes to New York and those I loved.

For one thing, Martin didn't make it. He was one of thirteen vampires who went to dust in Strawberry Fields. The Laundromat lost five members altogether. They decided to honor the fallen by renaming the nightly blood competition the Strawberry Fields Memorial Regatta. I didn't think it made much sense, but they liked it.

Charlie's lost eight bikers. The Bloods Club auctioned off their Harleys and threw a beer bash in the back court with the money. It went on every night for an entire week before the cops started sitting outside in squad cars because there was so much fighting and carrying on. The membership agreed that the lost vampires went out in a blaze of glory, kicking ass. What more could an outlaw biker want?

Shalid Khan, Captain Roger J. Worthington, and First Mate Gianni Amalfi all died that night. They remained with the ferry, making sure it stayed in the *Intrepid*'s path. They were honored as heroes. Their bodies were retrieved from the Arthur Kill. Khan's family shipped his home to Pakistan.

The remaining crew and captain of the *Intrepid* were found safe below decks.

Two weeks after the battle I came downstairs one evening to walk Jade and found Mickey in the lobby, manning the front door. His arm hung in a sling, but his back seemed a little straighter than it had been.

He told me they treated him "right royal" in the military hospital and didn't even charge him a dime. He muttered something about wishing he could have killed a dozen more of the murderin' Brits. If he saw any vampires that night, I think he would have lumped what he saw into the category of pink elephants. He certainly didn't look at me as if I were a monster.

I told him I owed him my life.

Mickey stood straight and said, "Erin go Bragh." Ireland forever.

Amen.

As for the ring . . . it's in my backpack, the Louis Vuitton one I carry everywhere. I haven't made up my mind what I will do about marrying Darius. I can't deny I love him. I still am not completely sure I trust him.

But I tell myself he's not just a vampire; he's a man. They're flawed creatures. I need to consider that before I make my final decision.

I am not talking to my mother.

I have not seen J.

I don't know if I'll be back with the Darkwings when they meet again.

ACKNOWLEDGMENTS

I often feel that being an author is a very lonely job, but in truth I never work entirely alone. I have many people helping me get my stories into print.

At the top of the list are my friend and agent John Talbot and my wonderful editor at Signet, Kristen Weber. This book wouldn't exist without either of them. I am an amazingly lucky author to have a truly great editor and a terrific agent who never lets me down. Both John and Kristen are consummate professionals—and compassionate human beings.

My gratitude also goes to Allen Davis, Det. (Ret.) of the NYPD, who patiently answered my questions: i.e., What did you carry around with you in an unmarked police car? What's the weirdest call you ever answered? Any authenticity I achieved is thanks to him; any errors are my own.

Thanks are given to my nearest and dearest for putting up with my short temper and frayed nerves as this book neared completion. Thanks to Hildy Morgan for listening; thanks to Priscilla Adams for lifting my spirits. Thanks to Susan Collini for having the Santa Margherita chilled. Thanks to

Flossy Finn for cheering me on. Thanks to Donna Wench at my local Barnes & Noble for believing in me too.

Thanks to all my animals for not caring whether I write or not.

Thanks to all you readers. You read. You understand. You care.

AUTHOR'S NOTE

My stories and my characters are entirely fictional. I dream them up. I don't know where the ideas come from. Jung's universal unconscious? My own subconscious? The Greek Muses? I really don't know.

And to answer the many readers who have asked me the following things:

Do I ever get writer's block? No. I just sit down and write.

Do I ever run out of ideas? No, I just dream awake—and the dreams become stories.

Yes, my stories are based on dreams, but New York City is real.

Terrorism is real.

And some of the most incredible events I write are based on situations that actually happened.

For one thing, it is possible to let a subway train pass over you and live to tell about it. In January of 2007 a Harlem construction worker named Wesley Autrey leaped onto the tracks in front of an oncoming subway train to save a complete stranger who had suffered a seizure and fallen there.

He covered the man with his own body, and miraculously both men lived.

Another true thing: Both British and American intelligence agents do kidnap and incarcerate "enemies" in secret prisons. Amnesty International's Human Rights Watch and other groups have drawn up a list of thirty-nine "ghost detainees" whom they say are missing and being held by the United States. One of the missing is Mohammed Omar Abdel-Rahman, son of Omar Abdel-Rahman, the "Blind Sheikh" who masterminded the bombing of the World Trade Center in 1993.

There have been many reported incidents of this kind of abduction. However, the most publicized might be the one that resulted in the Italian government charging twenty-six Americans and six Italians, including the former head of Italy's military intelligence, with kidnapping a Muslim cleric from the streets of Milan and transporting him to Egypt.

In 2006 President Bush admitted secret detention camps existed, but insisted they were empty. If you believe that, I have a bridge in Brooklyn I want to sell you.

True too—a hair of the prophet Muhammad is kept in the Hazratbal mosque in the Indian Kashmir.

On a lighter note, readers might want to know that since 1997 passengers have been able to ride the Staten Island Ferry for free. The five ferries in service run twenty-four hours a day, 365 days a year. The twenty-five-minute ride offers an unforgettable view of the harbor, Ellis Island, the Statue of Liberty, and the New York skyline.

You can spot all the foreign visitors riding the ferry because they're at the rail taking pictures. Most of the Americans are commuters who sit inside the ship reading the *New York Post*. But a Staten Island Ferry ride should go on every American's top-ten-things-to-do list. It's a national treasure.

Also the American Society of Indexers (www.asindexing.org) does exist. Many of their members are librarians. They are, without exception, unusually smart and resourceful people. However, ASI has *never* held their national conference in New York City, and they have never had a meeting crashed by vampire hunters, nor anyone else, to the best of my knowledge. They also have no gun-toting security committee—although in these troubled times, it might not be a bad idea.

Hugs and kisses to everyone,
Savannah

Penguin Group (USA) Online

What will you be reading tomorrow?

Tom Clancy, Patricia Cornwell, W.E.B. Griffin,
Nora Roberts, William Gibson, Robin Cook,
Brian Jacques, Catherine Coulter, Stephen King,
Dean Koontz, Ken Follett, Clive Cussler,
Eric Jerome Dickey, John Sandford,
Terry McMillan, Sue Monk Kidd, Amy Tan,
John Berendt…

You'll find them all at
penguin.com

Read excerpts and newsletters,
find tour schedules and reading group guides,
and enter contests.

Subscribe to Penguin Group (USA) newsletters
and get an exclusive inside look
at exciting new titles and the authors you love
long before everyone else does.

PENGUIN GROUP (USA)
us.penguingroup.com